PRO BONO

VERTICAL.

PRO BONO

SEICHO MATSUMOTO

TRANSLATED BY ANDREW CLARE

VERTICAL.

Published by Vertical, Inc., New York

First published in Japanese as *Kiri no hata*
by Cyuokoronsha Publishing Co., Ltd. in 1961,
republished by Shinchosha Publishing Co., Ltd. in 1972

ISBN 978-1-934387-02-6

Manufactured in the United States of America

First Edition

Vertical, Inc.
451 Park Avenue South, 7th Floor
New York, NY 10016
www.vertical-inc.com

PRO BONO

Chapter 1

Kiriko Yanagida left the inn in Kanda at ten in the morning.

She had wanted to leave earlier, but having heard that famous lawyers tend not to arrive in the office too early, she'd waited until ten.

Kinzo Otsuka was the name of the lawyer whom Kiriko had come all the way from Kyushu to see.

That he was the best when it came to criminal cases was not something that Kiriko, a twenty-year-old company typist, had reason to know about. However, she'd learned his name from her conversations with various people following the incident that had suddenly turned her life upside down.

Kiriko had left K-City in northern Kyushu two nights ago and arrived at Tokyo station late the previous evening.

She'd gone straight to that particular inn because she'd stayed there once before, on her junior high school trip, and its familiarity put her mind at ease. Also, since the inn catered to group visitors, it was likely to be inexpensive.

Although she didn't know him, she was confident about the prospect of meeting Kinzo Otsuka, and she was sure that once they'd met, he'd take on her case. She had, after all, spent twenty hours being buffeted on a steam train between Kyushu and Tokyo. Surely he'd recognise her determination at their first meeting.

When she awoke, the sky was clear and bright. Her ability to rise at such an early hour after a continuous journey of twenty hours was not due simply to her youth, but also had much to do with her raised spirits.

The inn was situated on a hill, and the quietness of the place seemed not at all like a morning in Tokyo.

Her impressions were different from the other time because this time she'd spent the night alone.

Just below the window was an elementary school. When she'd first woken and looked out there was nobody around on the sports ground, but gradually children began to arrive in their twos and threes like small black beans, so that by the time the maid had come in to change the bedding, there was quite a commotion outside.

"A very good morning to you," the elderly maid greeted her, the corners of her eyes wrinkling as she smiled. "I should think you are tired out, aren't you? Shouldn't you have rested a little longer?"

"But I was already awake," said Kiriko, moving over and standing next to a rattan chair on the veranda.

"Ah, that's because you're young. It's different for the likes of me..."

8

The maid had discovered during the course of the previous evening that Kiriko had come from northern Kyushu. She offered her some tea and red pickled plums on a small plate. The plums were small and wrinkled. Kiriko's eyes were drawn vaguely in their direction.

"I would love to visit Kyushu just once, you know. I hear that Beppu is a lovely place."

"You're right."

The maid wiped the tabletop painstakingly with a white cloth. "Would this be your first time in Tokyo? Are you here for the sightseeing?"

She'd clearly come to the conclusion that a young girl staying alone in an inn would not have relatives or friends in Tokyo. She must be here to look at something or else to find work.

"No, not really," replied Kiriko, sitting herself down in the rattan chair.

The maid began lining up the teacups on the table, and the white of the cups reflected in the red lacquer of the table. She bent down and laid the plates out in order. But it was obvious from her eyes that she was thinking about what the guest had said.

Kiriko took out her notebook. She opened it and read out the address of Kinzo Otsuka's office. "Room XX, X Building, M Annex, Marunouchi Ni-chome, Chiyoda ward, Tokyo. Do you know how I get there?"

"It's right next to Tokyo station. On the opposite side from the Yaesu entrance," explained the maid, adding in an

9

inquiring way, "It's nothing but company offices over there, though. Is it someone you know?"

"Yes, a little. I'm visiting a lawyer's office."

"A lawyer?"

There was a look of surprise in the eyes of the maid, who'd assumed that Kiriko was in Tokyo to find a job. "And you came especially all the way from Kyushu?"

"Yes, that's right."

"Well now, that is quite something," said the maid, looking over at the younger woman.

This young guest appeared to be carrying a great burden on her shoulders. The maid wanted to inquire further but held her curiosity in check.

"Do you know that area well?" asked Kiriko.

"I pass by that way often. There are lots of red brick buildings that look the same on either side of the road, and dozens of signs out in front. What is the name of the lawyer you are seeing?"

"He's called Kinzo Otsuka."

"Kinzo Otsuka?" The maid took a sharp intake of breath. "He is a very famous man."

"Oh, do you know him?"

"No. Not personally. But, well, when you do this sort of job you meet all kinds of people, and so naturally I know his name." She laughed lightly and added, "That's quite something, isn't it? Going to see such a well-known lawyer?" She looked at Kiriko with a serious expression and said, "Aren't there good lawyers where you come from?"

"Why, yes, of course, but…" Kiriko cast down her eyes. "I just thought it'd be better to ask a top-class lawyer in Tokyo, that's all…"

"You won't do better than that, I suppose." The maid regarded the younger woman with a look of amusement. "Is it a troublesome case?"

"Something like that," answered Kiriko, vaguely, abruptly closing the door on any further conversation. She got up from the rattan chair and knelt down in front of the neatly arranged cups. But her face, with its child-like lines, was unexpectedly cold, and there was a sudden distance between herself and the maid.

The Marunouchi X Building was located in an area with tall red brick buildings on either side of the road, and it was rather like walking around an old foreign town. It felt a little like looking at the old western buildings portrayed in Meiji period paintings, and under the early summer sunlight, many parts of the edifices lay hidden in dark shadow.

The entrances were narrow, and the corridors beyond appeared dark. If it weren't for the bright green leaves of the trees lining the sidewalk, the whole scene would have resembled a dark, one-dimensional copperplate engraving.

Inlaid into the front of the trading houses were little square black nameplates displaying in gold lettering the names of the companies. It was the sort of place that would not have raised an eyebrow had horse drawn carriages been travelling the streets instead of cars.

Having stopped to ask the way, Kiriko finally tracked down the sign for Kinzo Otsuka's law offices. Kiriko assumed that if she, a young girl from Kyushu, had heard of a famous lawyer, then people in Tokyo would know him for sure, but she was amazed to find that nobody did. Everyone she asked either nodded in a slightly perplexed way, or laughed and walked straight past her with a wave of the hand. She finally found out from the sixth person she asked—a student, who went out of his way and took her right up to the front door.

"It's here," he said, pointing.

This place also had one of those oxidized nameplates.

She stood in front of it and composed herself.

The objective of her twenty-hour train journey was before her in the form of a dark rectangular-shaped entrance.

Two young men appeared from inside and came energetically down the stone steps casting a cursory glance in her direction. One of them discarded his cigarette, and then both walked away.

Kinzo Otsuka was in the back of the office, talking to a client who was an unpleasant character.

The interior was divided by bookcases rather than walls. In the spacious area beyond were five junior lawyers, a clerk who was a former court stenographer and was more or less a permanent fixture, and the desks of young ladies employed to carry out a range of general tasks.

The younger lawyers' desks faced the rear and were arranged in a sort of keyhole formation. The stenographer's desk and the chair used by clients on their first visit were also there.

But that area was only visible through a gap. The full extent of the office could not be seen from where he sat.

The narrow section of the office was exclusive to Otsuka, and the only furniture in there were a wide desk, a large swivel chair, a simple reception desk, and a chair for visiting clients. The walls were the oldest thing in there.

The client sat in the chair, talking incessantly, amused by his own words. As he occupied the high status of a public prosecutor, even Otsuka could not bring himself to shoo him away.

The wily fifty-two-year-old lawyer displayed the onset of middle age, with his gray hair creeping up from his temples, ruddy chubby cheeks, and sagging double chin.

Otsuka had in fact one concern on his mind. Although judgement was soon to be rendered on a large and troublesome case, he had yet to put together any kind of evidence. It was largely because of this concern that his attention was now not fully on his guest's story. Nevertheless, he couldn't bring himself to be discourteous, and so he simply smiled and made the appropriate half-hearted responses.

He willed himself not to think any further about the case. And then suddenly he remembered he had a round of golf scheduled for two o'clock that same afternoon over at Kawana. He'd been invited by Michiko Kono, but he'd forgotten because he'd turned her down. It was a little late, but if he left now there was no reason why he couldn't make it in time. It did seem like a good idea, he thought, and then he began to glance at his watch.

The client noticed and at length stood up from the chair. Otsuka accompanied him out of the office and was relieved to see the back of him leaving through the door.

But then as he turned around he suddenly noticed a young woman, sitting talking in the chair in front of Okumura's desk. She wore a white suit, and her appearance was eye-catching. There were only two other lawyers in the room, both with their backs turned and sifting through great piles of documents spread out on the desks in front of them.

As Otsuka made to go back into his room, Okumura glanced in his direction.

It was just as he was thinking, *Please, don't come in here*, and clearing his desk of papers, that Okumura walked slowly into his room.

"There's a client to see you," he announced, watching Otsuka scoop up his papers from the desk and put them in his black briefcase.

"Oh really?"

Otsuka recalled the white-suited figure of the young lady who was sitting out in reception.

"Will you see her?" inquired Okumura.

"Isn't there another lawyer around?" he replied, locking his bulging briefcase.

"Three are out, and the other two have their hands full at the moment."

Lawyers made it a rule to see clients in person, and when Otsuka was busy, one of the younger assistants would take down a client's details for him. In this case, it was clearly his turn.

"What sort of issue is it?" he asked, looking at Okumura.

"Aren't you going out for the day?"

Okumura, noticing that Otsuka was preparing to leave, looked at him as if to say, *You should take care of it yourself.*

"No, no, I can hang on a while." Feeling that going out to meet a woman was a little questionable, he lit a cigarette.

"It's a murder case. The young lady is the defendant's younger sister," explained Okumura, reading the memo he'd taken with a rather indifferent expression on his face.

"Where, I wonder?" muttered the lawyer to himself, sifting through his memory of newspaper articles.

"It was an incident in K-City in Kyushu."

"Kyushu?" Otsuka's eyes bore into Okumura's face. "Kyushu, that's quite a distance from here."

"She says she's come all the way here especially to ask for your assistance."

The lawyer knocked the ash from his cigarette and massaged the nape of his neck with the fingers of his other hand. It wasn't unusual at all for his help to be requested. But Kyushu—that *was* far away.

"What would you like to do?"

"What would I like to do? You mean would I like to meet with her?"

Okumura moved his slightly built body in front of Otsuka, bent forwards, and said, in a low voice, "It seems she has no money."

15

Silence.

"The young lady is called Kiriko Yanagida. I understand she is a typist working for a small company in K-City. Her brother, the suspect, is a schoolteacher, and they've been living together. They do have an uncle, but it seems he won't give them any money."

"And you've already explained about the standard legal fee?" Otsuka stopped massaging his neck and began tapping the edge of the desk lightly with his fingers. He suddenly had a vision of Michiko Kono, bathed in bright light against a green slope with a golf club raised in her hands. Another man was standing next to her talking, and she was laughing at his remarks…

"Yes, I explained it to her. About the travelling expenses. Being Kyushu, you'll have to go by plane of course. And then there'll be accommodation expenses, in a good hotel, mind you, research and investigation expenses, photocopying charges. Added to which there'll be a legal fee of, in our case, five hundred thousand yen, for lodging a case in the district court of first instance. I explained that in the case of a business trip away from Tokyo, we charge a daily expense rate of eight thousand yen a day. Oh, and finally, in the event that you win the case for her, we'd normally expect to receive a success fee…"

Otsuka took a draught on his cigarette.

"I explained it all, and she seemed quite surprised. She wanted to know how much it would come to, to see the case through to its conclusion. I told her that it really depends on the nature of the case in question, but that, not taking into account, for the moment, any second and third round hearings, and including the expenses for the trip to Kyushu, it'd likely be in the region of eight hundred thousand yen for the first instance hearing. That was just my estimate, of course, but that's what I told her. And of course we'd need payment in advance for the legal fees. And you know what she said? I mean she is young of course, but she asked for a one-third discount, because she hasn't got that kind of money. She's ever so young. But she seems to know what she wants."

"Down to a third?" Otsuka gave a wry smile.

"And not only that. She asks whether we'd accept half the advance payment. She's after all come all the way from Kyushu and respectfully requests that you undertake her case."

"We won't make any money out of it, yes?" said Otsuka, speaking from experience.

"We won't make any money," replied the clerk, also speaking from experience. "It does seem an interesting case. Of course, it's an altogether different matter if you want to do it pro bono…"

"People come here seeking my help without the remotest idea of how much it's going to cost. All they know is that they want the assistance of a good lawyer. It's always that way. They don't know anything."

"Are you going to decline?" said Okumura. "After all, you are busy. You needn't get involved in anything like this."

"I did something like this some time ago. Similar case, too. Now that I'm this busy, I'm not sure I have the time or enthusiasm to undertake a case that's not profitable. I suppose I should turn it down…" Otsuka turned his wristwatch over.

"In that case I'll see her out."

"Just wait a minute. She has, after all, come all the way from Kyushu. Better if it comes from me. Show her through, would you?"

Okumura withdrew, and in his place a young woman entered the room. It was the same woman dressed in white that he'd glimpsed a little earlier. When he looked closely he saw that her suit was made of a coarse material.

The young woman looked at Otsuka and made a polite bow. She had a slender face with well-defined features. Her eyes had an intense look about them, and this was what struck Otsuka more than anything as he talked with her.

"So you're from Kyushu, are you?" he asked, with a smile.

"I'm from K-City. My name is Kiriko Yanagida." Her words were crisply spoken, and she confidently held the lawyer's gaze as she spoke. The contours from her cheek to her chin gave a youthful impression.

"May I ask why you came to my office for assistance?"

Kiriko Yanagida answered without hesitation, "Because I heard that you are one of the best lawyers in Japan."

"There are bound to be some first-rate lawyers in Kyushu, too." Otsuka took out a new cigarette and inserted it between his lips. "I don't think you needed to come all the way to Tokyo."

Being young, she almost spat the words out: "I just thought that if it's not you, then I can't do anything to save my brother." She stared with intense eyes at Kinzo Otsuka's face.

"Really? Is it such a difficult case?"

"My brother is the suspect in a robbery and murder case. It was a sixty-five-year-old lady that was killed. When my brother was arrested, he confessed everything to the police…"

"Your brother confessed?"

"Yes. He did when he was with the police. But, later, when he saw the public prosecutor, he changed his mind. Of course, I believe he is innocent. I think what he said afterwards is the truth, but the lawyer over there said that, because of some technicality, it'd be very difficult to prove his innocence. But I wasn't convinced, and when I asked around and found out about you, I came straight here to see you."

"How *did* you come by my name?"

"I heard it from someone connected with the court in Kyushu. I heard that, from time to time, you come to the aid of falsely accused defendants. And that's why I came here to see you."

Otsuka started to become anxious about the time again. "Well, that was a long time ago. Nowadays lawyers everywhere are excellent, the technical level has risen enormously. Tokyo or the provinces, there really isn't much difference."

"But won't you just listen to what I have to say?"

For the first time, Kiriko had a look of desperation in her eye.

Otsuka had the distinct feeling that once he listened to her story, he'd be unable to resist taking her on. He was also becoming more and more irritated at the thought of Michiko laughing and joking with some other man on the golf course.

"My fees are relatively expensive. The clerk explained the standard charges, did he?"

"Yes," she nodded. "I've already asked the clerk, but would it be at all possible to have a discount on your legal fees? I don't have much money to spare. My salary is quite low. What little money I have is really what I've managed to save from my bonus."

"It would surely be better not to put yourself through this," Otsuka advised. "I simply can't become involved. It's a little odd saying this about myself but, well, to tell the truth, when you get to my level, the legal fees far exceed those of a younger lawyer. The litigation costs—be it travelling expenses, my daily rate, or the costs of the investigation—certainly don't come cheap. All of that's separate and in addition to the legal fees. I appreciate you've gone to a lot of trouble, but I think it better if I don't listen to your story."

"You mean, I can't persuade you to take on my case?"

Otsuka was starting to feel a little oppressed. "I simply don't think it necessary to request the assistance of a lawyer whose fees are so expensive. To be honest, with us, you are paying partly for the name. In terms of actual talent, we are no different from other lawyers. I believe there are excellent lawyers outside of Tokyo, too."

"But I came from Kyushu especially to see you."

"I think that was a mistake. It is incorrect to think that the lawyers in Tokyo are the best."

"You're turning me down because I can't afford to pay the legal fees. That's right, isn't it?"

It was a forthright question for such a young woman to ask and, as Okumura had said, she certainly seemed to be sure in her own convictions.

"There may be an element of truth in that," replied Otsuka, deciding it best to give her an honest, straightforward answer. "In any case, I'm extremely busy with a full case load at the moment and I can't just take off on a business trip to the provinces. I would have to carry out detailed research and be available to attend court right from the outset. Needless to say, that is the representative lawyer's duty. Unfortunately, I don't have the time. Of course the money aspect is there, but first and foremost I simply don't have the time to spare."

Kiriko lowered her gaze and thought for a while. She sat stock still without so much as moving a muscle. Although her figure appeared soft, her posture seemed to Otsuka as if it were fashioned from steel.

"I see," she said. She lowered her head and made as if to get up from her chair. "There's nothing for it, I suppose." She stood and bowed. "I'm very sorry to have troubled you."

Otsuka felt a little flustered, and although it was a meaningless gesture, he walked her to the exit.

Kiriko paused by the door and muttered, "I don't know whether my brother will get the death penalty." Then she turned, and without looking back, her white form disappeared down the dark stairs. Her drooping shoulders stayed in Otsuka's mind's eye long after she had gone.

The clerk, Okumura, came out and stood next to him, but the only sound that reached their ears was the hard one of Kiriko's shoes descending the stairs below.

Chapter 2

Kiriko woke up at seven. She had slept fitfully, her night filled with dreams. Fragmented, confused and dark dreams. She seemed to recall tossing and turning all night long.

Her head throbbed. Her eyelids felt heavy with the lack of sleep and her eyes were stinging.

She got up, and when she pulled the curtains back sunlight flooded in from the window. It was a glittering, vibrant shaft of light.

She didn't feel like having a wash straight away and instead sat for a while in the rattan chair. She would have to go back to work the day after next. If she didn't take this evening's train she wouldn't make it back in time. Two nights ago, when she had arrived in Tokyo, she knew she'd have to board tonight's train, but now she felt heavy-hearted.

The slight warmth of the sunlight on one side of her face began to irritate her and she stood up. Taking off the gown provided by the inn, she changed into her suit. She started to become restless cooped up in the hotel room and decided a walk outside in the fresh air would do her eyes good.

As she went out into the corridor she bumped into the maid who was coming in with the breakfast tray.

"Oh!" The maid narrowed her eyes and smiled over the top of the tray. It was the same elderly lady from before. "Good morning. Are you on your way out?"

"Yes, I'm just popping out." Kiriko bowed her head slightly.

"I dare say I will see you later then. I will prepare your meal for when you get back," said the maid, kneeling down to open the sliding door of the next room.

Kiriko borrowed some wooden sandals from the inn and went outside. It was still early and there weren't many people about.

The road sloped away, paved with flagstones. A short, blackened cigarette butt lay twisted and broken in the mud. The crushed, mud-covered shape made Kiriko think of her brother's situation.

The leaves gave off a fresh luster, as if wet. The sunlight had only reached the tops of the houses, and very few shops were open. The steep slope eventually levelled out and led to the station. The only people doing any business were the old ladies selling newspapers and weekly magazines; the other stores all still had their shutters down.

Nobody came out of the station, but the entrance was thronged with businessmen, walking purposefully toward the ticket gates. Newspapers were being sold, but Kiriko wasn't minded to buy one.

From the bridge, the station platform that ran along the edge of the river below appeared long and narrow.

Kiriko had a bird's eye view of the trains and the passengers, who were moving around busily like insects.

The morning tranquility was sustained only by the surrounding scenery. A temple roof rose above the others, verdigris coating the edges of the ridge tiles.

She gazed around. It was like being in a dream. She was devoid of all real feeling. The whole of Tokyo was a pallid gray color, like a paper model.

There were a lot more people out and about on her return, but their faces all looked the same.

"Welcome back."

The maid came in with her breakfast. The menu was the same as the day before. Looking at the tray, Kiriko felt as though the day was simply a continuation of the one before. The uncomfortable time she had spent meeting with the lawyer Otsuka seemed but a strange and fleeting interlude.

"Your eyes look a little red, my dear," said the maid, looking up as Kiriko tucked in with her chopsticks.

"Yes?"

"Didn't you sleep very well?"

"I slept quite well, thank you."

She didn't have much of an appetite and had only a mouthful of her *miso* soup.

"What's this? Aren't you hungry?" asked the maid, a look of concern on her face.

"Not very."

"I see. But you should eat some more, a young woman like yourself."

"This is enough," said Kiriko, taking a sip of tea.

"As I thought. It's your first time in Tokyo. I expected you to be tired," said the maid, looking hard at Kiriko's face. "Did you go sightseeing? I wasn't working last night and didn't have a chance to ask you."

"I didn't go anywhere." Kiriko put her teacup down. "Thank you, that was nice."

The maid looked at her askance. This young woman had cut short the conversation once again. Something unyielding in her young eyes made that perfectly clear and checked the elderly maid from pressing the matter further.

"It wasn't much," the maid said, sliding the tray toward herself. As she moved the plates to one side, she said, almost as a parting shot, "You did come all this way to Tokyo. It would be a waste."

"A waste..." muttered Kiriko, once the maid had gone.

Going out in the fresh air and looking down at the trains did not dispel her feeling of unease, which seemed to be encapsulated in that one final word uttered by the maid. She tried to suppress it, but it wouldn't be suppressed, instead resonating in her heart like a distant echo.

She had often been described as headstrong by her brother—her brother, who now stood accused in an unsolved murder case.

When she was little, she'd gotten into a fight with a boy and made him cry.

Even now that she was working at a firm, she refused to ingratiate herself with her boss and the male employees the way the other office girls did. Men who asked once and were refused did not ask her again. Although Kiriko did not consider her behavior out of the ordinary, she'd developed a reputation for being strong-minded.

Having had her request turned down by Kinzo Otsuka the day before, she was now determined to take the noon express train and return to Kyushu; she'd even bought her ticket.

That was the way she always did things.

But the maid's words came back to her, and suddenly her eyes opened to what she was doing. *You did come all this way to Tokyo...*

Of course, it was nothing to do with sightseeing. But then, why had she travelled all the way from Kyushu to see Otsuka?

A strange kind of courage came to her. She'd never been so consumed by the desire to rely on anybody. It even seemed to give color to her bland surroundings.

Kiriko left the inn. It wouldn't do to use its phone. She couldn't be sure the switchboard operator by the front desk wouldn't listen in on the conversation. The operator in Kiriko's company knew many secrets about the employees there.

It was 10:30. Perhaps Otsuka was already in his office.

The morning sidewalk was flooded with pedestrians. The multitude of shops and businesses that had had their shutters pulled securely down were now doing a brisk trade.

A public phone caught her eye, but when she came closer she noticed that there was someone inside. It was a middle-aged man, and he was clutching the receiver and laughing and jabbering incessantly.

The conversation droned on. The man stood there on legs that seemed too tired to support him. Just when the conversation showed signs of coming to an end, it continued again.

At last the door opened and, without so much as glancing in Kiriko's direction, the man walked away.

She took up the receiver, and the mouthpiece was still warm with condensation. She took out her notebook and dialed the number of Kinzo Otsuka's office.

A man with a hoarse voice answered the phone.

"Hello, could I speak to Mr. Otsuka please?"

"May I have your name?" came the reply.

"Kiriko Yanagida. I came by yesterday…" she said in a soft voice.

The man appeared to be thinking. "Ah, the lady from Kyushu?"

Kiriko recalled the face of the diminutive desk clerk. Mr. Okumura. Yes, that was his name. "That's right. I would like to see the *sensei* once more."

"Is this concerning the matter we discussed yesterday?" asked Okumura after a slight pause.

"Yes, it is."

"But you should have received a reply yesterday."

"I did, but…" Kiriko felt that Okumura was standing in her way. "I can't accept his reply. I came all the way from

Kyushu especially to ask for his help. I'd like to see him once more. Please would you ask him when would be convenient to meet."

"*Sensei* is away from the office right now," came the reply. "I don't know whether he'll be in today."

Kiriko felt her legs stiffen. "I need to see him today. If I miss this evening's train I'll be in trouble at work tomorrow. Please would you tell me where *sensei* is?" she said, fully intending to call on him unannounced once she knew his whereabouts.

"Kawana," replied Okumura.

Kiriko didn't know the place.

Okumura sensed as much from the silence that followed, and said, "It's quite far away. It's not in Tokyo. It's near Izu, in Shizuoka Prefecture."

Kiriko waited six hours. She whiled away the time wandering up and down the streets of Tokyo. It was an absurdly tedious and irritating waste of her time. In the Ginza, there was nothing but irksome people and buildings. On the other hand, it was more or less as she imagined it would be. Nothing aroused her interest. She felt completely detached from all the people walking around her. Everybody looked as though they led well-to-do lives. The women smiled and laughed as if without a care in the world. In fact, judging from their expressions and their clothes, she was sure that if they became involved in a case, they could raise eight hundred thousand yen in legal fees without much hardship.

She also wandered around an open area laid out with fresh green lawns. Pine trees with gracefully shaped branches grew all around. In one direction was a row of buildings that looked as though they'd come straight out of an old photograph, while in the other stood a quaint old castle.

Cars flowed continuously like the fast moving current of a river. Flag-toting groups of sightseers formed lines and made their way towards the Imperial Palace.

I probably won't be able to remain with the company much longer, thought Kiriko, gazing absent-mindedly at the dull scenery.

The case had paralysed the small city with fear.

One day the police showed up and took her brother away. The way they'd come to arrest him—so casual, like friends coming to invite him out. But her life with her brother ended that day, and Kiriko's world was turned on its head. People round about were suddenly cold towards her.

At last it was half past four. Her body ached with fatigue, but also her spirits were down. Nonetheless, she walked towards town. She passed a tobacconist and noticed a red public phone in the storefront. Its lurid color seemed to revitalize her. As she advanced towards the phone a man came from the side and almost bumped into her.

"After you," offered the man, moving his tall body to one side and indicating that she should go first.

Kiriko apologized meekly and inserted a ten-yen coin. "Is this Mr. Otsuka's law offices?"

"Yes," came Okumura's hoarse reply.

"It's Yanagida." Kiriko had her back turned towards the waiting man. "Have you heard further from the *sensei*?"

Okumura had told her to call again at four-thirty when they spoke by phone the same morning.

"Yes, he called in," replied Okumura rather flatly.

"And what was his reply?" Kiriko's heart began to beat quickly.

"The same, I'm afraid. He said to tell you that you already have his answer," said the clerk in a monotone. "As Mr. Otsuka stated yesterday, he is unable to take your case."

The strength went from Kiriko's clenched fist. At the same moment, she felt a burning sensation race through her body. "So, because I haven't enough money, he won't take my case. That's it?"

"I should imagine the reasons were explained to you yesterday."

"A human being is suffering for a crime he didn't commit and may well be given the death penalty. Are you telling me that because I don't have any money, Mr. Otsuka won't help me?"

Okumura fell momentarily silent, probably on account of Kiriko's unusually sharp tone.

"Well," began Okumura, "it is up to Mr. Otsuka. I don't know why he decided the way he did. There's no point complaining to me."

"Look, I am poor. You are right, I can't pay the legal fees you told me about. But I came all the way from Kyushu for this. I believed Mr. Otsuka would help me and so I took four days' vacation from work and used what little money I have for train fare."

"So you keep saying, but I don't know what we can do about it. Please understand our position. There must be able lawyers in Kyushu, too. And in any case, ours are busy with a very heavy work load at the moment."

"Is it really impossible?"

"I'm afraid there is nothing we can do to help you," Okumura said as if he was about to hang up.

"Hello, hello!" said Kiriko in a surprisingly loud voice. "I heard that there are lawyers who believe in a righteous cause who will represent someone without making an issue out of legal fees. I heard that Mr. Otsuka was one such lawyer. Isn't there any way he can help me?"

"It's unfair to put us under moral pressure like that," replied Okumura calmly. "It is a decision which we must be allowed to make freely. And in any case, you were singularly unprepared when you requested Mr. Otsuka's assistance. Coming here without knowing our fees are considerably higher than elsewhere. Moreover, we are all very busy at the moment."

"I understand," said Kiriko. "I have to return to Kyushu on this evening's train. If I'm late by even one day, I really don't know what will happen. Even without this, my company hasn't been keen to retain me since they found out about the incident. If I lived in Tokyo, I'd keep on asking Mr. Otsuka for his help. But now I can't even do that. You told me to call back at four-thirty, and that was my last hope."

Okumura remained silent. From behind her came the noise of feet shifting restlessly. The man who was waiting for the phone seemed to be growing impatient with the long call. His pale cigarette smoke drifted past the side of Kiriko's face.

"Then please tell Mr. Otsuka," she said. "I don't know whether anyone can save my brother. If I had eight hundred thousand yen, perhaps he could be saved, but unfortunately I just don't have that kind of money. What I have come to realize is that there is no hope for poor people looking for help. Thank you. I am sorry to have troubled you. I won't request your help again."

There was no response. Kiriko replaced the silent receiver. The click as the line went dead seemed to signal in her heart the end of everything that could be done.

She turned away. The scenery was devoid of meaning. Everything seemed pallid and straw-colored, as if it had no color in fact. It was flat, two-dimensional, completely lacking in perspective. Her throat was parched. But she didn't feel like going into a shop to buy a drink. All she could think about was the journey back to Kyushu on the night train. She walked along parallel to the railway line, and the pedestrians coming from the opposite direction were bothersome. She felt an urge to go quickly to the countryside where there weren't so many people.

Suddenly there was a voice from behind. At first Kiriko didn't realize it was directed at her.

"Excuse me?" came the voice again, this time from the side.

Kiriko turned and looked. A young man in his mid-twenties stood there smiling and bowing. She realized it was the man who had allowed her to use the phone first a little while back. He had a shock of unkempt hair and wore a dishevelled-looking jacket. His necktie was twisted and his trousers had lost their crease and billowed about his legs. In short, he seemed to have an extremely casual dress sense.

"I'd just like a quick word with you." A smile came to the man's lips as he gazed at Kiriko with a reserved look in his eye.

"What about?" asked Kiriko, suddenly on her guard.

"It's awfully rude of me but, well, I overheard your conversation when you called that lawyer. Actually, it wasn't so much that I was listening. I could hear everything you were saying…"

The man took out a notebook from his breast pocket and handed her his business card. "Don't worry, I'm not a weirdo. This is me."

Kiriko took the card and looked at it. "Keiichi Abe, Editorial Department, *Comment*." She looked up and peered at the young man's face.

While waiting to use the phone, Keiichi Abe had been listening to the young woman's conversation. In his experience, women generally made lengthy phone calls, gossiping and laughing about trivialities. Thinking this call would be no different, Abe was beginning to regret letting her go first, but as the conversation continued he soon realized nothing could have been further from the truth.

It seemed that the person she had called was a lawyer named Otsuka but that he was out, and that she was speaking with someone taking his calls.

She said she had come to Tokyo from Kyushu especially to request this lawyer's assistance. It appeared she'd been turned down once before but was trying again to persuade the lawyer to change his mind. The woman's voice had become increasingly loud: her brother might be sentenced to death for a crime he did not commit; the lawyer would not take her case because she had no money; poor people could not rely on the law.

Abe had begun to listen in earnest mid-way through the conversation. Although he had a matter to see to, he left off making his call and followed the girl once she had finished her conversation.

Following on from behind, he could tell from the way she walked just how downhearted she was. But, for some reason or another, she was in an awful hurry. She faced front all the way, not once glancing to the side, her slender shoulders hunched forward. He didn't think he was imagining this based on what he'd gleaned from the phone conversation.

Although it was perfectly natural, when he called to her she looked at him with a puzzled look on her face. When he gave her his business card—perhaps she'd never heard of the magazine or its publisher—there was no reaction in her eyes. She looked exhausted.

He invited her to a coffee shop, but she didn't agree very readily. Bowing repeatedly, he finally persuaded her to join him in a smart little café nearby.

She ordered fruit juice and downed it in one gulp.

Wanting her to be at ease, he even refrained from smoking.

She sat there with her eyes cast down slightly and her mouth tightly shut as if she was chewing on her lip. Her nose looked slender and elegant.

"So you're here from Kyushu?" asked Abe, trying to keep the conversation as easygoing as possible.

"Yes," replied the young woman, her shoulders suddenly becoming tense.

"I hope you don't think I'm being too forward, but it seemed to me from the phone conversation that your older brother is in some sort of trouble?"

The woman nodded slightly without answering. She had something of the young girl in her face, with its soft lines curving round from her cheeks to her chin.

"What kind of case is it? Perhaps you could explain it to me, if it's no trouble, that is."

She looked up. Abe thought he saw a slight glint in her eye and, flustered, he was quick to add, "Ah, please don't worry—I'm not trying to turn this into an article or anything like that. I was touched by what you were saying on the phone, that's all."

The woman lowered her eyes again. Her eyelashes were neatly groomed, and her complexion was pale, almost translucent, and this, together with the soft lines of her face, seemed to accentuate her youthful looks.

"It seems you need a lot of money to involve a lawyer in a case like this. Isn't that right, for a top-class lawyer? As you said, poor people can't afford to place any trust in the courts these days. There are lawyers who will work without remuneration, but at the end of the day, that's up to the lawyer concerned. They're not all the same. If they're not inclined to do it then of course they'll turn you down." Abe paused, and then asked, "I also thought I heard you say 'Otsuka.' Would that be Kinzo Otsuka by any chance?"

The young woman remained silent. He wasn't sure whether she had nodded her confirmation. But deep down Abe knew it had to be.

"If it's Kinzo Otsuka, he's one of the best attorneys in Japan. In other words, he's very expensive. You asked him about his fees?"

There was no answer. The young woman chewed on her lip. A blue vein bulged slightly on her forehead. Abe was a little embarrassed and decided to try a different line of questioning. "Are you planning on staying in Tokyo very long?"

"No," she answered, this time without hesitation. "I'm returning home on this evening's train."

Abe was somewhat taken aback. "That's a little sudden, isn't it? Whereabouts in Kyushu are you from?"

"K-City," she replied quickly.

"And so you've given up all hope of persuading Kinzo Otsuka to help you?"

"I work, so I can't stay in Tokyo forever."

Abe thought it a shrewd answer. There was no prospect of help, and so she had decided to return home. "And what about the case?" he asked. "Won't you talk to me about it? Who knows, perhaps I can be of some assistance."

"I can't do that," she now flatly refused, and made as if to leave her seat.

"Would you tell me your name?" Abe prodded.

But the young woman stood up and bowing politely said, "Excuse me."

Abe stared in astonishment. He was speechless and felt as though he'd been dealt a stinging slap across the face. He quickly settled the bill and exited the shop. The young woman's shoulders seemed even narrower in the congested street, but something about her posture warned Abe, in no uncertain terms, against pursuing her.

Abe went back to his office and asked one of his colleagues who was well acquainted with the newspaper industry, "Hey, what's the leading paper in K-City, Kyushu?"

"That would be the *N News*," he replied.

"Do you know where I can get hold of a copy?"

"They have a branch office in Tokyo. If you take a trip over there they will probably show you. What is it you're looking for?"

"Oh, just something I need to look into." Abe replied in a vague sort of way and left.

He went straight over to the *N News* branch office and having given them his business card managed to have them show him their stock of archives.

"When are we talking about here?"

"Mmm," said Abe, scratching his head, "I don't really know for sure. It was a major case that happened in K-City."

"Give me the details."

"I don't really know those, either. I'll probably know it when I see it."

"In that case, I'll show you the bound back copies for last year and this year. If you'd like to follow me."

The newspaper employee was considerate and guided him over to a large stack of shelves that formed one wall of the room and started handing down bundles of bound, dust-covered newspapers. "Here we are. You can take your time and look at them here."

"Thank you. That's very kind."

The newspapers were bound by linen thread in monthly volumes on the cover of which, stamped in red ink, were the months January, February, etc.

In the dimly lit and dusty room facing the crowded buildings beyond the window, Abe furiously turned the pages of the newspaper bundles.

Chapter 3

Abe began by looking through this year's file of newspapers. Being a Kyushu publication there were, of course, many articles of local interest.

Obstructed by the building next door, the sunlight from the windows was rather dull.

Abe turned the pages, beginning with January, but the volume had nothing of any note. He cast his eye over the smallest of articles in the society section, but nothing matched what he was looking for.

He moved his attention to the February volume. There were a fair number of personal injury cases, but none gave him that certain feeling that he was on the right track.

The March bundle looked as though it would be the same. The newssheets were notably uneventful. They were full of reports about the splendor of the cherry blossoms in Dazai and carried large photographs to prove as much.

It was while he was about halfway through it, diligently reading the miscellaneous news items, that there suddenly appeared before him a headline in large eye-catching print.

"Aged Female Moneylender Clubbed to Death in K-City."

This is it, thought Abe, holding his breath. Suddenly the face of the young woman calling from the red phone came to mind—the woman who, shortly after the call, had stubbornly refused to answer his questions in the coffee shop.

A large photograph accompanied the article. It was of an ordinary dwelling house, but in front there was a crowd of people trying to peer inside. The police had cordoned off the entrance. To the right of the article was an oval photograph showing the old woman's face. It looked as though it had been taken by an amateur and was blurred, but the woman was clearly smiling. Her hair was sparse and she was quite thin.

Abe began devouring the text.

"At a little after 8:00 am on March 20, Tokie Watanabe (aged 30), wife of company employee Ryutaro Watanabe (aged 35), paid a visit to her mother-in-law Kiku Watanabe's (aged 65) residence in the township of XX, K-City. Tokie thought it suspicious that while the rain shutters were down, the front door was unlocked with only the paper sliding door shut. On entering the house, she discovered Kiku lying in the eight-mat *tatami* room on the ground floor, apparently dead, with blood coming from a wound on her head. She telephoned the police immediately.

"A number of police officers, including Station Chief Otsubo and Criminal Investigation Section Chief Ueda, were dispatched to the scene of the crime from K police headquarters. According to their investigation, Kiku had died having collapsed facing south in front of her chest of drawers positioned on the westerly wall of the house. She was covered in blood, having been repeatedly struck about the head with a blunt instrument.

"According to the preliminary investigation prior to autopsy, it was estimated that approximately eight or nine hours had passed since the time of death. Accordingly, the crime is likely to have been carried out between the hours of 11:00 pm and midnight on the previous day. From the position of the body, it would appear that Kiku had put up considerable resistance. Off to one side, an iron teakettle had tipped on its side in a brazier, spilling hot water and blowing ash onto the *tatami* mats. Kiku had not yet changed for bed and was wearing ordinary clothes at the time of the attack. Since she was known to be in the habit of retiring for bed relatively early, it is also possible that the crime was committed earlier than estimated. Furthermore, placed next to the brazier were two teacups, a teapot and container of tea, so it appears she was expecting a visitor.

"Kiku had lived in the house for the past thirty years. However, since her husband passed away fifteen years ago, she had been carrying on a money-lending business and living off the interest. She had been living entirely alone since her only son Ryutaro and his wife moved out five years earlier.

"Accordingly, officials leading the investigation are flummoxed that they cannot compile a list of missing valuables and cash if this was a robbery. There were signs at the scene of the crime that the criminal had been searching for something, as one of the drawers in the chest of drawers was left partly open with its contents disturbed.

"Although the murder weapon has not yet been found, the theory that this was a grudge killing is persuasive. Kiku was known to lend money to all and sundry at high rates of interest and was relentless in reminding her debtors to repay their loans. Chance meetings on the street would often bring forth a tirade of abuse. The crime is therefore being viewed as possibly a work of retribution by some aggrieved borrower. Furthermore, the authorities are continuing their investigation to see whether anyone suspicious was seen in the neighborhood of the Watanabe household at that time.

"XX Town is a quiet residential area located away from shopping centers and the more lively parts of town. It still retains a number of old samurai houses from its castle town days. Most of the residents retire early for bed, and there are no reports of anyone having heard screams or other noises in the vicinity of the Watanabe household.

"On the night in question, since Kiku had not changed for bed but instead kept a kettle on the brazier and prepared utensils for making tea, it would appear that she was expecting a guest and the identity of the guest is currently under investigation."

Tokie's statement was also included: "I went to see my mother-in-law on the twentieth of March to seek her advice about paying my respects during the equinox visit to the family grave. I thought it strange that although my mother-in-law was in the strict habit of locking the front door, on this occasion it was unlocked, with only the interior sliding paper door pulled shut. My mother-in-law was very strict about locking up on account of her business.

"I was so shocked when, upon entering the house, I found my mother-in-law lying in front of her chest of drawers, dead, in a pool of blood. Right now it's difficult to say without a thorough check whether or not anything was taken.

"My mother-in-law was a strong-willed woman with a sharp tongue who was in the habit of personally haranguing borrowers to repay their debts. I think somebody probably held a grudge against her.

"My husband is an only son, but he used to hate the way his mother did business and so we moved out and live by ourselves now. That said, she also had a more generous side to her and would on occasion take account of particular circumstances and lend large sums of money to unsecured borrowers."

The first newspaper article came to an end here. Abe read it through a second time and made a note of the important points. Then he turned to the next article.

It was a three-column article headed "Weapon Was Oak Rod; Murder of Old Moneylender in K-City."

"According to the criminal investigation section of K Police Station, who are looking into the murder of an elderly female moneylender, a rod made of oak, thought to have been used by the assailant, has been discovered in a ditch on waste ground beside a local temple two days after the incident occurred. The police confirmed that it was found in a water-filled ditch approximately 60 centimeters in width close to the temple fence on the east side of a weed-infested plot of some 500 square meters in an area located two blocks north of the Watanabe household.

"The police had carried out a thorough search of the area for the weapon when they turned their attention to the ditch. They dredged the bottom of the dirty water and found an oak rod measuring approximately 70 centimeters in length.

"The tip of the club was still coated with blackish blood. The victim's son Ryutaro (aged 35) testified that it was the stick his mother used as a precaution when closing up the front door at the end of the day. The criminal investigation department said they were greatly encouraged by the discovery of this physical evidence. Section Chief Ueda confirmed that this was undoubtedly the murder weapon. At present, the police are working to analyse the fingerprints, which may be difficult to detect as a result of immersion in dirty water. It is also thought that the blood on the end of the club matches that of the victim's blood type."

The next article read "Oak Rod Confirmed as Murder Weapon."

"Following analysis of the blood on the end of the oak rod found on the twenty-first in a ditch on waste ground by a temple two blocks away from the victim's house, it has been confirmed that the blood type is 'O,' matching that of the victim Kiku Watanabe. With regard to the fingerprints, having soaked in dirty water, they were only indistinct and accordingly not adequate for the purposes of identification. With regard to the loss suffered by Kiku Watanabe, her son and his wife confirmed that, following their own investigation, nothing at all had been stolen, and the theory that this was a grudge killing has gained weight. Furthermore, since Kiku was not known to have any relationships with men, the possibility that it was a crime of passion has been discredited.

"The police investigation section is said to be confident that it will arrest the perpetrator at an early stage in their investigation.

"According to Section Chief Ueda, the investigation is pursuing the grudge-killing line.

"Although a search carried out by the son and his wife revealed that nothing had been taken, clear fingerprints, thought to be those left by the criminal, were found on the chest of drawers. In addition, certain persuasive facts have come to light, which at this stage of the investigation are not being disclosed. The arrest of the murderer appears only a matter of time."

Abe quickly turned to the next page. Large print leapt out of the page at him: "Killer Is Elementary Schoolteacher; Pressured to Repay Loan, He Struck."

This was a four-column top story. Before reading the article, a photograph caught his eye. It was of a young man in his late twenties wearing a suit. The face resembled the one he remembered of Kiriko Yanagida.

Abe regained his composure and raised his eyes from the newspaper, and faced toward the building outside to his front. In the window he could see three office girls talking and laughing together. A male employee from the newspaper's research bureau passed behind Abe and looked at him curiously.

Abe bent over his newspaper once again. His concentration grew more intense.

"On the 22nd, the K Police criminal investigation section which has been carrying out a thorough investigation of the murder of an old woman moneylender finally arrested the perpetrator of the crime.

"Unexpectedly, the criminal has been identified as Masao Yanagida (aged 28), an elementary schoolteacher from the same city. The revelation has come as a considerable shock to local residents.

"The criminal investigation HQ believed that the crime was committed by someone harboring a grudge due to the harsh methods the victim used in collecting her high interest loans and accordingly concentrated all their efforts in that direction.

"When the victim's son and daughter-in-law checked around Kiku's body, they came across a notebook that they remembered contained the details of her debtors. When they compared it with the bundle of promissory notes kept in the cabinet of Kiku's chest of drawers, they found that one of the receipts was missing.

"The missing receipt related to a loan of forty thousand yen taken out on October 8 last year in the name of Masao Yanagida, a teacher at the XX Elementary School in the town of XX. According to Kiku's notebook, the deadline for repayment had been the end of the year, but Yanagida had made no more than two payments on his monthly interest of ten percent. At that stage, the criminal investigation section had made discreet inquiries about Masao Yanagida. They ascertained that he rented a second floor apartment in XX Town where he lived together with his sister, Kiriko (aged 20), a local company typist. He was a determined man who, not having parents to support him, came by his present job after working his way through college.

"Lately he had experienced money problems, and his worries didn't go unnoticed by his colleagues at work. There were also those who testified to the harsh reminders for settlement issued by Kiku. It seems Kiku had visited the Yanagida household on several occasions in order to encourage payment and, finally, had waited by the roadside and railed at him while he was on his way to the school. As a consequence, Yanagida had recently begun suffering from a slight nervous complaint.

"The criminal investigation section ordered Yanagida to attend an interview for questioning, at which point, it was noted, he turned a deathly pale color and began to shake with fear. During the conversation, the police secretly took his fingerprints. On finding that they were a perfect match with the prints left on the chest of drawers, the criminal investigation section concluded that Yanagida was the perpetrator of the crime, promptly issued an arrest warrant and detained him.

"During questioning, Yanagida denied carrying out the crime.

"According to Criminal Investigation Section Chief Ueda, Yanagida is without doubt the perpetrator. Not only do the fingerprints match, but he has no alibi. In addition, there is sufficient motive for the murder: having been pressed for payment and, on one occasion, abused to his face, he bore a grudge, and so went to Kiku's house. Using the rod she kept for protection, he clubbed her violently over the head and murdered her.

"Perhaps thinking that suspicion would fall on him if the promissory note were ever found, it is thought he searched it out from the chest he recalled seeing from his previous visit to the house and took it with him when he made his getaway, stopping only to discard the murder weapon in the ditch on the waste ground.

"Although the accused denies committing the crime, this is often the case, and it is thought he is close to making a confession.

"The principal of XX Elementary School stated: 'I was extremely shocked to hear that Yanagida was responsible for the murder of the old woman. He was a conscientious teacher and popular with the students. I have no idea why, or for what purpose, he borrowed forty thousand yen. I'm finding it all hard to believe, but we are considering a response. If he confesses to the crime, I would like to assume some of the responsibility for what has happened.'

"An eyewitness stated, 'On two occasions I saw Kiku, the murdered woman, accost Yanagida on the roadside. She harangued him mercilessly, and he apologized repeatedly with a troubled look on his face.'

"The accused's younger sister, Kiriko (aged 20), had this to say: 'I'll never believe that my brother committed such a monstrous outrage. I knew that Mrs. Watanabe had visited our house but, because I was there, my brother took her outside to talk. I didn't know the conversation was about repaying money. I had absolutely no idea that my brother had borrowed such a large amount. But, even if it's true that he was having difficulty repaying the loan, I do not believe for one moment he is the murderer.'"

While Abe was reading this, it seemed almost as if Kiriko's face was floating up from between the type print. With her shoulders tense and biting her lip, her eyes staring fixedly at one point off in the distance. A stubborn expression, and yet the line of her jaw youthful, fair. Then there was that view of her from behind as she walked defiantly through the crowd, her gaze fixed ahead of her.

The sun began to sink and the room became unusually dark. Abe took up his notebook and began turning the news pages once again.

"Yanagida Partial Confession; Murder of Old Woman."

"Former elementary schoolteacher Masao Yanagida (aged 28), currently under investigation by Criminal Investigation Section Chief Ueda at K Police Station, finally made a partial confession on the evening of the 27th to the crime he had been persistently denying. According to his confession, at the beginning of September last year, he had dropped and lost a deposit of thirty-eight thousand yen for a school excursion while taking it home for safekeeping. At a loss as to how he was going to repay the money, he made a number of visits to the house of Kiku Watanabe who he had heard was in the business of lending money at high rates of interest. Eventually he was successful in borrowing forty thousand yen on condition that it was repaid by the end of the year. However, subsisting on a low wage and with interest accruing at ten percent a month, he was never in a position to make repayments of the principal or the interest.

"After the deadline passed, beginning about February this year, Kiku made increasingly forthright demands for repayment and went as far as calling at Yanagida's apartment and lying in wait to accost him on his way to school.

"So pressed and in order to placate her for the time being, Yanagida promised that on the night of March 19 he would bring two months' interest to Mrs. Watanabe's residence and hand her the sum. This finally explains why Kiku Watanabe who normally retired early to bed had not changed into her nightclothes but instead prepared a pot of tea and appeared to be waiting up for someone.

"When Masao Yanagida called on Watanabe's home at about 11:00 pm on the 19th, he found that only the sliding paper screen had been pulled across the front door and that it opened without difficulty. Having called out to her and had no reply, he opened the screen and saw that she was lying on the floor, apparently already murdered.

"Yanagida was horrified and thought about contacting the police immediately, but it occurred to him that so long as the promissory note remained in the house, he would be pursued for the debt forever and that his public standing as a teacher would be damaged. He would sooner free himself of such anxieties and, knowing that Mrs. Watanabe kept the receipts in her chest of drawers, he made up his mind to take them and make good his escape.

"Yanagida claims that his fingerprints were left there when he stood in front of the chest of drawers which were to the side of where Kiku lay dead, searching through the bag of receipts.

"Having successfully located the promissory note corresponding to the loan taken out in his name, he took off with it in his possession. The following day he applied a match and incinerated the note. This much he admits, but he persistently denies that he was responsible for the murder of the victim Kiku Watanabe.

"The Criminal Investigation Section, however, maintains that Yanagida is the real killer, and they see his confession as being a partial confession made out of desperation at having been confronted with such irrefutable physical evidence as the fingerprints on the chest of drawers, and the fact that specks of blood on the cuffs of trousers confiscated from the suspect's residence and worn by the suspect on the 19th match the victim's blood group, as well as the fact that the ash on his trousers is identical to that spilled at the scene of the crime. Accordingly, it is considered purely a matter of time before the suspect makes a full confession to the killing of Kiku.

"Section Chief Ueda states that 'Yanagida has reluctantly acknowledged that he had the motive for and carried out part of the crime. This is a wholehearted attempt by the accused to avoid the serious crime of murder, and his story that Kiku was already dead when he arrived at her home is nothing other than a desperate attempt at extricating himself from liability. We are expecting him to make a full confession any moment now.'"

Abe turned over the next three or four issues. Again, bold headlines leapt from the page.

"Yanagida Confesses All; Old Woman Bludgeoned to Death."

"Masao Yanagida, the suspect in the murder of an elderly moneylender, finally gave in to police questioning on the 30th and confessed to the murder of Kiku Watanabe. Formerly he had admitted to the theft of a loan promissory note but consistently denied having any part in the killing. With this, the murder of the elderly moneylender that has gripped the Kita-Kyushu area has been solved eleven days after the incident took place. Masao Yanagida's confession is set out below."

Keiichi Abe turned his attention to the contents of the confession. His notepad and pencil were at the ready. The light coming in through the windows began increasingly to fail.

"According to Yanagida's confession, as a result of Kiku Watanabe's unremitting demands for repayment and the abuse she would hurl at him from the roadside as he would travel to school, he ended up harboring a deep grudge and murderous intentions. Having finally resolved to carry out the crime on March 19, he called Kiku the day before and promised to stop by the next evening at about 11:00 pm with the money.

"When Yanagida arrived at Kiku's residence at about 11:00 pm on the 19th, Kiku was waiting up for him. As Kiku busied herself preparing the tea while leaning over the charcoal brazier, Yanagida came from behind with the wooden club and bludgeoned her over the head. Although Kiku collapsed, being stout-hearted she fought back. At this point the iron kettle, which had stood on top of the charcoal brazier, was knocked to one side, spilling water and kicking up a cloud of ash. Yanagida continued his merciless onslaught with the club until Kiku breathed her last.

"Having made sure the job was done he went over to the chest of drawers and, taking his promissory note from the bundle of receipts, left from the front door with an air of composure. He discarded the club in a ditch by a vacant lot near a temple. He burned the promissory note the next morning close to his own apartment.

"Yanagida thought it best just to take his own promissory note, but his luck had run out, since Kiku had written the names of her debtors in a separate ledger. By comparing the remaining promissory notes with the entries in her ledger, the police were soon able to discover that Yanagida's promissory note was missing. This was the first step in the arrest of Yanagida by the criminal investigation department.

"Section Chief Ueda commented that, 'Although we did expect Yanagida to confess, we were relieved when at last he resigned to confess to everything. His confession matches perfectly our findings at the scene of the crime. The physical evidence alone—the fingerprints on the chest of drawers, the fact that the blood found on the turn-ups of his trousers,

trousers worn on the night in question, was the same "O" blood type as that of the victim, and the fact that also the ash on his trousers matched the ash from the brazier—all makes it very difficult for Yanagida to deny that he was the perpetrator of this crime.'"

Abe finished taking notes and leafed through the next dozen or so pages. As he did so, he came across a two-paragraph article, briefly written, in a corner towards the bottom of the page.

"Yanagida Retracts Confession before Prosecutor—'I Didn't Commit Any Murder.'"

"As previously reported, Masao Yanagida, the suspect in the K-City moneylender murder case, had been sent to the district prosecutor's office on April 5 and was questioned by Public Prosecutor Masuo Tsutsui. However, although Yanagida had already confessed to the crime at the K Police Station, when confronted with Public Prosecutor Tsutsui he suddenly retracted his confession saying that while it is true that he did enter the house and steal the promissory note for his 40,000-yen loan, he did not kill Kiku, and that she had in fact already been murdered when he got there. Yanagida appears to have reverted to his original story made before his full confession.

"Criminal Investigation Section Chief Ueda commented: 'I also anticipated that he would deny the murder charge when he met with the public prosecutor, and judging from his character it's no surprise at all. What I mean to say is that his intention was clear, right from the outset, that he wished only to somehow avoid the murder charge. This is why having once felt compelled to make a confession following the police interrogation he once again does his utmost to assert his innocence in the presence of the public prosecutor. According to the authorities investigating the crime, there was sufficient evidence to send him to the public prosecutor's office and, notwithstanding his retraction, we are confident that he is guilty of the offense.'

"The suspect's younger sister, Kiriko Yanagida, said: 'I am so pleased that, having initially admitted to the police the murder of Mrs. Kiku Watanabe, my brother has now informed the public prosecutor that this is not the case. I believe this is the truth. I believe my brother is innocent of this murder.'"

Abe once again found himself facing the young woman who stared intently at one point on the wall, her fingers laced together resolutely on top of her knees.

The sunlight, which had fallen across the newssheet, became weaker still. He read the last article and closed the heavy file.

"Yanagida Murder Trial—Not Guilty Plea Remains."

"Suspicion deepened around Masao Yanagida, previously questioned by Public Prosecutor Masuo Tsutsui in relation to the K-City moneylender murder. As the prime suspect in the case, he was indicted for murder on April 28."

This case appeared to have caused a real scandal in the area. The uproar was evident from the tone of the newspaper articles. A column had criticism from the area's so-called prominent figures that gave the impression that they already believed Yanagida to be guilty, stating that the fact that the suspect in such heinous a crime had come from the ranks of elementary school teachers was a clear sign of a general decline in morals. The principal of the elementary school where Yanagida taught resigned.

Abe left the research room of the *N News* branch office as the lights blinked on, and thanked the clerk as he left. The stairs in the building were dimly lit.

Outside, there was a hint of pale blue left in the sky, but the city had already transformed into a world of neon. Abe walked through the rush-hour crowds. He didn't feel like dealing with a train or taxi right away.

As he walked along he thought it highly likely that the only person who believed Masao Yanagida was innocent of murder was his sister, Kiriko. All he had seen was the newspaper reports, but it certainly looked as though Yanagida was the perp. Yanagida's retraction of his confession in the presence of the public prosecutor after having admitted his guilt to the police just sounded like an evasion. And then there was the physical evidence that appeared to be incontrovertible proof.

Kiriko had come to Tokyo and implored the attorney Kinzo Otsuka to represent her brother. Otsuka was the best, but he probably charged exorbitant legal fees. She was likely turned down because he assumed she couldn't afford to pay the fees.

The sound of Kiriko's voice as she gripped the red phone still lingered in Abe's ears. It was just something he overheard, quite by chance while waiting for the phone to become free. "A human being is suffering for a crime he didn't commit and may well be given the death penalty. Are you telling me that because I don't have the money, Mr. Otsuka won't help me?" She had leaned towards the telephone then and said, "I heard that there are lawyers who believe in a righteous cause who will represent someone without making an issue out of legal fees. I heard that Mr. Otsuka was one such lawyer. Isn't there any way he can help me?" And then her final desperate plea: "I don't know whether anyone can save my brother. If I had eight hundred thousand yen, perhaps he could be saved, but unfortunately I just don't have that kind of money. What I have come to realize is that there is no hope for poor people looking for help. Thank you. I am sorry to have troubled you. I won't request your help again."

While climbing the steps of Yurakucho station along with the throng Abe got it into his head to use this case for an article in his magazine. One might say it was just a sudden impulse. Or perhaps he instinctively believed what that determined young lady intuitively felt.

Around lunchtime the next day, Abe waited for an opportunity to talk with Tanimura, the editor in chief. Tanimura arrived for work just after 11:00 am. From the moment he sat at his desk he'd done nothing but read piles of letters. He would look at readers' letters with painstaking care, and since he read in excess of thirty letters each morning, this inevitably took some time. Letters that were of no use to him would be tossed into a large waste paper basket, while those items that looked useful for reference he would keep and jot down brief notes on them in red pencil. They would then be circulated to each sub-editor.

The editor in chief read his letters for a full thirty minutes before breaking off. He then made several consecutive phone calls. Since he was talking with contributors, the calls were all lengthy. He was on the phone a full forty minutes. Then he returned to the readers' correspondence, gradually reducing the bundle of unopened letters. He had immensely broad shoulders.

Keiichi Abe plucked up courage, stood up and walked over to the chief's desk.

"Excuse me, are you busy?"

Tanimura looked up with widened eyes, the light glinting off his spectacles. "What is it?" he asked in a thick, husky voice.

"I'd like to discuss a news report with you…"

"Oh really?" The chief dropped the letter he was reading onto the desk. "Let's hear it," he said, and picked up a cigarette from the top of the desk and eased back in his chair, signalling that he was ready to listen to Abe's story.

Abe took out his notepad from his pocket and explained the gist of the murder incident.

"Well, now." Tanimura folded his arms and cocked his head slightly to one side, the smouldering cigarette still between his fingertips. A faint smile came to his lips. "I wonder…" His bespectacled eyes regarded Abe's face with scepticism. "It's not the type of story that would fit with our magazine, you know." He rocked slightly. "It's more the sort of story a tabloid would carry."

Comment was an influential general magazine. Writers who were easygoing when contributing to other publications

60

felt they had to be much more conservative with *Comment*. Although the magazine hadn't been established until after the war, it was fast becoming an institution.

That was thanks to the extraordinary energy of Tanimura. Legend had it that in order to advance *Comment* into the lofty heights it now enjoyed, he went for two years on no more than three hours sleep a night. There were many tales about Tanimura. He had quarrelled with contributors, and actually came to blows with some of them. Tenacity and impatience coursed through his veins.

Tanimura had the strength of his own convictions. He was prepared to go to any lengths to improve the magazine. It would be no exaggeration to say that it was his enthusiasm and vigor that was responsible for creating the *Comment* of today. Even those who despised him had to credit him for that much.

Upon hearing his scoop was "more the sort of story a tabloid would carry," Abe felt dejected. "But," he insisted, "if he is innocent, I think it's a problem. His sister comes all the way from Kyushu to request the help of the lawyer Otsuka, but the lawyer turns her down because it doesn't look as though she can pay his fees. So, because she has no money, she can't hire a top-class lawyer, and thus her brother may get the death penalty. It raises issues about the inner workings of the current court system."

"But even if Otsuka fights the case for her, there's nothing to guarantee that he'll win," said the chief, rocking his body back in an exaggerated fashion. "Plus, even lawyers have to earn their keep. They can't just go defending people for nothing. It doesn't make sense to criticize the lawyers."

"It wasn't meant as a personal attack on Otsuka," replied Abe. "It's just one case that shows the phenomenon that people without means are precluded from access to a fair trial."

"That's not a bad idea." The editor in chief unfolded his arms and took a drag on his cigarette. "And you propose citing this Kyushu murder case as the basis for the article?"

"Yes, that's right."

"But, the whole success of the article stands on the premise that the school teacher is definitely innocent. If he turns out to be guilty it will be hugely embarrassing for the magazine. Do you have the nerve to assert that he is innocent?"

"That's precisely why I'd like to investigate it now."

"And just how would you do that?" asked the chief, narrowing his eyes in a sneer.

"I would go to the scene of the crime, read the investigation reports, survey the actual site. I would meet with as many people as possible, try and collect data that the police were unaware of or that had been discarded intentionally."

"I think you'd better give up on it," said Tanimura right away. "It's not something we want to risk the fate of our magazine on."

Abe stood in front of Tanimura's desk and watched as the chief suddenly stopped rocking. "Well, don't you agree? There's no social interest angle here. It's a straightforward robbery and murder. If we knew the thought processes and context like in that other case, it'd be better, but we haven't got that here. Our readers will get the impression that we're simply jumping on the band wagon and following the trend of criticizing the judicial system and the public prosecutor's office."

"But," said Abe, defiant to the last, "there is an issue here that people who can't afford it won't get a fair trial."

Tanimura's look said, *You still don't get it, do you?* "That's why you want to use this case as a concrete example, right? And I'm telling you I don't think it's appropriate. You say you want to go and investigate the scene of the crime. It will cost a considerable amount of money, and you'll be absent from the office at such a busy time for several days, possibly even weeks. That's quite a financial burden for a company like ours. What I'm really asking is whether this one case is really worth the risk to the magazine."

It's worth it, thought Abe, but he couldn't bring himself to say so. He didn't have the confidence to assert with any degree of certainty that Masao Yanagida was innocent, and he knew that there was little prospect of proving it if he went to the scene of the crime. There was the possibility that he would return having found proof that Yanagida was in fact guilty. The only basis for his vague belief in Yanagida's innocence was the resolute look in that young woman's eye and her piercing voice as she yelled down the mouthpiece of the red telephone. He hadn't one shred of objective evidence. Abe felt his defiance slipping through his fingers. He retreated from the editor in chief's desk.

Tanimura ignored him and bent over the documents on his desk, cigarette in mouth. Tanimura squinted as smoke got in his eyes. His expression transformed into a look of smug contentedness in Abe's mind.

On his way home from the office that evening Abe called in at his favourite bar.

"Hello there!" One of his work colleagues came over with a smirk on his face. His name was Hisaoka Sutekichi. "What did you say to the chief at lunchtime today?" he asked after taking a sip and narrowing his eyes like an elephant.

"Nothing much." Abe didn't really want to talk about it. Hisaoka's tone showed a hint of something more than casual interest in the matter. He had no doubt been at his desk when Abe's proposal had been flatly rejected by the editor in chief and must have watched as Abe retreated crestfallen.

Hisaoka was quite smart, always observing from the sidelines. He was the sort of person who criticized people's work behind their backs, and always wore a faint grin. He was very skillful at managing to avoid doing the difficult or annoying jobs.

"Come on, out with it," he persisted, tapping Abe on the shoulder.

"Well..." Feeling cornered, Abe reluctantly began to talk. His inability to say no had nothing to do with giving in to Hisaoka's persistence. Rather, having been turned down by the editor in chief, he felt the need to give vent to his gloomy feelings.

"I see," said Hisaoka Sutekichi, pulling the rim of his glass away from his mouth.

"Do you think it's interesting?" asked Abe.

"A little, yes. Although it's nothing to get too excited about, mind you." Hisaoka's sudden killjoy expression belied his opinion. "It's no wonder Mr. Tanimura said no. It's not the kind of thing he likes. If I were in his shoes, I probably would have rejected it, too."

"Why?"

"It's fairly interesting, but there's no value in the story. No matter how much you try and make it an exciting story, it's just not that fascinating. Even I wouldn't risk the expense of sending you all the way to Kyushu. A general interest magazine shouldn't be playing private investigator. It's absurd."

Abe regretted talking to Hisaoka. But the next words Hisaoka spoke stayed with him for a long time afterwards.

"But if you absolutely want to do it, then you should go to Kyushu at your own expense."

Abe left Hisaoka and thought seriously about what he'd said. *A trip to Kyushu.*

I'd like to go to K-City with my own money and gather the info I need. He became wrapped up in this idle fantasy. But it was just a daydream. Needless to say, he had neither the ten or twenty thousand yen necessary nor the time to spare. He could have taken time off from work under some other pretext, but an investigation carried out without the blessing of *Comment* was virtually meaningless. The job he had to do stood out in clear relief. He had to make this issue known through his journalism.

Abe took out his note pad and examined the circumstances of the case. According to the newspaper articles, there was no way Masao Yanagida wasn't the one who murdered the old moneylender. There was a motive: He was struggling to repay the high-interest loan of forty thousand yen. The old woman had doggedly pursued him, dropped by his apartment without notice, ambushed him en route to school, and hurling foul-mouthed abuse at him. He'd only paid the interest on the loan twice, so of course he had no rebuttal to the loan shark's reprimands. Abe could almost see the anguished face of the young teacher.

The evidence was overwhelming. His fingerprints were on the chest of drawers at the scene of the crime. Spots of blood matching the blood type of the old lady's, together with ash that had spilled onto her *tatami* floor, were found in the cuffs of the trousers he'd been wearing that night. The physical evidence alone was beyond reproach. It wasn't unreasonable for Chief Ueda of the K-City Police criminal investigation section to state that he was confident they had the right man. The public prosecutor was already in the process of serving the indictment.

Abe took his note pad out every day and read it. Slowly, he lost the conviction he originally had. He began to sense that even if he went to the scene of the crime in Kyushu he wouldn't be able to find anything to dispute the evidence that had been amassed against the suspect. He came to believe that Tanimura was justified in turning down his request after all. At the time, he must have been incapable of making a rational decision because he was too excited. Had he persisted and, against better advice, gone to the scene of the crime in Kyushu, it would surely have ended in a terrible failure. Perhaps his excitement was due in no small part to the particular impression he had of the young woman Kiriko Yanagida.

The only thing that made Abe want to believe in Masao Yanagida was what compelled him to borrow money from a loan shark in the first place. He had dropped and lost the 38,000-yen school excursion money that was collected from the students. To make up the loss, he had gone to Kiku's place intent on borrowing money. Oblivious of this, the children had probably completed their trip without incident. Yanagida accompanied the children and was surely relieved to see their happy, smiling faces. At that moment, the flames of debtor's hell started to burn in his heart. Nevertheless, this noble motivation was not persuasive enough to absolve Masao Yanagida of the crime for which he now stood accused.

Abe made up his mind and wrote a letter to the address listed for Kiriko Yanagida he'd seen in the newspapers.

```
I met you when you came to Tokyo some
while ago. I gave you my business
card, so you might recall me when you
see the name on the envelope. You were
talking on the telephone with someone
at the offices of the lawyer Kinzo
Otsuka, and afterwards I talked you
into going to a nearby café. Thinking
back now, I see that was incredibly
rude of me. At that time I was unable
to hear your story, but I later had an
opportunity to read some newspapers
from your hometown and I learned
about your brother's unfortunate
predicament. I, too, believe your
brother to be innocent. Accordingly,
I would really like to know how the
```

67

```
trial is progressing. You may refuse
my request, but I want you to know
I am not writing this letter out of
idle curiosity. Rather, I was deeply
moved by your conviction at that time
and I've been worried about the court
proceedings ever since. I would be
extremely grateful if you would advise
me of the above. Yours truly.
```

Abe posted the letter and waited several days for an answer, but he had no news at all from Kiriko. He sent another four letters after that, but none came in reply. Since his letters were not returned, he surmised that Kiriko Yanagida was in fact living at the address. Abe brought to mind the young woman's face as she sat in silence in the café gnawing on her bottom lip. Her lack of response to his letters felt like she was closing the door in his face, just as when she'd brusquely excused herself from the cafe.

Time passed. Abe became very busy at work. He buried himself in long hours and a heavy workload, never giving up nor forgetting about Kiriko.

December.

Kinzo Otsuka breathed out a white cloud of vapor as he went into his office. Three young lawyers were working at their desks, but when they saw Otsuka they got up from their chairs and greeted him: "Good morning."

"Morning," Otsuka replied and continued on past them to his own desk. The stove heater was lit. The area where the young lawyers worked was separated by a wall of book shelves. The clerk Okumura followed Otsuka in and, taking his overcoat from behind, said, "It's cold."

"Yes, it's gotten chilly again this morning."

"There's a strange postcard for you," said Okumura, changing the subject completely.

"Strange postcard?"

"I put it on your desk."

"All right."

In this job, lawyers occasionally received threatening letters, depending on the case they were involved in. It was by no means unusual. It was a little odd that Okumura had made particular reference to it.

Otsuka sat down in front of his large desk. The morning's mail was laid out in front of him. It was all addressed to him personally, as the other, more general office mail was sorted out earlier by Okumura. The post was divided into two piles consisting of books that had been sent as gifts and letters. The postcard lay on top of the pile of letters.

It must be this, thought Otsuka as he picked up the postcard. The sender's name was written on the card: Kiriko Yanagida, XX-town, K-City, F-Prefecture. He had no recollection of who it was. Of course, he had no reason to remember all the names on the correspondence he received each day.

He turned it over and read the reverse.

```
Dear Otsuka-sensei; My brother
received the death sentence at his
first trial. He appealed, but died on
November 21 in F-Prison while his
```

```
case was still in appeals. Since the
court-appointed lawyer was unable
to secure an acquittal, he requested
only that his sentence be reduced by
taking extenuating circumstances into
consideration. My brother died in
disgrace branded a common thief and
murderer.
```

The card was written in ink in bold, confident strokes.

That was all very well but Otsuka didn't understand what the message was supposed to mean. He hadn't grasped it at all.

"Okumura?" Okumura stood up and walked over practically before Otsuka called him. Otsuka waved the postcard in his direction. "What's this all about?"

"Sorry?" said Okumura, stopping in front of the desk. "Ah yes—sometime around May, I think it was… A young lady from Kyushu came to the office."

"From Kyushu?"

"Yes. Her name was Kiriko Yanagida. You met with her here in your office. She was about 20 years old. Her brother had been questioned in connection with a murder and she had come from Kyushu to request your assistance…"

"Ah," Otsuka's voice leapt from his mouth. "That one…"

His memory was good, and he remembered at once. She came here having heard that he was the best lawyer in Japan. She was still a young girl with a pretty face but had piercing eyes. He'd told her that surely there were good lawyers in Kyushu, too. But she responded with tense lips that she'd come to Tokyo because she believed he was the only one who could save her brother.

It was one of the cases he had turned down. Of course, he had been busy, but since Okumura had hinted she couldn't pay and they should therefore turn her down, he'd felt inclined to do just that. In the past he had fought and won cases using his own money. But that was when he was young. Nowadays, he was busy with big cases and had neither the time nor the energy to do that. "I accept your decision," she had said, and again by the exit, "I don't know whether my brother will get the death penalty." And then she had disappeared down the stairwell, her shoes ringing out on the hard surface of the steps.

"So, he died in prison, did he…" Otsuka was still staring at the postcard. But what really preyed on his mind were the words: "court-appointed lawyer was unable to secure an acquittal… My brother died in disgrace branded a common thief and murderer."

Depending on the interpretation, one could come away feeling that this event had come about because Otsuka had refused to give his assistance. Criticism and resentment nearly jumped out from between the lines of print. Refusing to take the case because of fees left Kinzo Otsuka feeling a bit ill at ease with himself.

"That girl," Otsuka looked up at Okumura's face as he stood there in front of him, "did she call again afterwards, while I was away?"

"Yes, while you were in Kawana," answered Okumura. "She telephoned and asked whether there wasn't some way she could persuade you to take on her case. I replied that we couldn't do it. So she ranted on about you not taking her on because she couldn't afford the fees and said she had heard that there are lawyers who believe in a righteous cause who will represent someone without making an issue out of money. I was annoyed, too, and told her something to the effect that it was unfair to pressure us on moral grounds. For someone so young she was quite forthright, you know."

"Hmm," Otsuka muttered, with a slightly dejected look on his face. "She was, wasn't she."

He was troubled. He remembered now—at the time he had played golf in Kawana with Michiko Kono and then gone off to Hakone. The day before, when Kiriko had come to the office, he had been conscious of the time, knowing that Michiko was waiting for him in Kawana, and hadn't been able to settle down. As a result, he hadn't paid any attention to what was being said in the meeting. He'd practically wanted to escape.

This was an unfortunate sequence of events for the young woman. If it hadn't been for that, he might have listened more attentively to the outline of the case and had one of the young lawyers do some investigating. In the end, he might just have undertaken the case pro bono. *However*, he thought, *even if I'd taken up the case, if he was the real culprit there's no way I could've gotten him acquitted.* But even with this excuse, the case weighed on his mind.

He couldn't escape from the thought of "what if." It was the sort of pious self-confidence that came from many years of experience, which had, on occasion, enabled him to prove innocent a defendant who was universally considered guilty.

It was the accumulation of such results in the area of criminal defense work that had earned him his reputation as the best in Japan.

Even that young woman from Kyushu would have accepted defeat if I had taken on the case and lost. But it was true what she said—the fact that she couldn't afford the fees meant that they had to rely on a court-appointed lawyer. "Poor people cannot hope for a fair trial." A young woman's hysterical voice came suddenly alive and resounded in his ears. An ever-louder scream seemed to emanate from between the lines on the postcard.

Above all, her brother had died in prison. Even though he was appealing the ruling he was considered guilty of murder at the time. Even the court-appointed lawyer seemed to assume he was guilty. One could even say the general impression of his death was the same as if he were executed by the state. It was clear from the young woman's postcard that she resented this aspect above all else.

"Okumura?" said Otsuka, lifting his chin from the support of his hands, "Horita went to F-City, in Kyushu, didn't he?"

Horita was Otsuka's junior.

"Yes, that's right," nodded Okumura in agreement.

"Send him an urgent letter. Can you please ask him to get hold of a copy of the court record from the Yanagida case and send it to me?"

73

"I beg your pardon?" Okumura's eyes were wide in amazement. "But *sensei*, the defendant is already dead."

"Do as I say," said Otsuka rather sharply. "I'd like to take a look at the transcript."

Chapter 4

The record of the first trial of Masao Yanagida arrived as requested from the lawyer in Kyushu. The case had been in appeal but, because the defendant had died while in custody, the record of the court-appointed attorney was loaned in its entirety. The lawyer who did Otsuka this favor was Horita. He was more than a dozen years younger than Otsuka.

Otsuka read the papers relating to the case at his home and in the office. As a result, his black briefcase was always heavy.

The crime was aggravated theft and murder. Masao Yanagida, an elementary school teacher, had murdered an old moneylender and made off with his promissory note.

The Public Prosecutor's written indictment stated as follows:

```
Defendant's registered domicile:
X District in XX Town, K-City;
Occupation: elementary school teacher;
```

SEICHO MATSUMOTO

Full name: Masao Yanagida;
Date of birth: X day, X month, 19XX

The circumstances of the prosecution were as follows:

On the X day of September 19XX,
the defendant, a teacher at the X
Elementary School and residing in
K-City, lost a deposit of 38,000 yen
for a school excursion while taking
it home for safekeeping. At a loss
as to how he was going to repay the
money, he had the idea of borrowing
money from Kiku Watanabe (then 65
years of age) who lived in the same
town and whom he had already heard
was in the business of lending money
at high rates of interest. Between the
end of September and the beginning
of October he made several visits to
Kiku's residence requesting a loan
and, eventually, on October 8, he was
successful in borrowing 40,000 yen
(the actual loaned amount was 36,000
yen, i.e., minus one month's interest),
repayable by the end of December. At
the same time the defendant handed
Kiku a promissory note in exchange for
the loan. However, since the defendant
was only earning a frugal salary of
11,000 yen a month, he was not in a
position to satisfactorily pay the
interest, let alone the principal,
by the due date. As a result, from
around February this year, Kiku began
making increasingly severe demands
for payment. The defendant became
anguished and resolved to murder Kiku
and take back the promissory note.

On March 18 he contacted Kiku and
informed her that he would call the
next evening in order to repay the
money. At around 11:00 pm on March 19
he visited her house, entering by the
front door. Kiku Watanabe was awake
and preparing a pot of tea for the
caller in the downstairs eight-tatami
room. As she turned to bend over the
charcoal brazier the defendant struck
her across the back of the head using
a 70-centimeter long oaken club, which
the defendant had noticed in the room.
The victim collapsed momentarily, but
then put up some degree of resistance.
In response, the defendant renewed
his attack, clubbing Kiku Watanabe
repeatedly on the left side of her
head and body until she died from
the attack. The crime is aggravated
robbery and murder as defined under
section 240 of the Penal Code.

Otsuka read the summary of the opening remarks of the public prosecutor's statement, but this was simply a full account of the written indictment.

There was a mountain of paperwork—a report on the factual circumstances surrounding the crime, expert opinions, the autopsy report, police investigation report, criminal investigation report, affidavits, witnesses' testimony, the decision of the court, summary of the defense prepared by the court-appointed attorney, etc.

Otsuka read these documents at home, warming his free hand over a charcoal brazier and smoking a cigarette. At the office, in between carrying on his real work, he would take the documents out from his briefcase and cast his eye over them.

Of course, this was an unprofitable case. He hadn't even been hired by anyone. And most importantly, the defendant was deceased.

The office clerk Okumura would come and go from Otsuka's office in performing his daily tasks, and each time he did so he would shoot a scathing glance at the Yanagida case paperwork spread out on the desk. But he never mentioned the matter. Otsuka suspected that Okumura joked about him behind his back with the younger lawyers. *What are we to do about the old man? He's so busy and yet he spends so much time messing about with this ghost of a case...*

Otsuka started to become a little wary of Okumura. He began spending a fair amount of his time looking at the documents in his study at home.

His wife would come into his study with a pot of tea and remark, "You're so busy, aren't you?"

His wife Yoshiko was the daughter of his late mentor. He had been a senior figure in legal circles, and since Yoshiko had seen and grown used to the way her father worked, she never asked questions about her husband's work. She discreetly took note of her husband's serious expression as he read his paperwork and left the room quietly. Naturally, she hadn't noticed her husband painstakingly reviewing the case of a dead defendant free of charge.

Otsuka could still hear the hard sound of the Kyushu girl's shoes as she forlornly descended the dark office stairwell. In his mind's eye, he could see her pallid complexion as she muttered the words, "I don't know whether my brother will get the death penalty."

But that couldn't be the only reason Otsuka found himself enthusiastic enough to have such a large volume of documents sent especially from Kyushu.

My brother received the death sentence at his first trial. He appealed, but died on November 21 in F-Prison while his case was still in appeals.

These words had wounded his heart.

The young woman seemed to be shouting that, because her brother died in prison during the appeal, it was in effect the same as being executed. She was practically accusing Otsuka, berating him for allowing this to happen by refusing to represent her due to her inability to pay his fees.

It was easy enough to disclaim responsibility. After all, it had been nothing to do with him. But the attorney charged with handling the case was a court-appointed lawyer who, he had later learned from Horita, was not especially competent. This was another source of regret for Otsuka. He couldn't help feeling that if he had taken on the case the defendant might have been saved. It was rather like the bad taste one had in one's mouth after hearing of a patient who died in the care of a mediocre medical practitioner after having been turned away by a competent doctor.

Plus, at the time, he'd been in an awful hurry to set off for Kawana to meet with Michiko Kono.

It was partly because he was in such a rush that he had declined the young woman before listening properly to her story. Had he not been so pressed for time, he might at least have listened to the gist of what it was she had to say. He might have discovered some inconsistency in the facts of the case and decided to take it on himself. The majority of the cases on which he had made his reputation and worked pro bono had started out in much the same way.

However, he didn't really know whether her brother was innocent. His desire to confirm that there were no inconsistencies in the documentation and thereby put his mind at rest was behind his eagerness to obtain and read through the record of the first trial.

The defendant was dead, and he didn't have the time to fly down to Kyushu in order to interview witnesses. He had to admit therefore that simply reading the court record was a less-than-thorough means of ascertaining the truth of the matter. But it would have to suffice. It would suffice to wash away that bad taste, if only incompletely. He was confident he would be able to prove wrong the young woman's view that her brother had died in prison because she had failed to secure his representation.

At the very least he wanted to be able to say his refusal to act on her brother's behalf was not motivated by his subconscious desire to leave quickly and meet Michiko.

Otsuka began to sift through the mountain of paperwork.

Report on the investigation at the scene of the crime.

In connection with the crime of aggravated robbery and murder,

committed by the suspect Masao
Yanagida, I carried out an inspection
at the scene of the crime as detailed
below.

Dated: March 20 19XX

K-Police Station.

Hiroo Fukumoto, Sergeant, Forensics
Section

Date and time of inspection: 11:00 am
until 12:50 pm, March 20 19XX

Location of inspection: The residence
of Kiku Watanabe and vicinity, XX
Town, K-City

Purpose of inspection: To collect
evidence and shed light on the
circumstances of the crime

Persons present at the inspection: (i)
Ryutaro, eldest son of the victim Kiku
Watanabe, (ii) [...]

Particulars of the inspection:

(a) Situation of the living room -
General Observations:

The building in question is a two-
story wooden structure with a floor
area of X and a south-facing front
entrance. The entrance faces a road
and the back door adjoins the wooden
fence of a neighboring house. A narrow
alley, approximately half a meter in
width, runs between the house and the
fence and passes across the back of
three other houses before emerging on
the road at the front.

At the time of the inspection the
back door was closed, the bolt on the
inside having been thrown across. The
entrance consisted of a sliding screen
and solid door, but at the time of the
inspection the door was open, with
only the paper screen pulled across.
[...]

Situation within the house:

In the eight-mat tatami room, there
was a chest of drawers against the
westerly wall. When I conducted my
inspection, I noticed the second and
third drawers were half open and
the clothing inside was in disarray.
The left side of the drawer had been
pulled some 10 centimeters further out
than the right. The lock on the left-
hand door of the small cabinet inlaid
in the lower right had been broken
off and the door left open, while the
right-hand door was still in place.

There were bloodstains on the tatami mat approximately 40 centimeters away from the chest of drawers. Bloodstains were also evident on the tatami approximately 50 centimeters south of a long charcoal brazier, which was positioned more or less in the center of the room.

An iron kettle had been placed on the charcoal brazier, but this was leaning over in a westerly direction at an angle of 30 degrees. The ash inside the brazier was wet, and ash had also spilled onto the tatami matting. On top of the ash there were faint signs of something abrasive having been dragged across the surface.

The body was not present at the time of the inspection, as it had been removed for autopsy.

Otsuka read the report with intense interest before moving on to the expert witness report:

The body removed for autopsy was that of Kiku Watanabe (then aged 65 years of age).

External examination revealed: height: 150 centimeters; weak physique and somewhat undernourished; injuries resulting in death conspicuous on victim's back.

There were no wounds to the neck, chest, abdomen or legs.

A contusion of approximately 10 centimeters in length reached as far as the periosteum on the right side of the back of the head; a jagged cut 4 centimeters in length ran diagonally top to bottom from the left side of the forehead, and a 3 centimeter cut extended from the left cheekbone to the outside corner of the eye.

Internal examination: In making an incision and drawing back the skin around the victim's head there was a slight depression and fracture about the size of a chicken egg, consistent with the contusion on the right side of the back of the head noted during the external examination. On the left side of the forehead there was a thumb-sized spot of subcutaneous bleeding, but no evidence of fracturing. Furthermore, there was similar internal bleeding evident between the skin and muscle of the left cheek. In addition, upon removing the victim's skull, it was noted that in the area of the right cerebral hemisphere there was acute swelling outside the dura mater measuring 10 centimeters by 8 centimeters by 2 centimeters, largely consistent with the depression

fracture. On removing the brain I
concluded that the base of the left
cerebral hemisphere indicated a strong
opposite blow.

I made an incision along the middle
of the abdomen and on opening up the
cavity found that the third rib on
the left was partially broken and also
identified signs of slight hemorrhaging
to the intercostal muscles. Other than
already stated, there were no injuries
of any note to either side of the
thorax. [...]

Cause of death: Acute swelling of the
dura mater and pressure on the brain
resulting from external force being
applied to the victim's head.

Suicide/Homicide: Conclusion: Homicide.

Time elapsed since death: Estimated 17
hours from the time of commencement of
post mortem (3:35 pm March 20).

Murder weapon/Method of assault:
With regard to the murder weapon,
I conclude that the wounds to the
right side of the back of the head,
the left side of the forehead and the
left cheek were inflicted using a blunt
instrument with a relatively smooth
surface (for example, an object such
as an iron bar or wooden club). With
regard to the method of assault, the

```
wounds to the right side of the back
of the head which caused the depressed
fracture are consistent with a strong
blow from the rear while turned away
from the attacker. The wounds to the
forehead and left cheek and also the
wounds to the third rib probably
resulted from blows delivered from the
front as the victim turned to face the
attacker.


Blood type: O


Further remarks: None.


Dated: March 20 19XX


F-Police Headquarters Forensics Doctor,
Sakae Suzuki
```

There were two more expert witness reports.

One of these concluded that, firstly, the bloodstains found on the bottom of the trousers that the defendant, Masao Yanagida, had been wearing on the evening of the 19th was blood type O and that this was the same as the victim's blood type, and that the fingerprints on the chest of drawers were a perfect match with those of the defendant; and, secondly, that the ash caught in the cuffs of the defendant's trousers was identical to that which had spilled from the charcoal brazier onto the *tatami* matting.

The second document was a psychiatric report prepared by a doctor and which concluded that at the time of the crime, the defendant's state of mind was normal.

Otsuka lit a cigarette and thought about the case. The fingerprints found at the scene of the crime, and the blood-stains on the trousers worn by the defendant on the night in question were decidedly factors unfavorable for Masao Yanagida. There was no getting away from the fact that he had illegally entered Kiku Watanabe's house and come into contact with her blood. The public prosecutor's written indictment and his opening statement appeared to present an air-tight case against the defendant.

And what of the defendant Masao Yanagida's statement? In the criminal trial hearing he had testified as follows:

```
First Trial Record

Aggravated robbery and murder

Masao Yanagida (present in court)

Statement relating to the Defendant's
case:

The Defendant contends that the
written Indictment is incorrect and
that the following points are the
correct facts of the case:

Sometime in October in the year 19XX I
borrowed 40,000 yen (actual amount of
```

36,000 yen due to deducted interest)
from Kiku Watanabe at a monthly
interest rate of 10%. The repayment
date was end of December and I signed
a promissory note to that effect.
However, after that I was only able
to make two payments of interest and
could not repay the principal. As a
result, from around February this year
Kiku Watanabe began to make severe
demands for payment.

The reason I visited Kiku Watanabe's
house at 11:00 pm on March 19 was to
make good my promise of the previous
evening when I telephoned to say
I would bring two months' interest
the following evening. However, I
was unable to raise the necessary
money that night and so I went to
her place to apologize and get her
understanding; I certainly didn't go
there with the intention of murder or
of retrieving the promissory note.

When I arrived at Kiku Watanabe's
house the front door was open and with
only the paper screen closed. I could
see a light on inside. Thinking that
Kiku was waiting up for me I called
out "Good evening" two or three times
but there was no reply. I thought she
might have been having a nap since she
was of age. When I opened the paper
screen doors I could see that the
screen doors to the eight-mat tatami
room on the left of the entrance hall
were open. When I looked more closely

PRO BONO

I saw that Kiku was lying on her back
in front of the chest of drawers but I
still thought she was asleep. However,
when I called out again she showed
no sign of waking up and not only
that, the iron tea kettle was over on
its side in the charcoal brazier and
there was ash on the tatami matting,
probably blown there from the brazier
when hot water spilled from the kettle.
I thought it a little odd, and when I
looked more carefully I saw something
red on the matting and knew then it
was blood. There was also blood on
Kiku's face. I considered notifying the
police immediately, but then guessed
the reason why she hadn't stirred at
all was because she had been murdered.
It was then that I decided to steal
the promissory note. If there were
a police investigation, it wouldn't
take long before the promissory note
came to light and everyone would know
about the high-interest loan. I would
lose face with the school, the PTA
and all my friends and acquaintances.
I removed my shoes and went into the
room — Kiku was lying dead, it was a
dreadful sight. I thought someone must
have been here before me and murdered
her. But I was concerned about my own
predicament and thought about making
off. I realized that if I didn't take
the promissory note it would not
go well for me if it were found. I
guessed it would be kept along with
Kiku's other valuables in a bag in the
bottom cabinet of her chest. The lock
was already broken and the left-hand

door open. I took only my promissory
note, left by the front door again and
went home. That night I burned the
promissory note on a lot in front of
my lodgings.

The facts of the case are as set out
above. I did not beat Kiku with an oak
club and murder her as the written
indictment alleges. Furthermore, I
did not open the drawer and rummage
through the clothing in order to give
the impression I had gone there intent
on robbery. With regard to the ash and
blood on the bottom of my trousers, I
believe I picked these up as I went
from the doorway past the chest of
drawers and back again.

When I looked into the room there were
two teacups, a teapot and a container
of tea placed next to the charcoal
brazier. There were also two guest
cushions, so perhaps Kiku was waiting
for me to arrive.

Judge: Do you recall ever having seen
this club? [The Judge showed evidence
item number 2 to the Defendant].

Defendant: No, I do not.

Judge: Do you recall ever having seen this? [The Judge showed evidence item number 3 - a bundle of promissory notes - to the Defendant].

Defendant: Yes I do. Kiku Watanabe kept them in a bag in her chest's bottom cabinet. I took the bundle out, retrieved only my own promissory note for the 40,000 yen loan and then stuffed the bundle back into the bag.

Judge: Do you recall ever having seen these? [The Judge showed the Defendant the confiscated trousers worn by the Defendant on March 19].

Defendant: They are mine. I was wearing them when I visited Kiku Watanabe on March 19. The following day I noticed blood spots on the trouser bottoms and, wishing to avoid suspicion, I hid them behind the ceiling in my room, where they were later found and confiscated by the police.

The sworn statement of Masao Yanagida, Defendant in the Criminal Trial.

Otsuka's initial thoughts were that the statement seemed to make sense. When Masao Yanagida arrived at Kiku's place at around 11:00 pm on March 19, Kiku had already been murdered by somebody else. It also provided an explanation for the blood and ash on the bottom of his trousers.

However, this seemed more than mere coincidence. The results of the autopsy also put the time of death at approximately 11:00 pm on the night of March 19, and Masao Yanagida himself testified that he was there at that time. It would be difficult to believe that the real assailant had arrived moments before Yanagida and killed Kiku Watanabe.

Given the irrefutable nature of the evidence—blood spots and ash on his trousers and his fingerprints on the chest of drawers—it did seem rather as though Yanagida had tried his best to make his story sound plausible. Otsuka was aware of the fact that the more intelligent criminals often tried to evade liability in this way.

Next Otsuka read the report of the questioning of the police officer who first interrogated the defendant following his arrest, but this turned out to be identical to the testimony given in court. It was on the sixth day of questioning that Masao Yanagida finally confessed to the charges against him. The testimony read as follows:

```
9th Interrogation Report


Suspect: Masao Yanagida


Until now I have stated that it was
someone else that murdered Kiku
Watanabe. However, now that it seems
your enquiries have come to an end
I wish to state the truth. In point
of fact, it was I who murdered Kiku
Watanabe.
```

PRO BONO

As I have previously stated, around
September last year, I dropped and
lost 38,000 yen - money I had collected
from the students as a deposit for
their school excursion. Realizing I
could not repay this money I borrowed
40,000 yen from Kiku. But because I was
unable to make the payments I began to
experience harsh demands from her to
settle the debt.

Kiku Watanabe was a greedy woman who,
not content with taking 10% interest
each month, was quick to accost me
on the way to school and come to my
lodgings to level abuse at me once she
discovered I was unable to repay the
loan by the deadline. As a result, I
became embarrassed with regard to my
position as a teacher, was unable to
concentrate in lessons and suffered
anxiety attacks. When I thought about
how this had all come about because of
Kiku, I felt a rage rising inside me
and wanted to kill her.

Around 6:00 pm on March 18 I called
on Kiku and she seemed pleased when
I told her I would return the next
evening and bring the interest owed to
date and part of the principal. When
I quietly entered her house at about
11:00 pm on the 19th Kiku was still up
and waiting for me. An iron kettle had
been placed on the charcoal brazier
and steam was pouring out of its
spout. To one side were two teacups, a
teapot and a container of tea.

SEICHO MATSUMOTO

When Kiku saw my face she said, "So
you actually showed up," and then got
up from where she had been sitting and
moved towards the brazier to pour me
some tea. I had already noticed the
oak club she kept in the house and
thought it would be a suitable weapon
with which to deal a solid blow. All of
a sudden I made a dash for it, picking
it up with both hands before bringing
it down hard on top of Kiku's head.
Kiku momentarily collapsed onto the
floor, but in the next instant she was
up again, grappling furiously at me,
and so I took the club in my right
hand and beat her across the face and
forehead. Kiku let out an awful scream
and then fell onto her back again and
stopped moving. Then I broke the lock
on the bottom cabinet of the chest
of drawers and forced open the door.
I took out the bundle of promissory
notes, found the one for my 40,000 yen
loan and fled the house, leaving by the
front entrance. I discarded the oak
club in a ditch on a vacant lot near a
temple and then went to my own house.
When Kiku first fell to the floor, the
impact on the tatami matting must have
caused the iron kettle to tip over
spilling hot water onto the charcoal
brazier and causing a cloud of ash to
blow onto the floor. In a lot near my
house I took a match to the promissory
note and burned it up. When I thought
about how much I had suffered on
account of that single promissory note
I felt a wave of relief, but now I

regret what I did and feel sorry for
Kiku.

Signed and thumbprinted at K-Police
Station in the presence of

Inspector Yoshio Adachi

10th Interrogation Report

With regard to my earlier statement
about the murder of Kiku Watanabe, I
couldn't remember yesterday which part
of her I struck, but today I do recall
and would like to make a statement.

The first place I struck her was the
back of her head. After she had fallen
and landed on her back I remember
striking her firstly on the left side of
the forehead and then across her left
cheek. Then I think I struck her on
the chest. Although I originally said
I hadn't touched the drawers, in fact
after I knocked Kiku down, I forced
open the cabinet, opening the left-
hand door and taking out the bundle
of promissory notes, then, to make it
look as though it had been a burglary,
I opened the second and third drawers
and rummaged through the clothing.

This was the final statement made by Masao Yanagida in the police station. It was revisited once again in court following the public prosecutor's examination, at which point Yanagida denied murdering Kiku Watanabe.

Question: Why did you state at the police station that you had murdered Kiku Watanabe?

Answer: Because the person in charge put me in a room and interrogated me. There was a detective in front of me, one on each side and one standing behind me. They kept saying things like, "Come on, you killed her, didn't you? It's no good trying to hide it from us. The investigation is totally done now, so just admit it. You've got a younger sister you're concerned about. But don't worry, we'll look after her." Nothing I said seemed to get through to them and I was exhausted physically and felt very dizzy. The fact is, I gave in and lied at the police station because I thought you would be sure to believe me once I told the truth in court...

From this point onwards Masao Yanagida was consistent in his acknowledgment of the theft of the promissory note and denial of the murder of Kiku Watanabe.

Otsuka set to work looking through the witness statements. There were statements from people such as the defendant's younger sister, Kiriko; the former principal of the elementary school where Yanagida had worked; his former colleagues at school; the landlord who lived downstairs from his rented apartment; and Kiku's eldest son and daughter-in-law.

Extract from the statement of Kiku's eldest son, Ryutaro:

> I didn't see eye-to-eye with my mother,
> and my wife didn't get on too well
> with her either, so we moved out about
> five years ago. Having said that, we
> didn't really fight. I hated my mother's
> line of business, and I've no idea how
> much money she had, as I never asked
> her. And so after the murder when the
> police asked me how much had been
> stolen, I really didn't know. I don't
> know how much cash she had on her
> either...

Extract from the statement of former elementary school principal A:

> Mr. Yanagida was a serious character
> who was enthusiastic about teaching
> and well liked by the pupils. I was
> aware that in about September of
> last year Mr. Yanagida had collected
> approximately 38,000 yen from the
> students as a deposit for a planned
> school excursion, but I must confess I
> knew nothing at all about him having
> lost the money. The school trip went
> ahead without incident and so I had no
> reason to think anything like that had
> happened. The first I knew anything was
> wrong was when this incident occurred.
> If only he had confided in me at the

time, I might have been able to get
hold of the money, but instead he took
it as his personal responsibility and
borrowed money at an extortionate rate
of interest — it's just unfortunate
that he brought this misery on
himself...

Extract from the testimony of elementary school teacher B:

I knew that Yanagida was having a hard
time with demands from Mrs. Watanabe
for payment of the loan. She would
wait by the roadside and accost him
on his way to school — calling him
all sorts of names. I saw it happen
three or four times. On days like
that Yanagida would come to school
with a pale face and seem really low-
spirited...

Extract from the testimony of landlord C:

Mr. Yanagida has been a tenant on the
second floor for the past three years
now. He is a quiet person and once
he'd returned home from school he
would seldom go out again. On Sundays
and other holidays he would have
about ten or so of his pupils around
and he and his sister, Kiriko, would
entertain them. Mr. Yanagida and his
sister get along very well and they're
well liked in the neighborhood. It
was from around February of this year
that Mrs. Watanabe began coming round

demanding repayment of her money,
mainly during the evening. When I
told Mr. Yanagida that she was here,
he went into a panic, went downstairs
and took her outside where they would
talk at great length. Mrs. Watanabe
spoke with a loud, insistent voice
as she told him she wanted her money
back or there would be trouble, and
she wanted the interest, too. Mr.
Yanagida would apologize repeatedly
and always managed to calm her down
before sending her home, but he looked
troubled and would sit there with his
head in his hands. I felt sorry for
him and pretended not to notice. I
remember Mrs. Watanabe coming round
perhaps four or five times...

Next Otsuka turned his attention to the testimony of
Masao Yanagida's younger sister, Kiriko. The voice of that
young, pale woman with intense eyes came to mind once
again.

Extract from the testimony of Kiriko Yanagida:

My father died from an illness 11
years ago, and my mother died also
from illness 8 years ago. My brother
looked after me right up until I left
school. He worked to keep a roof
above our heads and at the same time
finished high school and then went on
to graduate from the New XX University
and become an elementary school
teacher. When I left high school I
trained at a secretarial school and

then joined my present company. My
brother's monthly salary is 11,000
yen and mine is 8,000 yen. This was
enough for two people to live on. My
brother is a serious person who has
few pastimes and no girlfriends. I
had no idea he had lost the 38,000
yen for the school trip, nor was I
aware that he had borrowed 40,000 yen
from Mrs. Watanabe. My brother ought
to have known that I had some modest
savings, but he probably would have
found it difficult to ask me for money
I had worked for and saved. That's the
kind of person my brother is. If he
hadn't kept it from me then I don't
think things would have turned out
the way they have. I regret that he
was so kind now. I did notice that
Mrs. Watanabe occasionally visited
our apartment, but usually it was
while I was out, or if I was there my
brother would take her outside where
I couldn't hear the subject of their
conversation. I thought it a little
strange and asked my brother what was
going on, but he told me that Mrs.
Watanabe had come to discuss the child
of a relative who was sitting the high
school exam next year. It was strange
that Mrs. Watanabe never came upstairs
where I was, but then I thought there
must be a reason and didn't give it
much thought after that. I wish now
I had pressed my brother to tell me
what was really happening. However, he
always seemed unconcerned when he was
with me, in fact he was more cheerful

than usual and so I wasn't really
suspicious.

I recall that my brother returned home
at close to midnight on the evening
of March 19. He was pale and looked
exhausted and dazed. I was surprised
and asked him what the matter was.
He said his friend had forced him
to drink and he wasn't feeling well,
and then he climbed into bed without
saying another word. I thought it
peculiar that I couldn't smell any
alcohol at the time, but I didn't
pay it any heed. The next morning I
prepared breakfast and woke my brother
up, but he said he still wasn't feeling
so good and to let him sleep a little
longer, so I left him like that and
went to work. That night when I got
home from work my brother arrived soon
after. I read the evening paper and
told my brother that Mrs. Watanabe had
been murdered. He said he had read it
too, but he didn't seem interested and
facing his desk continued marking the
students' exam papers. When I think
back now, he was doing his utmost not
to make eye contact with me. And then
two days later he was arrested by the
police. I was so shocked I felt as if
my whole world had been turned upside
down.

I simply couldn't believe my brother
had murdered Mrs. Watanabe. I'm
convinced he's not the sort of person
who is capable of something like

```
that. Under the circumstances I can
understand, as my brother himself
conceded, why he took the promissory
note, but I absolutely refuse to
believe he carried out a murder...
```

Otsuka could almost hear the young woman's voice again. Her whole heart seemed to burst through that voice. Her intense eyes floated up out of the print on the copy of the testimony.

Otsuka smoked his cigarette while he read, placing his fingers against his temple and losing himself in thought. This was something he did with increasing frequency in the privacy of his own study at home and also at his desk in the office.

Of course, he couldn't hope to complete his review of all this documentation in such a short space of time. He was an extremely busy lawyer and had a lot of urgent business to deal with. There were also a number of pressing court cases to attend. It was not uncommon for him to have to spend half the night in preparing for some of the hearings.

Since he could only use the spare moments in between doing his job to work his way through the large volume of documents relating to Masao Yanagida's case, it dragged on. He certainly couldn't read it through in one sitting. He had to read and re-read it until he had all but committed the details to memory. And then he would have to establish logic from the facts of the case and discover unseen inconsistencies...

However, as far as Otsuka could see, there didn't seem to be any errors in the public prosecutor's observations relating to the crime. The physical evidence was certainly sufficient. There were the fingerprints at the scene of the crime, the defendant's trousers stained with spots of the victim's blood, and ash from the brazier, and the fact that he took the promissory note from the chest of drawers—all of which he had admitted. On top of which, there was a motive for the killing. Rather like assembling a prefabricated box, the physical and consequential evidence clicked into shape to form a solid, three-dimensional object, which seemed overwhelming in its size. It was hard to say that the guilty verdict in the first trial was the result of an incompetent court-appointed attorney for the defendant.

Otsuka understood the gist of the case, and wondered whether to abandon it. Whether he gave up on it or not was entirely up to him. There was, after all, no client. Had he researched the case right from the beginning he might have given it up after all. In short, this was a troublesome case with little prospect of winning. Even had he taken it on, he felt he would not have been able to prove the defendant innocent.

Masao Yanagida claimed that Kiku had been murdered by someone before he had arrived at her place. But the autopsy put the time of death at around 11:00 pm on the night of the 19th, when Yanagida had visited the Watanabe house. Was it possible that another person could have entered Watanabe's house, murdered Kiku and fled the scene coincidentally just moments before Masao Yanagida arrived? If it were possible, then it would be necessary to prove that another assailant had been there. However, from Otsuka's reading of the official court record, there was no indication of any such proof.

Otsuka considered forgetting this case. When he thought about how even he could have done nothing for Yanagida, the feeling of responsibility for refusing to represent the young woman should have lifted, giving him a sense of relief.

But it didn't turn out that way. He was still restless and couldn't relax. He couldn't help feeling that what the young woman said was the truth. The unease he felt at having turned her away on the grounds of inability to pay his fees stuck with him. He also felt that Michiko Kono was complicit in his refusal to act.

Sensei—my brother died in prison with a guilty verdict hanging over him. The menacing words uttered from a woman's dry throat came to him just as vividly as before.

Otsuka had taken his worries with him when he met with Michiko. While he was talking with Michiko, his face was dark, like the shadow of a cloud suddenly drifting across the sky. At the time, he had suddenly stopped mid-sentence, and his eyes stared dejectedly far off in the distance. Michiko, intelligent and perceptive, did not fail to notice.

"*Sensei,*" said Michiko, looking searchingly at Otsuka's face with her eyes like pools of black ink. "Are you worried about something?"

"Why do you ask?" replied Otsuka, tossing back the question and smiling.

"Well, you look preoccupied, is all."

"I can't help that," answered the lawyer. "I have a lot of work at the moment."

Of course, Michiko knew nothing of the indirect role she had played in this gloomy affair.

"You run a business. Sometimes you worry about your work, right?"

"Well yes, but…" Michiko replied rather flatly and smiled, revealing a row of perfect white teeth. Michiko was slim and tall. Even in a kimono, sitting alongside him, she cut a handsome figure, almost as if she were wearing splendid Western attire.

Otsuka suddenly brought to mind the Ginza restaurant that Michiko managed. It was famous for its quality French cuisine, and both its décor and prices were expensive. The restaurant had been established by her estranged husband, but it was during the last four years of Michiko's management that it had really taken off. She had a talent for making things work.

Otsuka had first made Michiko's acquaintance when she came to his law office to discuss divorcing her husband. Once the restaurant was up and running, her husband had begun to develop a taste for fast and loose living and this was something Michiko couldn't tolerate.

Her husband expressed his regrets and said he wanted to make up, but she declined his offer. One reason was a rumor that her husband's mistress was pregnant, but in any case Michiko refused to budge.

Around that time her husband had started another large, independent business venture, so he agreed to her demands and transferred the Ginza restaurant to Michiko in lieu of alimony.

At the time, the restaurant was not nearly as popular as now. Her husband had offered her seven million yen in cash, but Michiko had refused and stuck firmly by her demand for the restaurant. It was soon afterwards that she retained Otsuka and succeeded in settling the dispute to her advantage.

There followed a two-year courtship which turned into their current relationship.

Michiko's restaurant was flourishing and running smoothly enough that she didn't need to be there all the time. She had poached a manager from the restaurant of a first-class hotel and hired thirty staff so that everything was under control.

So there were no obstacles to Michiko taking off for a few days to play golf in Kawana or Hakone, and spending quality time with Otsuka in nightclubs and such never affected the running of her business.

When Otsuka had said, "Sometimes you worry about your work, right?" he was implying that even in a business doing as well as Michiko's she would occasionally experience irksome problems. But putting the question back to her in this way was simply a means of ensuring that his lover didn't notice his melancholy.

Before long Otsuka discovered an inconsistency in the court record. A barely visible kink had appeared in the tightly assembled prefabricated box. The discovery was all thanks to Otsuka's expert eye, and in this case it was partly due to an inner confidence.

The feeling of intimidation by Kiriko's voice wasn't the only reason Otsuka had taken it upon himself to look into the verdict of the Kyushu court. Although he wasn't especially conscious of it, he flattered himself that he could discover an error in the judgment. It was his experiences as a young lawyer that had shaped his pride and his early outstanding successes that had propelled him into the position he now enjoyed. Early in his career he had been a tough adversary with the police and the court.

The insight into an inconsistency in the court record was quite an episode in itself.

Once again, Michiko had been with him. They were in the restaurant of the T Hotel. Otsuka had gone to the hotel to see a business client who was staying there. Once they had finished their business, he'd telephoned Michiko and called her over.

The restaurant was pretty crowded and obviously popular with foreigners, judging by the numbers of them. There was an American family having a meal opposite Otsuka and Michiko's table. They were a couple with a daughter of about seven and a boy of about four. It looked a little odd from the point of view of Japanese practice, but the wife sat there with an unconcerned look on her face while her husband busied himself looking after the children. From time to time Otsuka couldn't help staring with a kind of admiration.

The father repeatedly chastised the girl. Otsuka thought he was probably teaching his daughter correct table manners. He also thought it curious that he was spending much more time dealing with his daughter rather than the younger child.

"Look," said Michiko in a low voice, "look at the little girl."

Michiko had also been watching them. Otsuka peered over towards the family again, and Michiko continued, "She's left-handed. Her father keeps on making her hold her knife in her right hand but every time she swaps it to her left hand."

Sure enough, the little blonde girl waited for her father to turn away and talk with her mother and then changed her knife and fork over. It was quite obvious she was more comfortable eating that way.

Michiko looked down at her plate and said, "It looks as if in the West, too, left-handed people have a tough time."

Otsuka nodded vaguely in agreement and wound spaghetti onto his fork.

It wasn't precisely that moment when Otsuka experienced the revelation. That took place while he was driving home alone after dropping Michiko off in front of a bank on a relatively dimly-lit Ginza street corner.

He was gazing towards the dark edge of the Imperial Palace moat when suddenly a bright streetcar passed by obscuring his view. It was then that it suddenly occurred to him. He remembered a sentence recorded in the autopsy report and another sentence from the report of the expert witness:

```
A contusion of approximately 10
centimeters in length reached as far
as the periosteum on the right side of
the back of the head; a jagged cut 4
centimeters in length ran diagonally
top to bottom from the left side of
the forehead, and a 3 centimeter cut
extended from the left cheekbone to
the outside corner of the eye.
```

Keiichi Abe finished work and looked at the electric clock on the wall of the proof room at the printers. It was just before 11:00 pm. Someone had said they had finished pretty early tonight. For magazines, usually they'd go in the day before the final proof day and wouldn't leave until after midnight the following day. Three of the younger employees decided to go out drinking in Ginza.

The editor in chief and female staff had already gone home and the deputy chief and a few others of a similar age had turned down the invitation with a smile. "I wish I were your age again!"

The three young men hastily made for the bathroom and shaved. Their faces were greasy and black with dust. They had been working solidly for three days with little or no sleep.

"Can we still drink in Ginza? Everything closes at 11:30 these days, doesn't it? It's no good if we can't take it easy and enjoy ourselves," said Yamakawa.

"Relax. It's thirty minutes from here by car, which means we'll arrive around 11:30. We'll just make it in time. We should be okay until a little after midnight," answered Nishimoto. "I've discovered a new bar, out of the way down a side street. They shut up the front so you can drink until late without any bother from the police."

"When did you find it?" asked Abe as he rinsed soap from his hands.

"About a month ago. The madam is a Kyushu woman. Half the hostesses are from Kyushu too."

"Is that right? You're from Kyushu as well, aren't you?" said Abe, looking over at Nishimoto.

"Enough," said Yamakawa, wiping his face on a towel. "I'm not gonna let you hog the ladies' attention. I'm Hokkaido born and bred, from Otaru, after all. Now of course, it might be a different matter if you pay half the bill…"

There was something special about that feeling of a job completed. They had been working flat out all month just for this day. Nothing else seemed to matter now. Public opinion would be the judge of how good the magazine was—all they could do was trust in fate and see whether it sold well.

The three of them took the company car and headed for the Ginza. Following Nishimoto's directions the car sped away from West Ginza.

"Hey, where are we going? Why are we headed in this direction?" said Yamakawa, a little dejectedly.

This area was poorly lit and with few people around.

"We don't have the money to go to West Ginza at the moment. But that day will come," explained Nishimoto.

"You're just helping her out 'cause she's from Kyushu," Yamakawa said. "You're bringing us there to drum up business."

"I'm a Kyushu man, I can't help it. All I can do is bring her some fat cat customers."

The bar didn't front the main street but instead was tucked discreetly away at the rear. A tailor's shop stood on the corner and a red sign was lettered with "Seaweed." Under that was an arrow. Nishimoto went ahead and rapped smartly on the oak front door.

"Hello there!"

"Oh!" came a voice in reply, but it was only after Yamakawa and Abe had followed Nishimoto inside that they met the owner of the voice.

A rather plump woman and three hostesses rose from a dark booth and came over to greet them.

"Come in, come in." The plump madam addressed Nishimoto as one would a regular customer, and then greeted Yamakawa and Abe more politely, "Welcome, please come in."

The hostesses steered Nishimoto over towards an empty booth in the corner.

"We haven't seen you for a while," said the madam, smiling at Nishimoto.

"Yeah, I've been busy."

Nishimoto wiped his face with a hot towel and, indicating Yamakawa and Abe, introduced them as company colleagues. The madam gave a formal bow.

"I hear you've a lot of people from Kyushu working here?" said Yamakawa to the madam.

"That's right. That's where I'm from originally. I brought a couple of girls with me when I set up the place, and then others got wind of it and ended up finding their way here."

There were several hostesses in the bar.

"Nishimoto's from Kyushu too, you know. If he gets fired from the company maybe you could take him on as an apprentice bar tender!" joked Yamakawa.

The madam and hostesses laughed. The madam then said as if it had just occurred to her, "Oh yes, Mr. Nishimoto, I almost forgot, we have a new girl from Kyushu. Nobu, go and call her over, would you?"

The young hostess sitting next to the madam stood up and went over the other side of the bar.

"Wow, you really only have Kyushu girls," marvelled Nishimoto.

The new hostess, a slender girl, was brought over by Nobu. She approached the table. Her figure appeared dark against the bright shelves in the background—decorated with gleaming bottles of foreign liquor.

"Rie, come and sit here," the madam moved over and offered the girl a seat and said to Nishimoto, "Here she is."

The girl sat down. The red cylindrical lamp standing on the table cast its light on her face.

Abe glanced casually at the girl, and then he stared in absolute amazement.

He found himself looking at the face of Kiriko Yanagida, the young woman who had used the public phone to call the offices of the lawyer Kinzo Otsuka.

Chapter 5

Keiichi Abe gazed in astonishment at Kiriko Yanagida. She sat rigidly next to the madam. It was probably due in part to the dull light from the narrow red cylindrical lamp, but she wasn't looking directly at her three guests. She must have still been unused to the job and not known where to look.

Abe's eyes were fixed on Kiriko's face. Her downcast eyes, the faint blue veins in her forehead, her slender, shapely nose, her clamped lips, and the youthful line of her cheekbones—each memory was reflected in the dim light of the table lamp.

"Your name's Rie?" said Nishimoto in a gentle tone. "Are you from K-City too?"

"Yes." Kiriko answered quietly.

It had been a long time since Abe had heard her voice in reality. He felt as if he was dreaming.

SEICHO MATSUMOTO

"Be gentle with her," said the madam to Nishimoto, bowing in turn to Abe and Yamakawa. "She's only just started and isn't used to it yet."

"Is this the first time you've done this sort of job?" asked Nishimoto.

"*This* sort of job? What a way to put it!" laughed the girl called Nobuko. She was one of the girls who had worked here since the bar first opened. She was tall, and always wore the collar of her kimono open in a sophisticated manner. "I asked her to come up from Kyushu."

"You did?" Nishimoto looked from one girl to the other. "How did you know her?"

"Her brother was my boyfriend a long time ago," she laughed. "Well, maybe that's going a bit far. Actually we used to live in the same neighborhood. That's how I know her. Her brother passed away, and so I invited her up here."

"Really? But what about her relatives?"

"She hasn't got any. So please, be nice to her."

"That's a real shame," said Nishimoto. "Well, we certainly would like to help. But first," he continued, looking at Kiriko's face, "did you say your name was Rie?"

"Yes." Kiriko nodded affirmatively, looking somewhat embarrassed.

"Now, don't let yourself be led astray by this Nobu, all right?"

"What? Don't you go saying such unkind things, Mr. Nishimoto," said Nobuko, holding her hands out imploringly.

Nishimoto leaned back and laughed.

Just then the highballs they'd ordered were brought over, and the girls raised their gin fizz glasses. Kiriko clutched a glass of juice.

"Cheers!"

As they drank a toast, Abe stole a glance at Kiriko, but her eyes were trained in Nishimoto's direction. Her expression suggested she didn't remember his face. Abe, too, feigned ignorance, but in his chest, his heart was beating like a drum. He expected her to recognise him at any moment. But from Kiriko's perspective, it was only natural that she wouldn't remember him. After all, more than six months had passed since he'd met her. They'd met by chance and they had talked in the coffee shop for no more than ten minutes.

So you're here from Kyushu? I hope you don't think I'm being too forward, but it seemed to me from the phone conversation that your older brother is in some sort of trouble?

He recalled that was how the conversation had begun.

What kind of case is it? Perhaps you could explain it to me, if it's no trouble that is. I thought I heard you say the name of Otsuka. If it's Kinzo Otsuka, he's one of the best attorneys in Japan. In other words, he's very expensive. You asked him about his fees?... And so you've given up all hope of persuading Kinzo Otsuka to help you?

But Kiriko had remained silent and stubbornly refused to answer any of his questions. She had sat there with her eyes downcast, so it was probably fair to say that she hadn't had a good look at his face. In the end she'd got up in a hurry and left the coffee shop without so much as looking back over her shoulder. When Abe, in a panic, had followed her outside she'd disappeared into the crowds and was walking briskly away to prevent him from following her.

Having hurriedly come from Kyushu to the unfamiliar surroundings of Tokyo, it would be little wonder that she had no recollection of talking with Abe. But even so, he still hoped she might remember him.

There was something she couldn't know: that Abe had researched the incident involving her brother in the newspapers. Kiriko doubtless would never have imagined that outside of people with local connections there was someone in Tokyo who possessed such a degree of knowledge and interest in the incident. He only knew her real name was Kiriko Yanagida from the news reports.

But more than anything Abe could never have imagined he would run into Kiriko in this bar, of all places. He knew that the madam was from K-City in Kyushu and that the hostesses were also recruited from there, but he was amazed at meeting Kiriko once again, after not having received even a single postcard in reply to his letters. He was so shocked it took a while for him to accept that this situation was in fact reality.

"Let me introduce my colleagues," said Nishimoto. "This is Yamakawa, and next to him is Abe."

The madam bowed her head and said, "Nobu, bring some business cards over, will you please?"

Abe swallowed hard. He had given Kiriko his business card, and sent her letters too. He thought she would look up suddenly when she heard his name. But she continued to keep her eyes averted, staring at the rim of her juice glass. She no doubt assumed that it was the madam that was supposed to do all the talking. Besides, the family name Abe was fairly commonplace and average.

"It's nice to make your acquaintance," said the madam as she formally handed her business card to Yamakawa and Abe. The card read *Bar Seaweed – Noriko Masuda*. Her name was written in small type. The madam had a plump, pale face, fine, plucked eyebrows and a small mouth and nose.

"Rie," said the Madam, "please go and talk with the customers over there."

Kiriko suddenly rose from her seat. The customers in the booth opposite were singing along raucously to the tune of a guitarist. The madam obviously thought Kiriko would feel more at ease entertaining the other group of customers.

"Isn't she lovely? Still so innocent…" Nishimoto followed Kiriko with his gaze. Abe looked on after her as well. He noticed her shoulders and recalled the view from when she had left the coffee shop that other night and disappeared into the crowd.

"Her brother, you know," began the madam, lowering her voice, "had something odd happen to him. Actually, I'm taking care of her now."

"Something odd?" repeated Nishimoto, moving his face closer.

Abe felt his heart jolt, but the madam just smiled and didn't say anything further.

"So is she living with you in your apartment?"

"No, she's staying with Nobu," she replied, glancing at Nobuko.

"We're sharing the same room in the apartment."

"So whereabouts is your apartment?" asked Abe, speaking for the first time.

"Oh, what's this?" joked Nishimoto, "are you trying to say you're interested in these young ladies? If you visit this place often enough maybe you'll get to find out. Right, Nobu?"

Nobuko laughed at Nishimoto's remark.

"But if you're living together with her, Nobu, it'll be incovenient when your boyfriend comes over." This time it was Yamakawa's turn at horseplay.

"Oh, no worries, I don't have a boyfriend."

"Liar," said Nishimoto, "I've seen you just recently strolling about with a handsome young man."

"Mr. Nishimoto! Don't say such things!" Nobuko slapped Nishimoto on the arm and everyone laughed.

It was a little after midnight by the bar clock and some of the hostesses in the corner were making discreet preparations to leave for home.

"Well, we'd better be on our way," said Nishimoto.

Abe looked across the room and noticed Kiriko's back in between two of the booths. There were a group of customers singing karaoke songs and looking determined to stick it out until closing.

The three of them stood up and the Madam shouted over, "Rie—our guests are leaving now."

Kiriko stood up and came towards them. Nishimoto went first, followed by Yamakawa and then Abe.

The madam and Nobuko were joined by Kiriko and two other hostesses as they escorted their customers out into the street. Right up until the end Kiriko didn't so much as glance at Abe.

Feeling reluctant to leave but finding himself unable to talk to Kiriko in front of the others, he followed on behind Nishimoto and Yamakawa and climbed into the car.

The car pulled away with the three of them rambling on drunkenly together. Keiichi Abe was determined to talk alone with Kiriko the next day.

The following evening at around 8 o'clock Abe took out the business card he'd received at Bar Seaweed the night before and dialed the number. When he asked to speak to Rie, the girl who answered seemed surprised. "What? Rie?" It was obvious then that Rie was so new she didn't have regular customers yet.

"Rieko speaking." Kiriko's familiar voice sounded in the earpiece.

"Is that Rie? This is Abe. I was in the bar last night—with two others."

Kiriko answered, "Yes." Her voice was cold.

"I met you once before, in Tokyo, quite a while ago. Do you remember?"

He couldn't hear Kiriko's voice. He thought the phone had gone dead, but he could hear music playing in the background.

"I remember," she said plainly, after a pause.

Abe was taken aback. "When did you realize it was me?"

"I knew right from the beginning, when you were sitting in the booth."

Abe should have known she would recognize him. She must have noticed him before he realized who she was. And the way she feigned ignorance right up to the end was very much her style, just as she had suddenly run away from him earlier, in the spring.

"Is that right? Y-You knew it was me?" said Abe, stuttering slightly. "If that's the case then is it okay if I say a few words? Do you know I sent some letters to you in Kyushu? Perhaps you read them?"

Kiriko remained silent for a while, and then answered in a dry voice, "Yes, I read them."

"I would like to see you, it's about what I wrote. We can't talk in the bar. There's a coffee shop nearby there—will you meet me there at about five tomorrow?"

He had decided on 5:00 pm, guessing that the hostesses would be on their way to work around that time.

"I can't," said Kiriko.

Abe had expected her to say that. "Just ten minutes. Please, I want to see you. I've been spending time, you see, looking into your brother's case. Of course, it's not about my work. Not that it's my hobby or anything like that. But like you, I also believe your brother is innocent. I want to ask you some more questions."

Abe was determined. Kiriko fell silent again, but this time it seemed as though she was considering what he had said. In the background he could hear the incessant noise of voices and guitar music.

"I really can't," repeated Kiriko, but her voice was less defiant than before.

"Is there no chance I can persuade you?" Abe thought he'd try one last time.

"No," answered Kiriko. "Excuse me." She said this as if ending a formal conversation and hung up. Her voice lingered in Abe's ear. Having taken it this far, he decided he had no alternative but to press for a meeting. He wasn't unaware of the fact that he was being rather stubborn, but he really wanted to get to the bottom of the case. Abe intuitively believed Kiriko when she had yelled down the phone that day that her brother was innocent.

Abe was the type who, having once determined to do something, lost no time in taking action. He would get impatient and not be able to settle down. The day after the final proof day was a company holiday and he found it tough killing time until 11:30 at night. He watched a movie, which wasn't very entertaining, and stopped in at a couple of dull drinking establishments.

Bar Seaweed was in a remote part of Ginza. There were a number of unlit buildings in the neighborhood and it was extremely dark. Abe lingered a while on the other side of the alley. A building with a bank or something provided useful cover with which to conceal himself. He smoked two cigarettes and was halfway through another when the dark figures of the hostesses emerged into the alley.

He stomped the cigarette out and strained his eyes. Five girls had come out—three walked ahead chatting noisily together. Two remained behind: one was Nobuko and the other Kiriko. Abe was confident he could recognize Kiriko's silhouette no matter how dark it was. He moved out from the shadow of the building. His plan was to make it look as though he had bumped into them quite by chance while returning home from a night out somewhere. It was even more convenient that Nobuko was there as well. If Abe asked Nobuko out then Kiriko would have little alternative but to come along too. After all, they were living in the same apartment, and Kiriko had come to Tokyo relying on Nobuko's support. They were still standing there and Nobuko was saying something to Kiriko.

He decided then to make his presence known. "Hey!" he said purposefully to Nobuko, "are you going home now?"

"What a surprise!" Nobuko turned around and saw Abe's face in the light of the street lamp. She remembered him as the guest Nishimoto had brought along the previous night. "Thank you very much for last night." Nobuko bowed in a friendly manner.

Kiriko looked surprised, but had no choice but to copy Nobuko and bow her head in Abe's direction.

Abe was determined that this was his chance. "Is the bar closed now?"

"Yes," answered Nobuko.

"Oh, I just missed out."

"You'll have to come again a bit earlier tomorrow night," laughed Nobuko in a well-practiced tone of voice.

"And I came all this way. How about we have a cup of tea? Rie too, of course."

"Thank you very much. But tonight I'm a little..." Nobuko smiled.

"What's this? Are you trying to get rid of me?"

"No, not at all. In fact I was just saying to Rie that I have plans. Rie, how about you, won't you take up his offer?"

Nobuko looked at Kiriko who cast her eyes down forlornly.

"He works with Mr. Nishimoto at the same company. He won't be improper, you know."

"Well now, that's a strange guarantee as to my behavior," laughed Abe.

"Honestly, Rie, if he were a weirdo I wouldn't leave you alone with him. Mr. Abe has asked you out so please go with him, Rie."

"Nishimoto is a man of many virtues," said Abe a little shyly.

The reason why Nobuko was so willing to entrust Rieko into his care soon became apparent. A taxi drew up and stopped in front of them. The door opened. A customer sat alone inside but rather than attempt to get out he moved to the edge of the seat and beckoned for Nobuko to get in.

"Nobuko."

The voice was deep but young.

Nobuko moved towards the open door. And then she looked back at Abe and Kiriko and said, "Goodnight." She hitched the front of her kimono up, quickly bent down and climbed into the taxi. The man slid over. She reached her hand out and closed the door with finality.

Abe stared absent-mindedly through the window at the face of the young man. Even under the dull light of the cab's interior lamp he could tell it was a young man in his late twenties. Possibly becoming conscious of Abe's scrutiny, the man turned his face away.

Nobuko waved from the window as the car disappeared around the dark corner with its red taillights blazing.

For a moment Abe stood there absent-mindedly and Kiriko stayed stock still. There was no sign of anybody else around.

"Is he Nobuko's boyfriend?" said Abe, seeing an opportunity to break the ice with Kiriko.

"Perhaps," she answered vaguely. "I don't really know."

Abe began to walk. Kiriko hesitated for a second and then followed behind.

Abe breathed a sigh of relief. "He's probably from some company or other. I suppose he's a customer, is he?"

Abe wondered aloud about Nobuko's boyfriend as they walked in an attempt to put Kiriko at ease. He had noticed that the man wore a high-quality overcoat.

"No. He's not a customer, he's the younger brother of the madam."

"Really?" said Abe, his voice registering surprise, but in fact he wasn't at all interested.

They reached the brightly lit front entrance of the café. Abe pushed the door open with his shoulder and they went inside. As he'd hoped, Kiriko followed him, and his heart fluttered.

Having read the public prosecutor's indictment relating to the murder of the old loan shark, Kinzo Otsuka's suspicions were aroused by a number of points.

The report on the investigation of the scene of the crime described the situation within the house as follows:

```
In the eight-mat tatami room, there
was a chest of drawers against the
westerly wall. When I conducted my
inspection, I noticed the second and
third drawers were half open and
the clothing inside was in disarray.
The left side of the drawer had been
pulled some 10 centimeters further out
than the right. The lock on the left-
hand door of the small cabinet inlaid
in the lower right had been broken
off and the door left open, while the
right-hand door was still in place.
```

Otsuka wondered why the drawers had been pulled out in an uneven way, with the left side protruding farther than the right.

Ordinarily, one would pull open a drawer evenly by applying equal pressure both left and right. But if someone were in a hurry or flustered, one would expect that the right side of the drawer would be pulled out further than the left. It would be normal for one's right hand to unconsciously pull with more force on the right-hand side. But according to the report, it was the left side of the drawer that protruded more than the right. What did that mean?

The culprit pulled the drawer open in a rush and the strength of his left hand must have prevailed. Whoever opened the drawer was, evidently, left-handed.

Furthermore, it was the left-hand door of the bookcase that was opened with its lock broken, while the right-hand door remained in place. The cabinet was positioned at the lower right corner. If the culprit had proceeded to open it after pulling out the drawers and without moving very far, he would have used his right hand to open the right side if he was right-handed. That would be the logical progression. But the evidence suggested quite strongly that the culprit was left-handed instead.

Otsuka considered this while reading the expert witness report, which stated:

> On the left side of the forehead there was a thumb-sized spot of subcutaneous bleeding, but no evidence of fracturing. Furthermore, there was similar internal bleeding evident between the skin and muscle of the left cheek.

And further:

> With regard to the method of assault, the wounds to the right side of the back of the head which caused the depressed fracture are consistent with a strong blow from the rear while turned away from the attacker. The wounds to the forehead and left cheek and also the wounds to the third rib probably resulted from blows delivered from the front as the victim turned to face the attacker.

In striking a person with a long stick or club it would be natural to hit the opposite side of the victim with a backhand blow, which allowed the greatest arc and amount of force. Therefore, a right-handed assailant would strike his victim on the left side, from the assailant's perspective. In this case, because the culprit was left-handed he would have struck the right side of the back of the victim's head when he attacked from behind.

In addition, judging from the drawing of the position of the body, the victim had fallen parallel with and about 40 centimeters from the front of the chest of drawers. The facial wound was not the result of a diagonal blow to the right cheek, but instead a diagonal line from below the left eyebrow down towards the right jaw. This would indicate that the blow had been delivered to the left side of the victim's face from the front, with the left-handed attacker striking on the right from his point of view.

The space between the chest of drawers and the body was extremely narrow. So if the victim had been struck by a club or something similar, the chest of drawers would undoubtedly have made it difficult to swing the club freely, which should have caused the attacker to swing from the side away from the drawers—attacking the right side of the face. However, according to the expert witness report, the blow to the left cheek had been delivered with considerable force. A roughly vertical blow to the head indicated that the assailant was standing at the victim's feet; it would be most natural to presume that he was left-handed.

Otsuka felt his cheeks redden as he considered his conclusions. According to the 9th interrogation report, the defendant had stated he was right-handed. He'd said: "I took the club in my right hand and beat her across the face and forehead." The more Otsuka thought about it the more he felt sure the true culprit must have been left-handed.

Otsuka turned the pages of each voluminous report, wading through the immense detail and making sure he didn't overlook any statements made by either the public prosecutor or the defendant.

What had turned events decidedly against the defendant Masao Yanagida was the fact he had entered the victim's house and come into contact with her blood. The blood had been found on the cuffs of the trousers he had been wearing. The statement of the expert witness verifying that Kiku's blood type was O and that this was the same as that found on the trousers amounted to indisputable physical evidence against Masao Yanagida.

However, thought Otsuka, the victim's blood was found only on the cuffs of Yanagida's trousers and, curiously, not on any other part of his clothing. The public prosecutor's speech concluded that "notwithstanding the victim had been struck with an oak club, it is by no means certain that blood would have discharged in the direction of the assailant, and in fact, since the blow was delivered to the head and cheek areas with a blunt instrument, it is likely that there was not much blood at all."

Otsuka felt he had to concur with this conclusion. If the weapon had been something like an oak club, it probably would not have severed any blood vessels, much less any arteries, and therefore there wouldn't have been a large quantity of blood that could have spattered.

However, there was an alternative explanation. In other words, didn't the fact that the blood was found only on the cuffs of Yanagida's trousers and not elsewhere on his trousers or other clothing prove that he did not in fact murder Kiku Watanabe? Blood on the *tatami* mats from the wounds on Kiku's head was small in quantity, which meant Yanagida inadvertently picked up the blood onto his cuffs from the floor when he entered the room immediately after she was killed.

After the assailant had struck Kiku's head and face, blood would not have immediately sprayed onto the *tatami* matting. After suffering a wound of this sort, most of the blood would, over time, seep from the body. Accordingly, it seemed illogical to argue that in the case of a blow delivered by a blunt instrument, as opposed to one with a sharp edge, blood would immediately spatter onto the defendant's trouser cuffs. This was further evidenced by the ash from the brazier that was also found on the cuffs. Someone had attacked Kiku, and from the impact of her body to the floor, the kettle, which had been resting on top of the brazier, had been knocked sideways causing a cloud of ash to issue and accumulate on the *tatami*. Yanagida must have walked on the *tatami* and picked up traces of blood and ash on his trousers. In short, Yanagida's trespass was, as he himself had originally testified, only after the victim had been killed.

According to the indictment, while waiting for the defendant to arrive, Kiku had set out two tea cups and two guest cushions and on the brazier she had placed a tea pot and tea caddy. Water boiled in the iron kettle.

However, the defendant had for some time past been subjected to a tirade of insults by Kiku Watanabe for failing to repay the loan, and Yanagida himself had repeatedly apologized for this. Even supposing Yanagida had communicated his intention of repaying the loan that evening, there was no reason to believe that Kiku would have been preparing to welcome him courteously as one normally would a guest.

It had been assumed that of the two guest cushions, one was for Kiku herself to use and the other for her guest, and that she was expecting only one visitor. However, would an old woman like Kiku really use a guest cushion herself when entertaining a visitor? Would it not be more customary for her to use an ordinary cushion, or simply forgo a cushion altogether and sit down on the *tatami*? It would surely be more natural to set out the better cushions to guests only. And if that was the case, she must not have been expecting just one guest—it would seem more likely that she anticipated two guests that night.

As indicated by the public prosecutor, citing the following extracts from the defendant's statement, it seemed extremely unnatural behavior on the part of the defendant to open the chest of drawers, filch the promissory note and then calmly return home, knowing all the while that Kiku was murdered.

PRO BONO

When I arrived at Kiku Watanabe's
house the front door was open and with
only the paper screen closed. I could
see a light on inside. Thinking that
Kiku was waiting up for me I called
out "Good evening" two or three times
but there was no reply. I thought she
might have been having a nap since she
was of age. When I opened the paper
screen doors I could see that the
screen doors to the eight-mat tatami
room on the left of the entrance hall
were open. When I looked more closely
I saw that Kiku was lying on her back
in front of the chest of drawers but I
still thought she was asleep. However,
when I called out again she showed
no sign of waking up and not only
that, the iron tea kettle was over on
its side in the charcoal brazier and
there was ash on the tatami matting,
probably blown there from the brazier
when hot water spilled from the kettle.
I thought it a little odd, and when I
looked more carefully I saw something
red on the matting and knew then it
was blood. There was also blood on
Kiku's face. I considered notifying the
police immediately, but then guessed
the reason why she hadn't stirred at
all was because she had been murdered.
It was then that I decided to steal
the promissory note. If there were
a police investigation, it wouldn't
take long before the promissory note
came to light and everyone would know
about the high-interest loan. I would
lose face with the school, the PTA
and all my friends and acquaintances.

```
I removed my shoes and went into the
room...
```

Masao Yanagida, an honest young man, was considered to be extremely trustworthy by his pupils and held in great esteem by the PTA. He had taken on a high-interest loan, which he was finding difficult to repay, and suffered the repeated torment of being waylaid by Kiku on the roadside who would assail him with all manner of verbal vitriol. For a serious and timid man like Yanagida, this level of abuse would have resulted in an unbearable degree of anguish. Shouldn't the court have taken better account of his psychological state at the time?

When he saw Kiku's corpse Yanagida no doubt pictured in his mind the start of the police investigation and the inevitable discovery of the promissory note. He probably simply wanted to conceal the fact that he had taken a high-interest loan from Kiku, as opposed to trying to make off with the funds.

Given Kiku's persistent demands it would be difficult to deny that Yanagida had an almost overriding compulsion to retrieve the promissory note. But, perhaps more than that, he was haunted by the fear and indignity of the police and general public becoming aware of the fact that he, an elementary school teacher, had borrowed so much money and then found himself unable to repay it when due.

If one could understand that, then one could also concede that in spite of his shock at finding Kiku dead, taking back his promissory note was not in fact unnatural considering his circumstances.

In his statements, Yanagida initially denied his culpability, then admitted his guilt, and then in court he retracted his confession. Why was it that he momentarily confessed to the crime? This appeared to cast doubt on whether the confession was given of his free will in the first place.

Otsuka knew that the court-appointed attorney hadn't recognized that possibility. If he had, then it would undoubtedly have appeared in the court transcript. But no such doubts were noted in the defense attorney's summary of proceedings.

The fact that Masao Yanagida had initially denied his culpability to the police, and then subsequently confessed to carrying out the crime, was recorded in the 9th interrogation report as follows:

```
Until now I have stated that it was
someone else that murdered Kiku
Watanabe. However, now that it seems
your enquiries have come to an end
I wish to state the truth. In point
of fact, it was I who murdered Kiku
Watanabe... I had already noticed the
oak club she kept in the house and
thought it would be a suitable weapon
with which to deal a solid blow. All of
a sudden I made a dash for it, picking
it up with both hands before bringing
it down hard on top of Kiku's head.
```

However, would an assailant intending to murder his victim really rely on an oak club placed by the door? It would surely be more usual for a criminal with murderous intent to go prepared with his own weapon.

According to the public prosecutor's summary, in this case, it was not a random attack but a pre-meditated one. If that were the case then it would seem rather odd for Yanagida to rely on using an object in the victim's house.

Again, according to the 9th interrogation report:

```
Kiku momentarily collapsed onto the
floor, but in the next instant she was
up again, grappling furiously at me,
and so I took the club in my right
hand and beat her across the face and
forehead. Kiku let out an awful scream
and then fell onto her back again and
stopped moving.
```

This was an extremely imprecise description of the crime. The real assailant would surely have given a more accurate and detailed account. In this case he was unable to say with any certainty where he had delivered blows, and he may simply have stated he "beat her across the face" after recalling reports of such details in newspapers and magazines.

It appeared the police had also noticed this as was evident from Yanagida's statement recorded in the 10th interrogation report:

```
With regard to my earlier statement
about the murder of Kiku Watanabe, I
couldn't remember yesterday which part
of her I struck, but today I do recall
and would like to make a statement.
The first place I struck her was the
back of her head. After she had fallen
```

```
and landed on her back I remember
striking her firstly on the left side of
the forehead and then across her left
cheek. Then I think I struck her on
the chest.
```

Why hadn't Yanagida disclosed this level of detail when he had first made his confession?

It was not completely implausible that he was following someone else's directions. It was from this possibility that Otsuka drew an inference.

According to Yanagida's first statement in the 9th interrogation report:

```
[I]n the next instant she was up again,
grappling furiously at me, and so I
took the club in my right hand and
beat her across the face and forehead.   .
```

The statement at this time did not say he struck her on the chest. In other words, certain details of the wounds had been given in the newspapers. It had been reported that there were wounds to the head and to the face, but nothing had been said about the victim's chest. So if it was the case that Yanagida learned of the victim's wounds from the press, then naturally he would not have been aware of the injuries to her chest.

The murderer had struck his victim's chest while she wore clothing, and consequently the damage was relatively light with only the third rib breaking. It would not have been obvious without closer inspection. Otsuka had heard previously from a forensic specialist that where the victim was of advanced age, a rib could easily be broken with the application of only moderate force.

The prosecution themselves had only become aware of the broken rib following their review of the autopsy report. A "confession" needed to be extracted that spoke to the matter of the broken rib. Therefore, in the 10th interrogation report, Yanagida added for the first time the statement, "Then I think I struck her on the chest."

And then there was the issue of the prosecution viewing the fact that the victim's chest of drawers had been ransacked as evidence of a deception perpetrated by Yanagida to give the impression that the promissory note had been taken in the course of a violent burglary. This rested on the premise that the loss had been limited to the promissory note. Indeed, the prosecution themselves seemed to recognize and accept that, other than the promissory note, Yanagida had not stolen anything.

However, it had not been established exactly which of the victim's belongings had been taken. She lived alone, separately from her son and his wife. According to the statement of her son, Ryutaro, he and his wife didn't see eye to eye with Kiku and had moved out five years before. He went on to testify:

> I've no idea how much money she had, as I never asked her. And so after the murder when the police asked me how much had been stolen, I really didn't know. I don't know how much cash she had on her either.

Since it wasn't known how much had been there, it wasn't clear what had actually been stolen. Even the victim's son didn't seem to know how much money she typically had on her and had no idea therefore if a large amount of cash had gone missing.

Precisely because the drawers of the chest had been pulled out, there was a possibility that a criminal had taken money and made his escape. That bit could just as easily prove Masao Yanagida's innocence. The real killer likely left the scene only moments before Yanagida had arrived.

If there was one thing that Otsuka had discovered from his painstaking review of so many voluminous documents, it was that all the evidence pointed overwhelmingly to Masao Yanagida's innocence.

The general good character and trustworthiness of the defendant was corroborated by numerous witnesses. Then there was the fact that he had only borrowed the money in order to discreetly make good the loss of the 38,000 yen earmarked for the school trip.

And, as the school principal had stated,

```
If only he had confided in me at the
time, I might have been able to get
hold of the money...
```

This tragedy had arisen because he couldn't bring himself to do that, and instead took it upon himself to make up the loss. This itself was an indication of Masao Yanagida's character.

Otsuka felt dejected.

If he had taken the case on at the time, he could have proved Masao Yanagida innocent. He was sure of that much now. He brought to mind Yanagida's sister when she visited his offices. A young woman with intense eyes.

He had told her, "There are bound to be some first-rate lawyers in Kyushu, too. I don't think you needed to come all the way to Tokyo."

But she had been insistent. "I just thought that if it's not you, then I can't do anything to save my brother."

And that seemed to have been the case. That was not to say that the court-appointed attorney from Kyushu was completely ineffectual. It was more the thought of "what if" that gnawed at Otsuka's conscience.

"You're turning me down because I can't afford to pay the legal fees. That's right, isn't it?" she had said, with heavy conviction. It had been a forthright question for such a young woman to ask.

"There may be an element of truth in that," he had replied, deciding it best to give her an honest, straightforward answer.

He had said more than was necessary, and now he regretted it. She undoubtedly resented him, believing he had declined her case because of money.

"I don't know whether my brother will get the death penalty," she had said as she paused before leaving his office.

Indeed, that was the verdict handed down by the criminal court.

This was the first dark arrow that Kiriko had shot in Otsuka's direction. The second volley had come in the form of that one particular sentence in her postcard: "My brother died in disgrace branded a common thief and murderer."

Otsuka took out a length of string and bundled up the mountain of paperwork. He decided that tomorrow he would have Okumura return the loaned court transcript to the lawyer in Kyushu. He closed his notebook, rested his chin on his hands and with a slight furrow in his brow, lost himself in thought.

"You look depressed," said Michiko, looking at Otsuka's face. "You ask to see me then sit there with a face like that. Can't you loosen up a little and smile?"

"I'm sorry," Otsuka apologized with a forced laugh. "I didn't mean to come here and be miserable."

The heated *kotatsu* table was draped with a colorful patterned blanket to trap the heat underneath. Several bottles of sake sat on top, but Otsuka wasn't feeling the slightest bit drunk.

It was the inn they always came to. They were on friendly terms with the owner and knew the maids too. They had come here ever since their relationship first started. They'd both changed into padded winter kimonos. It was quiet all around. The cold air from outside seemed to penetrate the paper screens and make its presence known inside. Unless they were summoned, the maids did not trouble them.

In one of the rooms not too far away they could hear a *shamisen* being played and the voice of a woman singing. From time to time a peal of laughter rose up.

"It sounds like they're having a good time," said Michiko, lifting a sake bottle to pour. "Come on, cheer up."

"I will, then." Otsuka raised his cup and said, "Shall we sing something as well?"

"Really? Now don't bite off more than you can chew." Michiko laughed prettily.

"I'll play the part of the audience."

"No fair!" Michiko fixed him with her stare. She had lovely eyes and she knew the effect they had. But then she began to sing. She had a thin yet penetrating voice.

Otsuka's ears were listening, but his mind turned back to the murder case. He suddenly noticed that the song had come to an end and gave a short round of applause.

"You weren't even listening," Michiko criticized.

"I most certainly was. It was lovely. I was captivated, enthralled. When a nice piece of music comes to an end it doesn't do to clap immediately."

"Please yourself," said Michiko, helping herself to a drink.

"Now, don't sulk."

"Well, what am I supposed to do? You come to see me then spend all your time thinking about work."

Otsuka thought her behavior childish, not at all what he would expect from the owner of a top-class French restaurant in the Ginza.

"No I'm not."

"Yes you are, it's written all over your face," retorted Michiko assertively. "It was the same the other day when we met. You had that bored look on your face."

"That's not true. I'm having a great time with you."

"Well, thank you very much. But I can tell when you have something on your mind. It's the same case you were thinking about the other time, isn't it?" Michiko stared at Otsuka.

"No, it isn't. Actually it's not even a case I am formally involved in," admitted Otsuka at length.

"You're not involved in it? Then why worry about it? How very odd of you."

It had nothing to do with him and yet he had rarely, if ever, been so bothered about a case before. It wasn't as if he had taken it on and then given up halfway through, either—he'd legitimately declined it in the first place.

He had had similar experiences in the past, but none had weighed as heavily on his mind as this case.

He knew only too well the reason why—because the defendant Masao Yanagida had died while in prison.

If he were still alive, Otsuka could have taken the first available flight and been there to do what he could. Be it Kyushu or wherever, he would go and investigate. But since the defendant was dead, he was denied any possibility of remedying the situation. This fact was something he couldn't change, and it cast a dark and chilling shadow across his heart.

Otsuka nodded his head and said, "It's been a while. I think I'll go and play some golf."

"Yes, why don't you?" agreed Michiko. "You've been spending far too much time in your office wrapped up in your own thoughts."

"Why don't you come along too?" said Otsuka, taking hold of Michiko's hand and sidling up to her.

"All right, I will."

"What about your restaurant?"

"Well, there's actually a bit of an issue right now. But for you, I'll come along any time."

Otsuka stroked her cheek with his finger.

Otsuka went to the office. Just before lunchtime, a young man arrived requesting a meeting for his opinion regarding a certain case. His business card announced him as Keiichi Abe from *Comment*.

Chapter 6

Okumura was the one who brought the business card in and placed it on Otsuka's desk.

"What's this?" said Otsuka, looking up.

"Someone's asking for an opinion about a case. I offered to take a look, but he says he wants to discuss it directly with you."

Otsuka stared again at the lettering on the business card. "Something to do with the magazine, I wonder? Or perhaps it's a personal matter."

"He said it was personal. But then he is a journalist. Who knows—maybe it's just an excuse so he can see you and get some information."

Otsuka was in good spirits this morning. When he was in a bad mood, he would think nothing of turning people away on the pretext of being too busy to see them. But he had only just arrived in the office and didn't feel like diving straight into the heap of bothersome papers that stared back at him from his desk. He didn't think it so bad an idea to meet with this unknown person to fill in some time while he settled into the day.

"All right, I'll see him."

Okumura left the room and was replaced a few moments later by a tall young man.

On first sight, Otsuka thought he seemed like a pleasant young man. Otsuka met with upwards of ten people a day and very good or bad first impressions were important to him. If he felt ill at ease with someone, he would feel less than hospitable towards them.

But the young man who now appeared before him seemed to contradict the stereotypical image of the worldly-wise, cocksure journalist, for he was turned out smartly and had an extremely cheerful expression on his face.

"Mr. Otsuka?" Abe smiled as he greeted the attorney. "As I explained just now to your office clerk, my name is Abe and I'm from *Comment*."

"Have a seat." Otsuka pointed to the guest chair in front of him. Then he took another quick look at the business card which he'd placed on his desk.

"You want an opinion about a case?" he asked, raising his eyes.

"Yes, that's right. I thought it would be a good idea to ask you about it."

Otsuka took out a cigarette and drew on it slowly. Light purple smoke drifted up through the stripes of bright morning light as it cascaded in through the window.

"I gather from talking with my clerk that this has nothing to do with the magazine?" Otsuka scrutinized Abe's face. The younger man had an extremely eager look about him. Even his eyes belied excitement.

"It's nothing to do with the magazine," replied Abe.

"That being the case, it must be something you're involved in?"

"I'm not sure I would say it concerns me exactly…" Abe hesitated for a moment and then said, "It concerns an acquaintance of mine."

"I see." Otsuka swivelled in his chair and leaned his body slightly so that he was facing Abe diagonally across the desk. "Let's hear it," he said, having now made himself comfortable.

"The case," began Abe, pulling a notebook out from his pocket and looking at it, "relates to the murder of an old woman."

Otsuka was startled. His swivel chair creaked as he found himself suddenly sitting upright. Without thinking, he put his cigarette in his mouth. His eyes narrowed and he blew out smoke in the hope of camouflaging his surprise.

"I'll explain the sequence of events for you. The old woman was 65 years of age. She had saved up a tidy sum of money and made a living lending it at high rates of interest. The case came to light on March 20, the body found at around 8:00 am by the deceased woman's daughter-in-law who quite by chance had decided to pay her a visit. The police estimated that the body had lain undiscovered for eight or nine hours, which would put the time of death at around

11 pm or midnight on the 19th, the day before the body was found. Judging from the appearance of the body, the old woman looked to have put up a fair amount of resistance. To her side, an iron kettle had been knocked over on top of a charcoal brazier and had spilled hot water, sending up a cloud of ash that settled on the floor. She had been beaten repeatedly about the head and face with an oak club which she had kept for security purposes, and died as a result of severe injuries."

Otsuka felt his lips turn pale. When Abe had begun to talk about the case, he had wondered, but now there was no doubt whatsoever that it was the same Kyushu murder investigation he had been looking into.

Otsuka was not normally one to believe in coincidences. Yet this was one occasion where he couldn't help but feel he had some kind of strange connection with the young man who now sat before him.

Otsuka failed even to notice the ever-lengthening column of ash forming on the tip of his cigarette and he listened not just with his ears but his whole heart as the young man continued his explanation.

"The old woman ran a moneylending business and since she was extremely unforgiving when it came to collecting her dues, she'd earned herself a good deal of enmity. With regard to the losses she suffered, the police investigation indicated that a promissory note had been stolen, and clothing in the chest of drawers had been rummaged through. It's difficult to say how much money had been taken as the old woman lived alone, but it can be assumed to have been a fairly significant amount."

The young man's eyes followed the lines of writing in his notebook.

"However, it was the promissory note that provided the police with their first breakthrough in finding a suspect. Said suspect was a young male elementary school teacher who had borrowed 40,000 yen from the old woman. However, his salary was quite small and he was unable to make the repayments as he had intended. It seems he was very upset by the old woman's relentless demands for payment. Moreover, not only did the young teacher not have an alibi that night, but stains of the same blood type as the old woman's were found on the cuffs of his trousers, together with particles of ash from the charcoal brazier."

Abe paused at this point and looked at the lawyer.

"The police subjected the teacher to a rigorous interrogation. At first he stubbornly denied committing the murder. He reportedly told the police that he had borrowed 40,000 yen from the old woman, admitted that he was unable to repay it and had gone to the old woman's home on the night in question and taken the promissory note. However, he was adamant that he was not the murderer. He maintained that his reason for visiting the home of the deceased on the night she died was to apologize for not repaying the loan, and when he arrived at her home as promised, the old woman had already been murdered by somebody else."

Otsuka listened to the words of the young journalist and felt as if he were reviewing his own findings of the case in detail. Of course, his own research was much more thorough and detailed. Nevertheless, hearing the train of events from someone else brought a sense of reality to the matter that he didn't feel when looking through the paperwork.

The young journalist continued:

"According to the teacher, he had been in torment for some considerable time over the 40,000-yen loan and, despite having promised to repay it, he had actually gone there that night to explain he hadn't managed to raise the money. However, when he saw the corpse, it suddenly occurred to him that if the promissory note were to 'disappear,' he would be released from his torment. Without so much as a thought for the consequences of his actions, he took his promissory note from the bundle of notes kept in the chest of drawers, and made his escape."

Abe looked up at Otsuka to gauge his reaction. But the lawyer had turned his head to one side and was exhaling smoke, so he lowered his eyes to his notebook again.

"Of course, there was no reason why the police should have relied on a partial admission of this sort. The teacher subsequently caved in under intense interrogation and confessed to the murder. His confession was in line with the police's own view of what had happened—namely, that he had broken into the old woman's house that night and beaten her to death with the oak club, before taking the promissory note and rummaging through clothing in the chest of drawers to make it look as though a burglar had been responsible. However, when the young teacher was examined by the public prosecutor in court, he retracted his confession and instead insisted that his original statement was true in that he stole the promissory note, but he certainly did not murder the old woman. Notwithstanding this about-face, it seemed clear to everyone that he had committed the crime, especially in view of the physical evidence presented by the blood stains and ash found on his trousers. And in fact, the criminal court found him guilty and handed down the death sentence."

Here again Abe looked at Otsuka's face, but the lawyer was still facing the wall lined with bookcases. The lettering on the spines of legal precedent books gleamed gold in the sunlight.

"However, this young teacher maintained his innocence until the very end. Several months into the appeal case, the teacher died of illness in prison. There is just one person who will always believe he was innocent—his younger sister."

Otsuka's eyes flickered for the first time. But he maintained his composure by blowing cigarette smoke out and watching it drift through the stripes of sunlight.

"I'm not sure whether my summary of the case is enough for you to form an opinion but, well, I also believe in the teacher's innocence. If you need to see more documentation I'm sure I could arrange to have it sent up from the local court. Could you possibly give me your thoughts on the facts I've explained?"

Abe stared intently at Otsuka's face. But Otsuka kept quiet and looked as though he intended to stay that way.

In the adjoining room a telephone rang, and the clerk and young lawyers could be heard discussing the various cases they were assigned.

Otsuka remained motionless, as if he were listening to the goings-on in the room next to his. Abe gazed at the lawyer, his own attention drawn to the telephone conversation.

"Are you able to give me your opinion based on what I've told you?"

Otsuka spoke for the first time in a while. He looked at the young journalist and spoke calmly. "I will do my best."

"Thank you very much," replied Abe, bowing his head slightly. "It's just that, well, I've only explained the gist of the case for you. I'm not sure you can form a proper view based only on what I have told you. What I'm trying to say is that, if you are interested in looking at this case, I could obtain the necessary documentation and come and see you again."

Again, Otsuka didn't answer immediately. As before, he moved his body diagonally to one side and transferred his gaze to the far corner of the room.

Just then a whirring noise from outside filled the air around them. Gradually the noise dissipated and, as if he had been waiting for it to come to an end, Otsuka answered Abe's question.

"I appreciate you have come here especially to see me, but it is going to be difficult to give my opinion on the facts you have told me. To begin with, the defendant is already dead. That fact alone would make a re-examination of the case troublesome."

"But..." Abe was shaking his head. "I really don't believe the issue is whether or not the defendant is dead. I'm asking you to look into this for the sake of the bereaved family and those who feel he was innocent."

With a deeply reluctant expression on his face, Otsuka stubbed his cigarette out in an ashtray. Placing his elbows on the desktop he made a bridge of his hands and rested his chin on his interlaced fingers.

"In any event, it doesn't look as though it's something I can take on," he said plainly.

"But *sensei*, haven't you proven defendants to be innocent of false charges like in this case?"

"Well yes, but…" said Otsuka with a wry smile. "Just because I won some cases like this in the past doesn't mean to say that all guilty verdicts are incorrect. Even from what you have told me it is entirely possible that the defendant's plea was false and that the prosecution and verdict were in fact justified."

"If that's the case, then fine. All I am asking is that you carry out an investigation and try and establish the truth of the matter."

"But," Otsuka pointed out, "didn't the defendant have a lawyer?"

"Yes he did," replied Abe. "This may sound rude but he was only a local lawyer appointed by the court to represent the defendant and didn't have anywhere near your level of skill. If you had taken on the case, then who knows, the defendant may have been proven innocent. I also happen to believe what he said."

Otsuka looked for the umpteenth time at the business card. He held it by the edges and then placed it carefully to the side of his desk.

"In any case," said Otsuka, with an ill-concealed look of irritation, "it's not a case that especially interests me, I'm afraid. Plus, we're pretty busy at the moment and tend not to give out opinions. Please don't take it personally, you understand."

"Perhaps I didn't explain myself properly," said Abe quietly. "I should think it difficult to appreciate the complexities of the case simply from my explanation. If you were to review the detailed paperwork, I'm sure you might feel differently. Can't I persuade you to change your mind and take a look at the case in more depth?"

The lawyer answered in a restrained, measured tone of voice, "I have already tried to tell you several times that I do not wish to look into this case. I'm sorry but that is my final decision. I am extremely busy right now."

"But *sensei*," Abe looked at Otsuka for the first time with a searching intensity in his eyes, "haven't you heard of this case before?"

The lawyer's face colored as he stared back at Abe. "What are you trying to say?"

"The defendant's younger sister told me she had travelled up from Kyushu to see you. She must surely have explained the gist of the case to you at that time."

"That's not true!" shouted Otsuka. "Okay, look, I do recall seeing the woman you are talking about but, as I said, I am extremely busy just as I was then. I believe I asked her to leave without listening to her story."

Abe looked again at Otsuka's face, "His sister said that the reason why you declined to represent her was that she couldn't afford your legal fees."

Otsuka's eyes shone as he looked at Abe directly and fixed him with his steely gaze. "Now I will ask you a question," he said. "What is your relationship with the defendant's sister?"

"There is no connection," said Abe with an air of certainty. "I will say that we're on friendly terms. She felt bitter that you didn't listen to her case because of the issue of legal fees. She said that if you'd agreed to take the case on then maybe her brother would not have died in prison, branded a common thief and murderer."

"It seems I am being unfairly accused," said Otsuka with a faint smile on his lips. "I'm free to decide whether to take on a case or not. I don't know what impression both of you have formed of me, but the problem certainly wasn't only fee-related. As I have said, I was also very busy at the time. I didn't even have the time to listen properly to the summary of the case. Of course it's unfortunate that she came from so far away especially to see me, but it was a sudden request without any prior communication and I felt I had no option but to turn her down."

"I see." Abe put his notebook back in his pocket. "I'm sorry to have taken up your time when you are so busy. I had come here today to ask your opinion on the case, but listening to your reply I understand why you are unable to do as I request."

"Did the defendant's sister," asked Otsuka, looking up, "ask you to come and see me?"

153

"No, it was my idea to come here. I felt sorry for her and wanted to help and so I began poking around a little. When I heard the story, I wanted to find out more. I'm sorry you feel you can't help me. But I won't give up. I may have to bother you again and I hope I can count on your cooperation at that time."

"Thank you. Goodbye." The lawyer rose from his chair and gave a curt bow.

Abe's youthful form left the office. Otsuka moved away from his desk. He looked out of the window at the bare treetops waving in the wind on the street below. The street was like a valley, with little natural light reaching the surface. People walked with hunched shoulders along the shadowy sidewalk. As Otsuka was gazing at the scene below, Keiichi Abe's dark figure emerged from the building. Abe thrust his hands into the pockets of his overcoat and began to walk away. His long, unbound hair soon tangled in the wind. He raised his arm and hailed a cab.

As he was about to climb in he turned around and looked back in the direction of the office, but he was too far away to notice Otsuka standing in the window looking down on him.

Abe's taxi moved out of the window frame and disappeared from view.

Okumura came in behind him. Otsuka returned to his desk and listened to the clerk's legal briefs, but his mind was still consumed by Abe's words.

After researching the case of the old woman's murder Otsuka thought the facts were clearly in the defendant's favor.

If he were to look into it more thoroughly he might find further evidence pointing to Masao Yanagida's innocence. His gut feeling from years of experience told him that Yanagida had been falsely indicted.

However, he didn't feel at liberty at this point to announce his views to the young journalist. He'd actually considered saying as much to him, having heard his story. Yet he was reluctant to do so because he'd flatly refused to agree to work for the defendant at his sister's request. The issue of legal fees had become caught up in a strange manner in the debate and was proving unnecessarily irksome. Be that as it may, Otsuka was left with a bad taste in his mouth and couldn't calm down.

Okumura continued to explain the day's schedule. Unlike most days, today the clerk's voice sounded like the incessant buzzing of a fly to Otsuka's ears.

That night Abe sent a letter to Mr. R, a lawyer in K-City, Kyushu. He had learned the court-appointed lawyer's name from the newspapers he'd seen. He was requesting, if it were not too much trouble, to borrow for a week the court records relating to the case of the murder. The case was already closed as a result of the defendant's death, and he hoped that the lawyer would simply acquiesce to his request.

Abe waited for a reply while dealing with the backlog of work at the office. The reply came five days later. It was a simple postcard:

    Thank you for your letter. With regard
    to your request, I am not sure how you

intend to use the court records as the
case has already closed as a result
of the death of the defendant. While
I understand from your letter that
the intention is not to use it for the
purposes of your magazine, I am afraid
I am not able to lend the records to
you. However, I would like to inform
you that a month ago I was approached
by a Tokyo-based lawyer named Kinzo
Otsuka in regards to this same case,
and I lent the records to him. If you
wish to learn more details of the case
in question, might I suggest that you
make inquiries of Mr. Otsuka.

Abe felt the wind knocked out of him at the sight of
Otsuka's name. Up until now he was under the impression
that Otsuka had not the slightest interest in this case, but
according to the court-appointed lawyer's postcard, Otsuka
had already requisitioned the court records and already read
them. What was more, there hadn't been the slightest hint of
this on Otsuka's face when he had met and talked with him
in his offices the other day. The lawyer had simply looked
on with an air of indifference, all the while drawing on his
cigarette.

Why on earth hadn't Otsuka mentioned it at the time?
Why had he flatly denied having any interest in the case and
pretended as if Abe's telling of it were the first he'd ever heard
the details? When Kiriko Yanagida had first gone to see him,
Otsuka naturally had no knowledge of the case. Yet the fact
that he had gone to the trouble of having the Kyushu lawyer
send the records to him clearly indicated that something had

piqued his interest in the case. It was more than just a passing interest—something had undoubtedly moved him to obtain the records.

The fact was that Otsuka had obtained the court records and read them. In all probability, being Otsuka, he probably studied the documents thoroughly. Why had he kept quiet about all of this when Abe went to see him?

Abe could still see in his mind's eye Otsuka's impassive expression as he stared sideways at the wall. His words had been cold and from the outset he had done his best to be uncooperative.

However, Otsuka knew all about the case. Why had he feigned indifference in an attempt to hide what he knew? Abe wondered whether his own attitude had in some way irritated Otsuka. After all, arriving unannounced and abruptly demanding an opinion the way he did may well have appeared rude to a first-rate attorney. But he couldn't begin to fathom such cool indifference from someone who was clearly interested enough in the case to get the records from Kyushu.

Abe considered making another impromptu visit to Otsuka's office and confronting him with the postcard from the court-appointed lawyer. But an approach like that, when Otsuka's guard was already raised, would be unlikely to produce the desired results.

Even though Abe was busy with his job, he couldn't help speculating as to Otsuka's state of mind. Why had he kept quiet about researching the court record? Why had he pretended ignorance?

Abe arrived at a particular conclusion that prompted him to call Kiriko. He met her around 2:00 pm at the usual coffee shop. Kiriko had arrived first and was waiting for him. When he arrived she greeted him with clear eyes.

There was a smile on her thin lips, but she didn't look as pleased to see him as he had hoped. This young woman's expression had been pretty much the same since he had first met her. Granted, there had been a slight change since she had started working in the bar, but she had a look that showed there was something which she stubbornly cherished and refused to let go of.

"Are you tired?" said Abe sitting down opposite her.

"No, not especially," replied Kiriko, lowering her blueish eyes.

"You work late every night?"

"Yes, usually until around midnight."

"You're not used to the job yet. That's why you're tired. Are you feeling okay?"

"I'm okay." Kiriko stretched her slender shoulders slightly as she spoke.

"I paid a visit to the lawyer Kinzo Otsuka the other day."

Kiriko suddenly raised her eyes and stared at Abe's face.

"Otsuka told me he didn't know the details of the case because he hadn't asked you to explain them to him when you met. I'd gone there to ask his opinion on the case and even though I explained the gist of it, he didn't show any interest at all. In fact he told me he didn't feel inclined to look into it and that it was pointless to even hear about it."

Kiriko sat motionless, staring at Abe. She was pretty, but her eyes were fixed with a penetrating intensity and gave off that hint of blue like a child's.

"But I think that was simply an excuse on Otsuka's part. He said he wasn't interested, but there is evidence that he had in fact thoroughly investigated the court proceedings."

"What?" Kiriko broke her silence with a timorous voice. "What do you mean?"

"I wrote a letter to Mr. R, the court-appointed lawyer in K-City, to the effect that I was thinking of hiring a local lawyer to look into the case and would it be possible to borrow the court transcripts. But guess what? He replied saying he couldn't lend them to me but that he'd previously loaned the records to Otsuka."

Kiriko swallowed hard and continued to stare fixedly at Abe's face, her gaze increasing in intensity.

"I was shocked as well when I saw the reply. After all, when I met with Otsuka, he appeared to know nothing about the case and affected complete ignorance. From his reaction at the time I'd never have guessed the real extent of his knowledge."

"But why did Otsuka suddenly take it upon himself to investigate the case?" asked Kiriko forcefully.

"My guess is that what you said to him weighed heavily on his mind—you know, about not taking the case because of legal fees."

"But if that's true," said Kiriko, her eyes wide like saucers, "why didn't Otsuka tell you he had investigated the court records when you saw him in his office?"

"That's the thing," said Abe. "I've been thinking a lot about that too. And, well, this is just my guess but, I think the reason why Otsuka kept things to himself is that he knows the truth behind the case."

Kiriko held her breath and waited for Abe to continue.

"Basically, I think Otsuka discovered proof that your brother was innocent. Being Otsuka, once he started looking into it, he would have researched it thoroughly and I'm convinced he came across something. Even in reading the same court records, his powers of discernment would be much keener than your average lawyer. If he hadn't found something, then there would have been no reason to be as cagey as he was when I met him. If the records supported the court's guilty verdict then surely Otsuka would have told me as much. The fact that he was unable to say that and simply remained silent must mean he uncovered something in the records which led him to the opposite conclusion from what the court arrived at."

Even without Abe's explanation, Kiriko apparently understood the reason why Otsuka had not announced his discovery to Abe. She cast her eyes down, lost in thought. Motionless, she looked as though she had been turned suddenly to stone. She gazed down at her coffee cup with wide-open eyes.

Abe looked at Kiriko, the very same woman who in the spring had walked out on him at the coffee shop. It was her, yet she was more defiant than she had been before. He had to admit, he was slightly unnerved by her.

Kinzo Otsuka climbed out of the bath, steam from the hot water still clinging to his flushed body. Too warm for a padded jacket, he stood facing the window dressed only in a thin cotton dressing gown.

The Hakone mountains in the distance faded and began to blend into the night sky. The hotel stood on high ground overlooking a myriad of lights shining from dozens of inns scattered around the valley below. The lights appeared and disappeared as the fog rolled through, skirting the base of the mountain range and partly shrouding a clump of cedar trees in white.

The white fog became steadily thicker. Otsuka watched its movement and wondered whether it was true what people said about heavy fog giving off sound. The headlights from several cars could be seen travelling up and down the slope below.

The sound of water came suddenly from the bathroom. It sounded like Michiko had just come out of the bath. Otsuka was still standing by the window gazing out at the scenery when he heard the door slide open.

"You'll catch a cold like that," said Michiko from behind.

Otsuka turned to see her dressed neatly in the hotel gown, face flushed red from the heat of the water. She held Otsuka's padded gown in her hands and slipped it over his shoulders. "What are you looking at?"

"The fog," replied Otsuka. "People say it makes a noise. Have you ever heard that?"

"No. I don't know. I wonder if it's true," said Michiko as she sat down and looked at her own face in a three-sided mirror.

Otsuka was quiet. He lit a cigarette and sat down in a rattan chair. Relaxed, he now realized for the first time that day just how tired he was from playing golf. He let slip a sigh.

Michiko looked up from doing her makeup. "Are you tired?"

"Yes, I am. I'm all in today," he replied, extending his arm and tapping his cigarette on the rim of the ashtray.

"Really?" said Michiko in a low voice. "You can't be so tired, surely. You've been in such good spirits today."

"I must be getting old," laughed Otsuka, "to have to take a nap right afterwards."

"The bath must've soothed away your aches and pains."

"When you're getting on a bit like me it takes a full night to recover from such an exertion. But you wouldn't know about that yet, eh?"

He gazed at Michiko's profile as she continued to apply her makeup. The oiled skin on her neck above her collar gleamed under the lights.

"Stop talking as if you were already an old man," laughed Michiko and she pursed her lips at the mirror and applied rouge. "I was a failure today," she continued, turning her powdered face towards Otsuka and joking about her golfing prowess.

"No, really, you've improved a lot," laughed Otsuka. "You'll soon be passing my handicap."

"I doubt that very much," said Michiko staring long and hard at Otsuka. "You were exceptional today. I'm blaming my poor performance on the wind. I couldn't get the ball to go where I wanted it to."

"When you've been doing it as long as I have, you learn to take the strength and direction of the wind into account." Otsuka laughed good-naturedly. Michiko moved to sit in the chair opposite him, but she stopped suddenly after catching sight of his bare feet protruding from the bottom of his gown.

"Your toenails need trimming," she said and wandered back to her suitcase. She was only wearing the hotel's cotton gown, but it suited her slim figure. She crouched down in front of Otsuka's feet, laid a sheet of paper on the floor and began clipping his nails. "The bathwater has softened them," she murmured.

The sound of clipping continued for a while. Michiko's hair was not yet dry and appeared glossy as she crouched in front of Otsuka. The hair at the base of her earlobe was plastered down with water.

Otsuka was still gazing out of the window. As darkness came on, the lights from the inns in the valley below grew in intensity.

"Shall we have supper? I'm getting pretty hungry," said Otsuka.

"Yes, let's."

Michiko took hold of his other foot and began clipping again. Nail clippings began to amass on the soft white parchment.

"We'll have to get changed into proper clothing if we go down to the restaurant. That's the only problem with a place like this."

"We can have them bring it here," said Michiko, looking up.

"I'd rather go downstairs," insisted Otsuka. "I think it's better eating in the restaurant in hotels like this."

"How rare," said Michiko, expressing her surprise at Otsuka's pronouncement. From her experiences with him at inns to date, he'd been wholly indifferent to such matters.

Otsuka stood up and Michiko helped him with his clothes before changing into her own suit. Only top-class hotels had lavish restaurants. It was dark outside now, and the lights inside were dazzlingly bright. It was dinnertime and the restaurant was full. At length a waiter found them a free table. Most of the guests around them were foreigners. Michiko looked at the menu and placed her order with the waiter. Not wanting to bother with the menu, Otsuka ordered the same. The restaurant was heated by steam.

The foreigners sitting next to them were laughing in a lively manner.

Michiko glanced at Otsuka's face. "What time are you going to Tokyo tomorrow?"

"Umm," said Otsuka, lifting his eyes and considering the question. "If I'm back around noon it should be fine."

"That's perfect," said Michiko.

"So we can relax and take things easy."

Michiko's face was radiant and beautiful—so much so that the foreign guests next to them glanced furtively in

164

her direction from time to time. She even managed to turn heads with her conspicuous good looks walking through the crowds in Ginza. She was excited this evening as it was the first time in a long while they'd managed to get away from Tokyo to stay in a hotel. This accounted also for her unusual talkativeness. Her well-formed lips moved constantly as she engaged Otsuka in conversation.

Then it happened. One of the waiters stopped beside Michiko. He bent down and whispered something in her ear. She seemed startled. The hand holding her fork stopped in mid-air and she cast her eyes down. But then she nodded and sent the waiter away.

"What's the matter?" asked Otsuka, looking directly at her.

"Somebody has come from the restaurant," she said in a flat voice.

"Somebody from the restaurant?" Otsuka too was surprised. "From Tokyo?"

"Yes. Oh, how disagreeable, turning up unexpected like this." Michiko knitted her brows.

"Maybe something urgent has come up. Hadn't you better go over and find out straight away?"

"Probably." Michiko moved her chair back and stood up. The exit was behind Otsuka. She left and he assumed she'd gone into the lobby. He continued with his meal for a while but then suddenly turned around and looked behind him. It was then that he noticed Michiko talking to a young man who was standing to the side of the ornate entrance. He was tall and young, in his mid-twenties. He spoke to Michiko in a hushed voice with an extremely serious expression on his face. He couldn't see Michiko's face but it was plain from her stance that she was tense.

The young man suddenly looked in Otsuka's direction. Their eyes met and the young man bowed deferentially. Michiko turned around and looked over towards Otsuka with a frozen expression. Michiko and the youth exchanged a few more words and then the youth walked towards Otsuka and bowed once again.

"Hello," he said.

Otsuka rose from his seat and removed his napkin from his shirt. Michiko came alongside and introduced the young man.

"This is Mr. Sugiura, the head waiter at my restaurant."

"Oh, really?" said Otsuka, smiling at the youth. "How very good of you to come all this way."

"Yes, thank you very much." The youth bowed his head again. He had large eyes and a clean-shaven face, and wore a well-tailored suit of the type in fashion among young men.

"I'm afraid I'm in a hurry. Please excuse me," the young man said clearly and then bowed politely once again.

"Please, won't you join us for a while? After all, you've come a long way."

"No. That won't be necessary," Michiko intervened. "He has to return straightaway."

Otsuka looked on idly as Michiko accompanied the head waiter to the exit. A short while later, Michiko returned to the dining table. She had calmed down by now and took up her fork again. She looked down and carried on eating her meal. But as he looked at her, her shoulders seemed to sag.

"What is it?" he asked, taking out a cigarette. "Has something serious happened?"

"No, it's nothing really," she answered quietly.

"Nothing? He came all the way from Tokyo to Hakone to talk to you. Has something unusual happened at the restaurant?"

Michiko continued to stare down at her plate and prod at her food with her fork. "It wasn't anything important. He could have easily told me by telephone. It was a little extreme coming all this way. I told him as much and reprimanded him for it."

"I feel sorry for him," said Otsuka. "I'm sure it wasn't necessary to send him straight back again. Couldn't you have offered him a cup of coffee at least?"

"It would become a habit," said Michiko firmly. "When I reprimanded him I told him he shouldn't have come all this way for nothing. He just doesn't think, that's his trouble."

Michiko showed a glimpse of her character as proprietress.

"But if he came here from Tokyo, it must have been something important. Do you want to return early in the morning?"

"No, it's okay." Michiko carelessly scraped the knife across the surface of her plate, "It's nothing to worry about, really. I told him to leave everything to the manager."

Otsuka didn't feel he had any right to probe further into the matter. It was, after all, a private conversation concerning

Michiko's restaurant, and he had to respect that. Nevertheless, Michiko had evidently been affected by whatever news she had received. She'd suddenly gone from lively conversation to stony reticence. Even her complexion seemed wan. It seemed to him that something untoward must have happened at her restaurant. Michiko's reluctance to share her burden with him was no doubt out of consideration for his feelings. They had come away to Hakone to enjoy their time together and she was probably trying not to spoil the trip. He was appreciative of this, but her sudden change of attitude concerned him.

"Something has worried you, hasn't it?" said Otsuka as they returned to the hotel room.

"No, I'm not worried about anything."

Michiko didn't change into her nightwear immediately and stood looking out of the window. It was dark, yet one could still see the white fog that had grown even thicker than before. Illuminated by the swathe of artificial lighting outside, the fog drifted like plumes of smoke.

"But there's something on your mind, isn't there?" persisted Otsuka, sidling up to Michiko's chair. "You look different all of a sudden."

"Let's not discuss it any more," said Michiko. "I've already told you I'm not worried about anything. You don't know anything about my restaurant, so there's nothing for you to be concerned about."

"Thank God," laughed Otsuka. "Running a business on your own is hard work at times. Even though you can leave it to the manager, there are always things that don't get done if you don't do them yourself. I should think it's the same for anyone in business—having to deal constantly with endless worries."

"And it's those daily worries I came here to forget about," said Michiko, turning to face Otsuka. Her eyes shone with a fiery light, the likes of which he'd never seen in her before.

It was approaching 11:30 pm and the last of the customers in Bar Seaweed were getting ready to leave. A lone customer pushed the door open and came in. Nobuko turned around intending to inform the individual that the bar was closing, but she stopped short when she saw who it was. The customer was a tall young man, and he strode purposefully over to the bar. Nobuko followed on from behind.

"You're pretty late tonight, eh, Ken?"

Nobuko started to take his overcoat but he shrugged his shoulders and sat with his coat on, elbows propped up on the bar. The bright lights shone on the customer's face. It was the same young man who went to see Michiko at the F Hotel in Hakone, the man with the clean-cut face in his mid-twenties with clear bright eyes.

"Good evening." The bartender bowed to the youth.

"Give me a highball," ordered the youth in a loud voice. "Is my sister here?" he added, scanning the room.

"She's just left with a customer."

The young man snorted. Nobuko came over and sidled up to him, sitting in a chair to his side. "Ken, have you already started drinking?"

"Only a little," he replied, facing away.

"What's up? Did you finish early at the restaurant today?"

"The restaurant?" he repeated, still facing the bar. "Yeah, I took off from noon."

"Oh, you skipped out? So where've you been wandering around since then?"

"All over."

He took the highball from the bartender and turned ever so slightly towards Nobuko. "Do you want a drink?"

"Yes please," she answered in high spirits, "I'll have a gin fizz, Chief."

"Coming up," smiled the bartender, winking at Nobuko.

The young man's name was Kenji Sugiura. He was the younger brother of the bar's madam. He also worked as the head waiter at the Ginza restaurant run by Michiko.

Kenji drank his highball with a look of displeasure on his face. Suddenly biting his lip, he began digging around in his pocket.

"What do you want, a cigarette?"

Kenji didn't answer Nobuko. Instead he pulled a notebook out of his pocket and began to leaf furiously through its pages. Just as one of the hostesses wandered past he called out to her and without looking up he ordered, "Hey, make a call for me." With his eyes still on the notebook he read out a number.

The hostess was Kiriko. She knew the customer's face. It was the young man she had seen in the car with Nobuko the other night. And before that, she had seen him two or three times in the bar. She had heard he was the younger brother of the owner and that he had something going with Nobuko.

Kiriko dialed the number Kenji had read out, her finger picking out each number in turn.

What's this? she suddenly noticed. It was a number she had dialed before now, not recently, but she was sure about it. It had been in the spring. She found herself staring intensely at her own finger. She found herself holding her breath as she realized what it was—she was dialing the number to the law offices of Kinzo Otsuka. She remembered the exact sequence of numerals.

The ringing tone sounded in Kiriko's ears. The number she had called that spring was ringing.

"Hey!" Kenji suddenly countermanded, "Don't make the call, hang up!"

When Kiriko looked around, the young man was holding his head in distress. Kiriko replaced the receiver and regarded his anguished look with abject amazement.

Chapter 7

Kenji's screaming command to hang up the phone shocked Kiriko, but she was perhaps more surprised by the way he dug his elbows into the surface of the bar and ran his fingers feverishly through his hair. It was done with such violent emotion that he looked as if he was gripped by a drunken frenzy.

Kiriko began to take an interest in the young man from the instant she realized she had been asked to dial the number of Kinzo Otsuka's offices.

Kenji hadn't said a word since his outburst, but simply fixed his eyes on the glass in front of him.

"What's the matter?" asked Nobuko, clearly alarmed by his behavior. Kenji chose not to answer this question and instead gulped down his glass of alcohol.

Nobuko had no reason to suspect that the telephone call had been made to Kinzo Otsuka. She seemed to think it had been made to some friend, and he'd just changed his mind before the call had connected.

"You're acting pretty crazy tonight, Ken," she said, in an effort to calm him down. "Come on, won't you dance with me? Rie, can you put on a record?"

"Stop it," said Kenji as Kiriko reached for a record. "I don't want to dance," he said despairingly.

"You seem very odd," observed Nobuko, still not able to get a handle on him. "What on earth happened?" she asked, half coquettishly.

Kenji responded by physically pushing her away. "I want to be on my own for a while. Stop chattering at me."

Nobuko nearly fell sideways off her bar stool from his push. "That was unkind of you," she said with a laugh, now deciding to placate his mood rather than become angered by it. "You're being weird, Ken."

Even the bartender looked on at Kenji's forlorn figure and laughed along. But Kenji of course was not any old customer, far from it—he was the owner's brother. Aside from his relationship with Nobuko, everyone who worked in this bar treated him as such.

"Chief," said Kenji, looking up, "give me a bourbon."

Nobuko spoke without hesitation, "Don't! It's like poison to him. Stop, Chief, he's plenty drunk already."

"What?! Mind your own business," Kenji scowled at Nobuko. Usually Kenji's hair was neatly combed and he was very conscious of his well-groomed appearance, but now his hair was an unkempt mess. "I wanna drink tonight. Let me do what I want."

Kenji's constitution was such that his complexion turned pale when he drank. This evening was no exception. He regarded Nobuko with a fierce look on his wan face. Nobuko held her breath and fell silent.

"Okay, Ken, but just a little bit, all right?" the bartender said, taking down a bottle of American whisky in an effort to diffuse the tension. He poured the golden liquid into the glass.

"Fill it up," said Kenji.

The bartender stopped pouring. "It's bad for you, Ken."

"Just shut up and pour already," Kenji insisted.

The bartender looked at Kenji's altered complexion and, perhaps not wanting any trouble, did as he was told and poured another glassful. Nobuko watched nervously from the side as Kenji knocked the whisky back as though it were diluted with water.

"No, stop!" she screamed and ran over grabbing at his hand. "Chief, take the glass off him."

"Hey! What are you doing?" Kenji brushed Nobuko aside and slugged the remainder of the whisky.

If a customer hadn't come in just then, Kenji might have become more violent. But a few businessmen came into the bar and Kenji, true to character, quieted down and let his head loll onto the counter top.

"Hey, Nobu," called one of the newcomers. Since it was one of her regulars, she couldn't very well pretend not to have noticed his arrival.

"Oh! Good to see you," said Nobuko, putting on a forced smile. Then she looked over at Kiriko, who had been standing all the while next to the telephone, and indicating with her eyes said, "Rie, please keep an eye on him."

This was the first opportunity Kiriko had to be next to Kenji. She regarded the young man, slumped face down on the bar with his hair in disarray. What, she wondered, was his relationship with Kinzo Otsuka? Was his violent outburst just a little while earlier connected with the lawyer? Or was his ill-tempered behavior brought on by something else entirely? She sat on the stool vacated by Nobuko and stared at him. Having downed the neat whisky, he lay across the bar, his fingers still wrapped around the stem of the glass, his hair covering his face.

The bartender busied himself preparing drinks for the new customers.

After a little while, Kenji raised his head. Kiriko said, "I think you've had a little bit too much to drink."

Realizing that it wasn't Nobuko's voice, he suddenly turned to face Kiriko. "What? Why are you here?" he muttered, his eyes pulled wide open and his face pallid.

"I'm sorry. Nobu has just gone to greet some customers over there. She'll be back soon."

"I don't care if she comes back or not." Kenji looked at Kiriko's face.

"Well, that's not a very nice thing to say."

"You gonna take that kind of tone with me, too?"

"It's just that, well, it's not like you to say things like that, is all."

"And you think you know me?" Kenji let go of his glass, folded his arms and turned slightly towards Kiriko. His hair hung down just above his eyes.

"Yes, I've seen you a few times since I started working here. This is the first time I've spoken to you in person, though."

"Is that right?" said Kenji nodding. "Actually I knew you'd started here. How long is it now? About two months already?"

"You've got a good memory. It's been exactly two months."

Kenji fumbled around in his pocket, fished out a cigarette and put it in his mouth. Kiriko struck a match and leaned towards him. She wanted to get closer to him. She felt she needed to know him better.

The cigarette burned and Kenji blew out wisps of pale smoke.

"You were in a bad mood before, weren't you?" said Kiriko, laughing.

Kenji made a dismissive face. Kiriko took in his profile. He had well defined, clear-cut features and youthful skin.

"What did you say your name was again?" asked Kenji suddenly. His eyes still had that young sparkle about them.

"It's Rieko," replied Kiriko.

"Oh yeah, that's right. I thought I heard it before."

"Mr. Sugiura, you're the brother of the owner, right?" asked Kiriko.

"Yeah, I suppose I am," spat Kenji.

Over in the corner, Nobuko was joining in a toast with her three new customers. She glanced over at Kiriko and noted that Kenji's mood had evidently improved. Her look seemed to say that she'd be over shortly. But Kiriko wanted to talk longer with Kenji. No, she had to.

"Mr. Sugiura, why don't you work in this bar?" Kiriko's tone suggested that since he was the owner's brother, it was a little odd to have to work elsewhere.

"Why?" Kenji's curiosity was aroused by Kiriko's fresh face and the unpretentious naivety of her inexperience in her new job. His attitude was quite different from that shown to Nobuko. "People do things for all kinds of reasons," he said, as if talking to a child.

"But it's your sister's place, right? I would have thought it convenient to work here together."

"Convenient?" repeated Kenji with a sneer. "Maybe. There are times when it's convenient being in my sister's place. But there are also times when it's not. And if anything maybe it's better that way."

Kiriko didn't really understand what Kenji meant by that. But then he was drunk, and it wasn't surprising that he wasn't making a lot of sense.

"So where do you work?"

It was the bartender who answered, having finished serving the drinks. "It's a restaurant in the Ginza called Minase. It serves high-end French cuisine. Since you're so new to town, I'm guessing you don't know it?"

Kiriko shook her head, "No, I don't."

"It's very well known," explained the bartender. "Expensive, but it has a reputation for serving delicious food. It has a top-class clientele, too. And the owner, well, she's extremely beautiful. Her pictures are sometimes featured in magazines, you know."

Kenji was still slumped against the bar, but during this explanation, his back twitched several times.

"Knock it off," he said, interrupting the bartender. "Don't go telling her where I work. If you were telling her that I own the restaurant then I wouldn't mind."

"I'm sure if you did you'd make a fine owner," said Kiriko.

"Thank you," laughed Kenji, pursing his lips slightly. "Let's drink a toast to that, shall we?"

"No, we shouldn't," replied Kiriko. "I can't drink, and you have had far too much already. It's a little sad that we can't drink to your success, but I wish you luck with your future all the same."

"Chief," bellowed Kenji, "give this young lady something light."

"Certainly sir. Coming up." The bartender leaned over the bar and asked Kiriko what she would like. Since she didn't really drink he mixed her a cocoa fizz, the weakest drink he could think of.

Nobuko watched all of this in glimpses from the booth in the corner. She had witnessed Kenji's mood improve and been greatly relieved. She looked as though she'd dart back to the bar as soon as the opportunity presented itself.

Kiriko had to grab her chance. She took hold of her cocoa fizz and raised her glass, said "Cheers," and took a sip. Kenji hadn't ordered anything for himself this time. He simply nodded in acknowledgment of her toast.

"That's delicious," said Kiriko.

"It was? Then bottom's up."

"No, I'd better not," said Kiriko, her eyes sparkling with laughter. "It wouldn't do to get tipsy now, would it?"

"Nonsense, it's good to get drunk occasionally," replied Kenji. "Alcohol is the best medicine when you're feeling gloomy."

Kiriko put her glass down, and nonchalantly slid toward Kenji. "I know the lawyer, Kinzo Otsuka." She spoke softly but in that instant there was an unmistakable look of horror in Kenji's eyes.

"The lawyer, Kinzo Otsuka?" stuttered Kenji, repeating the words he had just heard.

"Yes," said Kiriko, keeping her voice low. "When you asked me to dial that number earlier, I realized it was the number of Otsuka-*sensei*'s office. I knew it from before."

Kenji's face suddenly became very serious. Until now he had been in a light-hearted frame of mind, even smiling slightly. That spirit had disappeared in an instant.

"But how?" stammered Kenji. "How do you know Otsuka-*sensei*? What's your connection with him?"

"Well, I'm certainly not family," she answered. "I'm not even a close friend of Otsuka-*sensei*. Perhaps the opposite," continued Kiriko in a low but forceful voice. "I hate him," she said while looking towards the rows of sparkling liquor bottles lined up on the shelf behind the bar.

Kenji stared fixedly at Kiriko's face. He was about to say something but Nobuko managed to make her excuses and came over from the booth.

"You've cheered up a bit, yes?"

Nobuko smiled at Kenji, but it was Kiriko that answered in an evasive sort of way. "Yes, finally."

Out of deference to Nobuko, Kiriko gave up her seat next to Kenji. Nobuko sat next to Kenji who in turn stared, as if transfixed, at Kiriko's retreating figure as she walked over to the booth in the corner.

Just then the front door opened and in came the madam. The hostesses welcomed her in unison:

"Hello."

The madam returned the greeting and bowed towards her customers before moving over to the bar. One of the girls took her coat from her shoulders, revealing a flamboyant kimono beneath. She was clearly overweight. She regarded her brother, still slumped over the bar, with a sour look and called out to him, "Ken!" But he didn't hear her. If he did, he chose not to answer.

She proceeded behind the counter and the bartender showed her the evening's receipts. She scrutinized them while glancing from time to time at her brother. When she finished, she moved in front of Kenji's slumped form and said, in a loud voice, "Ken!"

"Uh?" said Kenji, looking up at length.

"What is wrong with you? What's going on?" She spoke reprovingly, as an elder sister is wont to do. Kenji brushed his bangs back with one hand. His eyes were clouded.

"You look terrible. You've been drinking before you came here tonight, haven't you?"

"I've been drinking here, mostly," said Kenji sulkily.

"What happened at the restaurant today?"

"I took the day off."

"You mean you played hookey, don't you?"

"Why not call them and find out?"

The madam stared at her brother for a while. Kenji looked like he wanted to bury his head in his arms again in order to avoid his sister's critical gaze.

"How's business going over there anyhow?" asked his sister, sounding concerned.

"Oh, you know," began Kenji, suddenly sitting upright. He took out a cigarette, placed it between his lips and searched in his pockets, eventually producing a box of matches. Nobuko had deferred, moving away slightly when the madam had arrived and so she was unable to light Kenji's cigarette for him.

Kenji lit his own cigarette and tossed the box of matches onto the counter. The matchbox bore an attractive design and the madam's eye picked this up immediately.

"Oh?" she said, picking it up. "You went to Hakone?" She looked Kenji full in the face, "Isn't this F Hotel in Hakone?"

Kenji looked defiantly back at his sister. He scratched his head casually and replied, "Yes."

"When did you go?"

"Today," he answered without looking at his sister.

She stared at his profile and said at length, "So, you skipped off work and took a trip to Hakone, did you?"

Both the madam and Nobuko, off to his side, stared at him, their eyes full of amazement and curiosity.

"Why did you go to Hakone?" the madam asked.

"I just went to hang out, that's all." With an irritated look about him Kenji put the matches back in his pocket.

"What do you think you were doing just wandering carefree around Hakone? You won't get anywhere if you don't work hard in the restaurant, you know," she rebuked.

Just then one of the customers called from the booth, "Hey, Madam?"

"Coming."

The madam looked as though she'd wanted to say something else, but bustled through the half-swing door set in the counter and walked towards the customer.

"How good to see you again," she said amiably, lavishing her charm on everyone.

Nobuko moved closer to Kenji. "Ken, did you really go to Hakone today?" Her attitude had suddenly changed and she pressed the question home. Her complexion had also changed.

"Yeah, I did," answered Kenji bluntly.

"Who did you go with?"

"I went on my own."

"That's a lie!"

"You think I'm lying? What if I didn't go alone?"

"You wouldn't go to a place like that alone. Tell me who you went with!"

"Shut up," said Kenji, contorting his face. "You can believe what you want to, I don't care."

Nobuko twisted her mouth and pressed herself still closer to Kenji. Unfortunately, as she did so a new customer came in through the door.

The customer was a man in his mid-twenties. He was tall and had the appearance of a *yakuza* gangster, a trend currently popular with young men of his age. He had a menacing glint in his eyes—also a popular affectation of certain young toughs.

"Hey," he said as he came in and playfully slapped Kenji's shoulder.

"Oh," replied Kenji as he turned around. For an instant his face stiffened.

"I've been looking for you. I went to the restaurant, but they said you had the day off. So I thought maybe you were in here. And, sure enough, here you are."

"I see." Kenji pushed Nobuko rudely from the bar stool and pointed at it. "Here, have a seat."

Nobuko greeted the customer politely, yet her expression was murky. The customer had been to Bar Seaweed on several occasions before now, and always together with Kenji.

"Please, have a seat, Mr. Yamagami," said Nobuko, indicating the barstool.

Yamagami grinned at Nobuko and sat down next to Kenji. Even the way he took the proffered seat was arrogant. He ordered a scotch with water.

"How are things?" asked Kenji of his friend.

"You're pretty drunk aren't you? How long have you been here?" Evidently Yamagami could smell alcohol on Kenji's breath.

"I've only just arrived," explained Kenji shaking his head.

"Meaning you've been drinking somewhere else before you came here. So business must be pretty good, eh?" returned Yamagami. "Things have been pretty tough for me lately. I've been meaning to talk with you for a few days now. Shall we take a walk later?"

Kenji's eyes flickered slightly, but his voice remained even. "Yeah, why not."

"Relax, have another drink."

Kenji looked around for a distraction. He noticed Nobuko glowering at him and avoided her gaze. He called out to Kiriko who happened to be walking by at that very moment.

"Rie, come here," he said, beckoning with his hand. "Let me introduce you. This is Takeo Yamagami. He's from Kyushu, too."

"Really?" said Kiriko, approaching the young man.

Kenji turned towards his friend and said, "This is one of our new girls, from K-City, of course. She's a friend of Nobuko's. Been here two months now."

Yamagami glanced at Kiriko and bowed, ever so slightly, without saying a word.

"Rie, if you're from K-City then you probably know this person. He had a bit of a name for himself as a baseball player at K High School. His name's Yamagami."

Kiriko had heard of the school. It was legendary for its very strong baseball team which was well-known nationally. That said, she didn't follow the game. "Oh really? So, are you from K-City too?" she asked the man who faced away from her.

"No. I'm from a place that's a bit removed from the city," he replied flatly.

"I wonder if you know it?" said Kenji, seeing that Yamagami was reluctant to continue the conversation. "It's a small place called N Village, near K Town."

"Yes, I know N Village. I've a friend from my high school days who lives there."

"That's where Yamagami is from too."

"In fact," said Kiriko, "isn't it pretty close to K-City?"

While these questions were being asked, Yamagami continued to drink his amber-colored whisky.

"When did your friend arrive in Tokyo?" asked Kiriko, feeling the need to keep the conversation with this customer going. In reality she didn't care at all when this man had left Kyushu. She sensed her opportunity to talk further with Kenji was becoming more and more distant.

"What? I've been in Tokyo for ages," answered Yamagami suddenly. "It's a bore being stuck out in the middle of nowhere, so when I graduated from high school I came straight here."

"That's right," Kenji elaborated, "in baseball he's well-known as a southpaw pitcher from his high school days.

When he graduated, he came straight to Tokyo and joined a professional baseball organization."

"Wow! So you're a pro baseball player?" said Kiriko with a look of admiration.

"No, he isn't a pro anymore," answered Kenji. There was something about the way he said it, something not immediately obvious to the casual observer, that seemed spiteful. "He was in the second team. There were great hopes for his future but it seems he had a change of mind."

"Oh, that must be disappointing," said Kiriko.

"It's not disappointing at all," cut in Yamagami abruptly. "It simply wasn't to be. They flattered me in high school and so I thought I could become a pro. But that was a mistake. I realized I would never achieve my potential stuck in the second team forever, so I decided to quit."

"But," said Kenji, this time to Yamagami, "if you'd toughed it out a bit longer it might have happened for you." He said this not in a caring, friendly manner but in a slightly sneering tone.

"There's no point staying somewhere where you're not going to develop, so I'm glad I decided to cut my losses and give up early on."

"No, you're wrong. I'm sure if you'd stuck with it you could have been a great southpaw pitcher right up there with the likes of Kaneda and Yoshihara."

Kiriko listened quietly, but she couldn't begin to guess what this man Yamagami was doing now that he was no longer a pro baseball player. That was the only mystery that emanated from Yamagami's person. At a glance, he had something of the gangster about his appearance, but, strangely, he also looked as though he might be engaged in a respectable occupation. It was impossible to tell.

The two men drank companionably for a while.

"Shall we head out?" said Yamagami, breaking the silence. He finished his second whisky with water and slapped Kenji on the shoulder.

"Yeah, let's," answered Kenji forcefully, midway through his last highball. He looked up at the bartender. "Chief, add it to my tab, please." He shot a grin at Yamagami.

"Hey, how much is it? It might be your joint but I'll pay my share, you know." Yamagami asked the bartender to reckon up the bill and pulled out some money from his pocket. Kenji turned away and didn't try to stop him.

"Hey, sis!" Kenji called out to the booth where the madam sat. "We're leaving now."

She stood up, bowed to her customers and came straight over. "Leaving so soon?" His sister looked at him as if she wanted him to stay a little longer.

"This gentleman," Kenji indicated with his chin, "wants to talk to me about something."

"Ah, Mr. Yamagami," said the madam to her brother's friend. "It's still early. Why don't you have a few more drinks before you leave?"

"Thank you," said Yamagami. "But I've a few things to attend to." He slid down from his seat.

"Chief," said Kenji to the bartender, "I'll pay what I owe next time I'm in. Put it on my tab, please."

Nobuko, who had been watching them from a discreet distance, now approached Kenji and said, "Aren't you coming back later?"

"Uh, maybe. But it's late now so I'll probably call it a day and go home."

Nobuko looked at Kenji reproachfully. She couldn't very well say anything with the madam and the other girls within earshot.

Yamagami left first, pushing the door open with his shoulder.

"See you soon," said Kenji, turning in the doorway to face his sister.

"Behave yourself," she called from behind as he turned to leave.

"Don't worry, I will." And then he disappeared into the corridor beyond the door.

Several hostesses went out with them to say goodbye. Nobuko made as if to follow, but she was chastized by the madam.

Kiriko was among the girls who had gone to see them off. They stopped, as always, on the corner by the bar, and watched as the two young men walked away, cheek by jowl. They looked for all the world like the best of friends.

"It's cold," muttered one of the girls next to Kiriko as they headed back inside the bar.

Kiriko stayed, looking down the street. The light from the street lamps was bright on the corner and so she concealed herself under the eaves of a building. Kenji had his back to her. Even on this street, which in the early evening was crowded with people, most of the shops and bars were closed after eleven o'clock. The light from the street lamps only sporadically lit the street.

The two men walked away, their shoulders bathed in artificial light. As Kiriko looked on, they suddenly stopped. They seemed to be quarrelling. They were arguing in fairly loud voices, although she couldn't hear exactly what it was about. It certainly wasn't a friendly exchange of words. Kenji was evidently very angry about something, and it looked as if Yamagami was trying to appease him. They got into a tangle on the sidewalk, pushing and shoving one another. Kiriko wanted to get a better look, but the door to the bar opened and Nobuko peeped outside. Kiriko turned around and went back into the bar just as Nobuko ran outside.

That was the last Kiriko saw of Kenji. She'd been looking forward to seeing him again but he never showed up. Nor did his friend, Yamagami. It was as if the two had orchestrated their disappearance that night outside the bar. She worked on Nobuko to try and get information out of her. She lived in the same apartment as Nobuko. It was a small place with one six-mat room. The arrangement worked because they were friends from the same hometown, but Kiriko had the feeling that before she arrived, Nobuko had allowed Kenji to stay there. She hadn't known it at first, but as time wore on she felt that had been the case.

There were times when after the bar had closed for the night Nobuko sent Kiriko home alone. She made a variety of excuses to Kiriko, but Kiriko figured they were all lies.

She felt sure Nobuko would spend the night with Kenji and returned the next day as if nothing had happened. She looked upset a good deal of the time and her clothes began to look a little dishevelled.

"Is it a nuisance to have me here?" Kiriko would ask Nobuko from time to time.

But Nobuko would just shake her head in annoyance. "I invited you to come here, didn't I? You don't have to stand on ceremony with me. Stop assigning me thoughts."

Nobuko had always been a good-natured girl and she had shown genuine concern for Kiriko's well-being. But when it came to Kenji, she seemed to forget herself. That much was obvious that night in the bar. Even the other girls alluded to Nobuko having a special relationship with the owner's brother. As with all women the world over, nobody said this in quite as many words, but it was apparent from the way the girls referred to them.

There was just one thing that Kiriko wanted to ask Kenji: What was his relationship with the lawyer Otsuka? First telling her to call Otsuka's office at such a late hour and then suddenly telling her to hang up and then showing such utter anguish certainly wasn't normal. She intuited that there was something there, a connection between Kenji and the lawyer. Perhaps it was her imagination, but she needed confirmation. But as long as Kenji, the key person, was on the lam, there was no other means of learning what she wanted to know. She had no alternative but to try and coax information out of Nobuko, Kenji's intimate partner.

"Why doesn't Kenji work in his sister's bar?" she had asked Nobuko on one occasion.

"Sibling rivalry. Kenji felt he wouldn't get the experience and training he needed there, so he decided to work elsewhere," explained Nobuko, siding with Kenji. "Kenji wants to have his own restaurant some day. He works at Minase to get some training. It's his dream to own a restaurant of his own like that." Nobuko's look suggested she'd like to be manager of such a restaurant.

"Has Kenji ever studied law?" probed Kiriko.

Nobuko dismissed the suggestion out of hand. "Law? He's had nothing at all to do with that. Why do you ask?"

"Oh, no reason in particular," laughed Kiriko, shaking her head innocently. This was a question she decided would better be put to Kenji directly.

"Kenji doesn't come by much these days, does he?" said Kiriko.

Nobuko made an annoyed face. "I'm sure he's just busy."

But Kiriko knew Nobuko still met with Kenji secretly. She could pretty much tell from Nobuko's behavior. Since moving in with her, there were occasionally days when Nobuko couldn't settle down and she clearly had something on her mind. Kiriko felt intuitively that these instances coincided with her seeing Kenji.

However, Nobuko was becoming more and more depressed. There were signs that she saw Kenji as before, but she no longer had that look of pure pleasure in her face. Perhaps they were experiencing relationship problems, but that wasn't something Kiriko could ask about. Her concern was limited to Kenji's connection with Otsuka.

Then one night the phone rang in the bar. Kiriko just happened to be passing as the phone rang so she answered it, "Hello, Bar Seaweed."

The caller then abruptly asked, "Is Kenji there?" It was a rough, drunken voice.

"No, I'm afraid I haven't seen him," answered Kiriko, her heart pounding.

"Oh? Okay, never mind," the voice said and hung up.

Kiriko replaced the receiver. She felt she recognized the caller's voice. It had to be Yamagami, the man who was with Kenji that night. She knew it was him.

The madam had been behind the bar as the telephone rang. "Who was it?" she asked.

"Somebody asking whether Kenji was here tonight. He didn't give his name."

"Oh?" The madam said nothing more and simply raised her eyebrows.

It had been twenty days since Kenji had stopped by on his way back from Hakone. Kiriko received a call from Keiichi Abe after not hearing from him for a while, asking to meet with her the next day around 4 pm at the usual place. Kiriko had asked a particular favor of Abe.

Kiriko met Abe at the same coffee shop they usually went to. She always met him before she went to the bar, in the twilight hours.

"One of my friend's sister works at Minase, so that was useful for looking into the matter you asked about," began Abe cheerfully.

When they last met, Abe had asked why Kiriko wanted to know such a thing, but she wasn't forthcoming with details. Abe had remarked that it was odd at the time. However, after Kiriko asked him to look into it, he had immersed himself in this research. He took out his notebook and told Kiriko what he had found.

"Apparently the proprietress of Minase is an attractive woman in her early thirties. I don't know which, but it seems a certain magazine featured her. I checked out her connection with the lawyer Otsuka, as you requested. It seems there is quite an intimate relationship between them, and not just that of customer and restaurateur either," explained Abe.

"It seems the employees in the restaurant are vaguely aware of the relationship. Even the sister of the friend I asked knew about it. The owner is an attractive woman, and it seems that she has had a number of would-be suitors approach her. However, the relationship with Otsuka apparently goes back a long way, since even the staff is aware of it."

Kiriko considered what she'd just been told. Abe gazed at her. Her contemplative look was very much like herself, eyes fixed on some point in the distance, chewing absent-mindedly on her lip.

"What's on your mind?" asked Abe, placing his elbows on the table. In fact Abe had no idea what she was thinking about. It wasn't that he didn't understand her desire to learn more about the lawyer Kinzo Otsuka, but it was unexpected

194

of her to suddenly ask about the owner of Minase. Abe had the feeling that Kiriko was always one step ahead of him.

"I just wanted to know about it, that's all," answered Kiriko with a smile. She'd changed since she had begun working in the bar. Before, she was too straight-laced and standoffish, but working in the bar had softened her edges.

"I know you have a special interest in the lawyer, I understand that," said Abe, gauging Kiriko's expression. "But, well, perhaps I have the wrong end of the stick here, but wouldn't it be better to concentrate on finding out more about your brother?"

"My brother?" Kiriko looked up. Her eyes assumed that characteristic defiant look.

"Yes. After all, he died with a slur on his character. Wouldn't it be better to concentrate your efforts on clearing his name? It's fine to be aware of Otsuka's involvement, but it's surely more important to investigate the circumstances surrounding your brother's death."

Despite herself, Kiriko listened attentively. If she had been her old self, she would have hurled back some stinging retort. "Of course I'm thinking about my brother," she said quietly. "But my brother is dead, and there's nothing more I can do."

"Oh really!" said Abe, his eyes wide in amazement. "That's certainly a change of mind. That's not how you saw things before."

"You think so?" nodded Kiriko meekly, but she didn't really care. "Mr. Abe?" she said, appealing to his better nature, "will you let me think about things as I please? And can you listen to me when I ask you to do things?" As always, her intense eyes sparkled brightly as she gazed at Abe.

He fell silent for a moment. "All right, I'll do as you say."

"I would like to ask another favor of you."

"What is it?" asked Abe, leaning forward to hear her instructions.

"There is a young man called Kenji Sugiura working at Minase. I'd like you to investigate him for me."

"Why? What has he to do with anything?" asked Abe, after making a note of the man's name.

"He's the younger brother of the madam at my bar. He works at the restaurant as the head waiter. I'd like to know what his reputation is over there."

Abe clearly thought this an odd request. In spite of himself he looked searchingly at Kiriko's face.

"Mr. Abe, I assume you want to know what I'm thinking," said Kiriko with a knowing smile. "I have a plan. You'll know about it soon enough."

Two days went by. Two days which proved to be monotonous for Kiriko. Neither Kenji nor his friend showed up at the bar. Nobuko continued to look depressed and became increasingly melancholy. Kiriko wondered why her roommate was so listless.

Then the call came from Abe.

"I've found out the information you wanted," he said.

"Really? Thank you very much."

"Shall we meet at the coffee shop?"

"Perfect."

"Fine, I'll be waiting there at the usual time."

"Thank you again."

Kiriko felt she had put Abe to a lot of trouble. When exactly, she couldn't recall, but he had once said to her:

"I'm sure your brother is innocent, and the lawyer Otsuka knows that. I'll continue to sound out his views for a while, and I'd like to run an article in my magazine proving your brother's innocence."

Abe's words had been full of passion and sincerity. They weren't spoken merely out of consideration for her feelings, but rather expressed a public-minded sense of what ought to be done to see justice prevail.

"Please stop it," Kiriko had said.

"Why?" asked Abe.

"I have a plan. But I can't tell you what it is just now. You'll know soon enough."

You'll know soon enough. That seemed to be her only answer to his questions recently. It was the same when they met again.

"I asked about Kenji Sugiura and it seems he is reasonably well thought of," Abe reported while he drank coffee.

"Really? I'd like to know more."

"As you said, Kenji is the head waiter at Minase. He's got a reputation as a hard working and conscientious individual. The senior staff apparently tend to be afraid of him. I don't know why exactly, but they keep their distance. My friend's sister said that Kenji is the only one who has the restaurant's best interests in mind."

Kiriko cast her eyes down and listened. But inside, her mind whirled with endless machinations. *The senior staff are afraid of him… Kenji is the only one who has the restaurant's best interests in mind.*

Why?

Kiriko recalled Kenji's strange behavior the night he returned from his trip to Hakone. Why had Kenji, of all people, suddenly taken off and gone all the way to Hakone? What was it he wanted to say when he had asked Kiriko to make the call to Otsuka's office? And why did he stop her? His subsequent aggressive behavior was also difficult to comprehend. There had to be a reason behind it all. It didn't seem entirely unrelated to Nobuko's melancholy moods of late, but it was useless asking Nobuko. Besides, Kiriko didn't feel inclined to talk to her about it.

In her mind's eye Kiriko could see Kenji and his friend Yamagami, the pro baseball player, as they grappled beneath the street lamp outside the bar that night, Kenji cursing while Yamagami continuously apologized. There was something she was missing, there had to be. Something involving Otsuka.

Abe regarded Kiriko as she stared off with a terrifying look in her eyes.

Chapter 8

Kiriko stood on the corner near a large restaurant. Bright lamps shone through its windows, the thin curtains engulfed in glaring light.

It was cold outside. Even for Ginza, this street was very busy and the pedestrians pulled their overcoats closer around their hunched shoulders. Standing in the cold outside, the lamps in the window looked even warmer and more inviting. Kiriko had been waiting here since about 7 pm. The street corner where she stood was opposite the restaurant. Behind her was a shop selling women's accessories; she didn't look out of place standing in front of the display window. Next to the accessories shop stood a clothes store and next to that a shop selling watches, jewelry and the like. Now and then Kiriko would wander up and down the row of shops looking at the items for sale.

Her eyes however were constantly drawn towards the restaurant—not to the windows but rather in the direction of the employee entrance off to one side. In contrast to the lavishly decorated main entrance, the dimly lit side door appeared drab and out of place.

Directly opposite was a coffee shop and a tobacconist. Kiriko moved along the sidewalk so as not to attract the attention of the old shopkeeper sitting in the tobacco shop. Her new position faced a bank, which stood inconspicuously in the dusk light.

Kiriko had come here at Nobuko's request. Kiriko shared the same room as Nobuko and was from the same hometown and had come to Tokyo at Nobuko's behest. She didn't have sufficient money to rent her own room and relied upon her friend's good nature to help her out.

Kiriko had been asked by Nobuko to watch Kenji Sugiura. In exchange for Kiriko's cooperation, Nobuko had explained everything to her. As Kiriko had suspected, Kenji was Nobuko's lover. He was the younger brother of the madam and he worked in this restaurant. Occasionally he would stop by at his sister's bar. Nobuko had become deeply involved with him.

According to Nobuko, Kenji had been treating her very coldly of late and she suspected he was seeing someone else. She said she had begun to notice it some time ago, but that it had become much worse recently. Kiriko agreed that this was a possibility given his behavior in the bar the other night when he had been extremely boorish towards Nobuko.

Nobuko told Kiriko that she had arranged to meet Kenji last night but that he had cancelled at the last minute. He had been unfriendly in the extreme and wouldn't listen to her entreaties. She was forced to conclude that he broke their date suddenly in order to meet another woman.

Nobuko's voice was choked with emotion: "If Kenji came out of the restaurant and caught me standing there waiting for him he'd be very angry. So can you take a day off from the bar and watch him for me? If he looks as though he's going somewhere then follow him. It doesn't matter how much it costs, I'll pay you back for your taxi fares and anything else you spend."

Nobuko also said she would see to it that Kiriko's absence from the bar that night didn't cause any problems. She was desperate. "I know it's a lot to ask, Rie, but please do it for me, I beg you."

Kiriko had agreed. She felt she couldn't refuse her friend. Actually, she was positively enthusiastic about doing it once she'd heard all the details. Of course, Kiriko had her own reasons for being interested in Kenji. His behavior in the bar the night he had returned from Hakone had drawn her attention.

How did Kenji know Otsuka? That also interested her. However, what she wanted to know about most of all was the reason why Kenji had been so troubled that night. His unruliness wasn't simply the result of excessive drinking. According to Abe, Kenji worked far more conscientiously than anyone else at the restaurant, so much so that he seemed totally devoted to it. Apparently Kenji wanted to own his own restaurant one day and that was why he'd gone there to learn the trade and worked so diligently. But she couldn't help feeling there was another reason why he was obsessed with toiling so hard for the sake of that particular restaurant. She had agreed to Nobuko's request and now found herself standing on the street corner because her own curiosity about Kenji had compelled her to do so.

People walked past her continuously. Some came back the same way and passed her again. She ambled about, appearing for all intents and purposes as though she was waiting for someone. A girl selling flowers and children selling chewing gum walked past. All of these people passed her again and again, yet none paid her any attention.

She looked at her watch. 8 pm. She had been standing there for an hour already. From time to time staff people would go in and out of the side door, but there was no sign of Kenji. Nobuko had told her that the restaurant closed at 9 pm, but it seemed that Kenji was in the habit of getting away earlier when he could. That was why Kiriko had felt the need to wait there starting at 7 pm.

She wandered along the line of shops for the umpteenth time. It was when she stopped in front of the tobacco shop that it happened. The glaring light from the clothes shop made the approaching person seem even more lively. She suddenly found herself looking into the eyes of a young man who was walking toward her.

Before she had a chance to say anything, the man was standing in front of her. "Hey," he said smiling. "You're the girl from Bar Seaweed, aren't you?"

Kiriko realized immediately that it was Kenji's friend, the young man called Yamagami. She remembered him from the other night as the man who had arrived at the bar a little after

Kenji and then left together with him later. She had watched them leave from the street corner, wondering what it was he had been so apologetic about.

"What's going on tonight?" said Yamagami as he peered at Kiriko, clearly puzzled since she was not at the bar.

Anxious not to miss Kenji while talking with Yamagami, Kiriko shifted her position slightly so she could see the restaurant.

"I'm taking the night off," replied Kiriko.

"Oh, really?"

Yamagami took a pack of cigarettes out of the left pocket of his overcoat. He placed a cigarette in his mouth, fished out a lighter from the same pocket and bent his head slightly as he lit the tip. The lighter bore an intricate design. The light from the dancing flame shone on his hollow cheeks.

"Are you doing anything interesting?" said Yamagami, blowing out smoke. He had high cheekbones and unfriendly eyes and his thin lips were twisted into an unpleasant smile.

Kiriko was stuck for a quick reply and blurted out, "I'm just on my way to the movies." She desperately hoped that he would go away and leave her alone.

"So are you waiting for someone here?" he said smirking.

"No, no, I'm on my own. I was just gonna wander about and find a theater."

"Well, if you're on your own and you need some company, I've nothing else to do right now." A predictably wry grin appeared on Yamagami's face as he spoke. Kiriko couldn't tell whether he was joking.

"No, really, I'm fine. Perhaps we could do that another time."

Kiriko really didn't want to get stuck talking to Yamagami outside the restaurant.

Yamagami laughed loudly. "Okay, I'm sorry to have bothered you. Let's make it a date next time, then." He turned his back on her and disappeared into the crowd.

Kiriko breathed a sigh of relief. She had managed to keep her eye on the side door most of the time while talking with Yamagami, but she hadn't seen Kenji.

She suddenly noticed that the woman in the tobacco shop was staring at her. Perhaps she had been listening to their conversation a few moments before.

Kiriko waited another twenty minutes. The side door opened and a tall man wearing an overcoat came out. Kiriko glanced at her watch again. 8:30 pm. She set off in pursuit of Kenji. Even when she was in the taxi, she didn't take her eyes off the car in front and she urged the driver not to lose sight of it.

The ride from the Ginza took thirty minutes. The car turned left, off a deserted street with electric tram lines set into it, into a narrow road hardly wide enough for one car to pass. Kiriko quickly searched for a landmark. There was a public bathhouse across the other side of the street from the tram. Two managerial-type ladies were ducking under the curtain hanging over the entrance. Kiriko made a mental note of the place.

The red taillights of the taxi in front illuminated the dark alleyway and moved slowly forward. The headlights of her own taxi revealed desolate houses on either side. They passed a number of small crossroads and Kiriko counted each of them.

It was when they had come to the fifth crossroads that Kiriko noticed the lead taxi's taillights had been turned off.

"You can set me down here," she said quickly to the driver. "Can you back up a little please?" She didn't want Kenji to notice she was tailing him.

She alighted from the taxi and pressed herself up against one of the buildings at the side of the alleyway. Her taxi reversed. The door of the taxi in front opened and it looked as though Kenji was paying the driver. There was a street lamp on the corner and its light shone down on his singular shoulders. Having paid his fare he took off down a side street. Kiriko followed from behind. Apartment blocks towered on either side of the street. Kenji walked along bending slightly forward.

They passed the apartment blocks and the street became darker. Kiriko tried walking as far from him as she could.

Kenji entered a small, ordinary house. The house next door, by contrast, was very big, and had a long fence running around its perimeter. On the other side was an office-like building constructed of red brick. Sandwiched as it was between the two larger buildings, the house was terribly inconspicuous. Kiriko was sure Kenji had gone into this house from the noise made by its lattice door as it closed behind him.

Although the alleyway was narrow, there were a number of large houses to the front as well. The neighborhood was shrouded in silence. Few people passed by this way. In the dark, the shrubbery at the front of the house Kenji entered looked like a black mass protruding from the fence.

Kiriko approached the house, intending to read the nameplate, but it only had the block number. Of course, this wasn't Kenji's house. But the way he had entered the building suggested he was very familiar with the place.

There was no sign of anyone around to ask and no bell to ring.

Suddenly, an idea came to mind. It might have been the position and location of the house, or it might have been the familiar way in which Kenji had entered the front door, but it suddenly occurred to Kiriko that it might be Kenji's secret hideout.

She wondered who lived there. If, as Nobuko had said, Kenji did have a lover, might this be her house? Being an ordinary house, Kiriko couldn't just go in and look around. Plus, all the houses in this street appeared to have their doors firmly shut and there wasn't a soul about to ask.

Kiriko stood idly around for some twenty minutes wondering what to do about her predicament. Suddenly she heard the sound of wooden clogs coming from the direction of the house she had been observing. She quickly concealed herself and watched as a middle-aged woman emerged onto the sidewalk. Kiriko guessed the woman wasn't just going on a local errand from the fact that she was dressed in warm outdoor clothes and carried a handbag.

She came out from her hiding place and caught up to the woman. "Can I ask you a question?"

The woman turned about and gave Kiriko a suspicious glance and then quite literally looked her up and down under the light of a street lamp some distance away.

"Excuse me but does a Mr. Tanaka live in this neighborhood?" asked Kiriko abruptly.

"No, there's no one here by that name," said the woman as she turned and started to walk away.

"But I'm sure I was told he lives in that house. Mr. Tanaka and his wife and children. Don't they live in your house?"

"No, I told you, there's no one by that name here," repeated the woman rather bluntly.

"I see. I'm sorry to have troubled you."

No sooner had Kenji gone into the house than this middle-aged woman had come out, by herself. She was dressed as if she were going some distance.

From these observations, Kiriko surmised that Kenji must be using this house as his hideaway. Perhaps the woman was a housekeeper employed to look after the place while he was away and now that the owner had returned had no need to stay.

He had gotten rid of her intentionally. Kiriko wondered what Kenji did while he was here. She thought about him meeting another woman, and suddenly the middle-aged woman's hurried departure made sense.

But that was the limit of her intuition—she could do no more to confirm her suspicions at the moment. She was not free to enter the house. There seemed no alternative to waiting and watching for Kenji to reappear. Would he come out alone or with another woman? Or perhaps the other woman would see him off and bid him goodnight. Kiriko could only hope to catch sight of the woman's face.

Even so, this was likely to require a good deal of time. She looked at her watch. 9:30 pm. She guessed Kenji wouldn't come out in the next thirty minutes. She moved off and started to make her way back, partly because there was no one around to ask, and partly because she was beginning to feel the cold.

The apartment blocks she had passed earlier loomed large on either side of the alleyway. Light escaped from the windows in the tall buildings and she could hear laughter. She left the apartment blocks behind and the alleyway gave out onto a deserted street.

Kiriko came to the place where the taxi had dropped her off. The road was on a slight downhill slope, at the bottom of which was the street with the tramlines and where, if memory served, the public bathhouse ought to be.

She emerged onto the street and was greeted by a dull scene. She killed ten minutes at that location. People walked to and fro.

Suddenly Kiriko looked back towards the entrance to the road and beyond, the alleyway. It was some distance away. A man came out onto the street and walked hurriedly away from the tramlines.

Forty minutes had gone by since she first arrived. By and by Kiriko returned to the alleyway. The deserted houses ran along the sidewalk as before.

It was while Kiriko was walking back this way that it happened.

Headlights from a car behind lit up the road ahead of her. The alleyway was narrow and Kiriko avoided the searching glare of the lights by pressing herself up against a fence. Until the car had passed her, the lights were dazzling and she couldn't see the vehicle's occupants. But as the taxi drew past she could see that its lone passenger was a woman. Kiriko stood and stared after the car even after its taillights grew smaller in the distance.

She had no idea who the woman could be. But for some inexplicable reason she had sensed the need for caution when the car had turned into the alleyway. The car stopped some way ahead—more or less the same spot Kenji's taxi had stopped earlier.

The door opened and the figure of a woman could be seen stepping out onto the sidewalk. The area was dimly lit by a street lamp and difficult to see properly. The woman cut across the front of the car and disappeared from view across the other side of the alleyway. From a brief glimpse, Kiriko took in a slim, shadowy figure wearing a black overcoat.

Hearing the sound of the car door close, Kiriko moved cautiously forward. She wanted to see where the woman was heading.

She rounded the corner and saw by the light of an apartment the woman's back as she walked away. The woman moved into darkness and then the distant light of a street lamp threw her slender form into faint relief. Next to the red brick building was the small house. While Kiriko was gazing at the woman she disappeared inside. Just as she thought! Her hunch had proved correct.

The woman Nobuko had talked about had not been in the house at all. Kiriko surmised that Kenji and this woman had arranged to meet there all along.

A cold wind blew about her feet. A small piece of white waste paper came tumbling along the alleyway in the wind. Other than that, nothing moved in the neighborhood.

In the house, black shadows merged into the darkness, and a deathly silence permeated the air. Kiriko went on through the small gate. To her front was an entrance hall with a lattice door. From the dull porch light she could see that it was old and with low eaves. Kiriko made another discovery. From here she could see a separate wooden door, off to one side of the entrance. It wasn't locked and appeared to lead around the side of the house, probably to a garden at the back. But it was no use, she couldn't see inside because the lattice doors had been firmly secured. Her one opportunity had been a moment earlier when she heard the doors opening and then an instant later closing again.

The middle-aged woman was unlikely to return soon, thought Kiriko. She heard the distant sound of a radio. There were no stars in the sky above the bare branches of the trees. Kiriko crept stealthily towards the entrance hall.

For the first time she heard a noise from inside. She strained her ears and listened, and the noise suddenly became louder. In an instant the lattice doors were thrown open. Before Kiriko could turn tail and run the woman in the black overcoat appeared before her.

Kiriko let out a low-pitched, involuntary squeal. But it was the woman in black who cried out loudly. For an instant she stood rigid in front of Kiriko, but then her shoulders began to shudder.

"I didn't do it!" she screamed.

Kiriko was dumbfounded.

"You have to be a witness. I didn't do it I tell you!" The woman screamed again, her lungs laboring for want of air. Her whole body seemed to be shaking. Kiriko had never seen anyone tremble so hard. The woman stared at Kiriko, and for a moment fell quiet. Her breathing became more erratic. Kiriko knew then that the intensity of her emotions had rendered her speechless.

The woman was tall and she had a beautiful face, but under the electric light her complexion looked pale. Her eyes were wide with fear. Her well-formed lips were open and she was gasping for breath.

Kiriko finally understood what the woman had been trying to say after she had suddenly grasped Kiriko by the arm and dragged her into the parlor.

The entrance hall, three *tatami* wide, gave way onto a six-mat room, which in turn led to an eight-mat room beyond. Kiriko was able to recall the layout of the rooms well after this night.

A portable brazier stood in the eight-mat room, and to its side, lying face up, was the body of a man. Blood stained the brazier's coverlet and lay in a pool on the surface of the *tatami*. The vivid red blood looked almost like a picture, as if applied with brush and paint. The man's unkempt hair was soaked in blood and his fingers were clenched tightly into fists. Kenji Sugiura stared wide-eyed towards the ceiling.

Kiriko stood rooted to the spot.

"He was like this when I got here," said the woman, gripping Kiriko tightly by the shoulders. "I've only just arrived. I didn't murder him. He was already dead when I got here."

The woman's voice was hoarse as though her throat was dry. Kiriko understood the situation. She had seen with her own eyes that this woman had only just entered the house. It was clear to her that Kenji had been murdered well before her arrival. She simply wouldn't have had the time to kill him, and furthermore, the condition of the body suggested that some time had passed since it had happened.

"Please, you must be a witness for me," repeated the woman, her voice shaking with fear.

Kiriko had never seen anyone as shaken as this. She appeared as though seized by a violent fever and her teeth chattered audibly.

Kiriko didn't answer straightaway and instead stared at the body. Kenji's blood had soaked through his shirt and flowed from a wound in his chest down to his stomach. His hand spasmed once as they watched.

"You believe me, don't you, when I say I didn't do it?" said the woman after a pause.

Kiriko nodded.

The woman stared at her, eyes open wide, and pleaded, "When they accuse me of this, you need to be my witness."

212

She shook Kiriko's shoulders. "It was just bad luck, coming here just after he was murdered. You're the only person who can save me. Please let me have your name, I beg you."

The stench of blood filled Kiriko's nostrils. It was mingled with the expensive perfume this woman wore about her person.

"I'll tell you my name. And I'll be your witness," replied Kiriko, speaking for the first time. "But first I need to know who you are."

The woman didn't answer immediately. She seemed choked with indecision.

"Who are you?" Kiriko repeated forcefully.

"My name is Michiko Kono," the woman confessed.

Kiriko wasn't particularly surprised. She had guessed as much when she first saw the woman. She was the owner of the restaurant where Kenji had worked. This house was where they had conducted their secret liaisons. She realized that in an instant.

"There, I've told you my name. I'm the owner of the place where Kenji works," she said, so out of sorts that she forgot to explain that "Kenji" was the name of the man who now lay dead before them. This gave Kiriko some scope.

Kiriko's imagination constructed a picture around the blanks in a moment.

Recalling how upset Kenji had been after he countermanded the call to Otsuka, Kiriko guessed there was a relationship between this Michiko Kono—Kenji's lover—and Kinzo Otsuka. Kenji's anguish was the result of nothing other than the relationship between Michiko and Otsuka.

But why had Kenji tried to speak to the lawyer? There had to be something else between Michiko and Otsuka, something that gave Kenji deep cause for concern.

This supposition on Kiriko's part formulated itself in an instant.

Her eye swept the room. It was sparsely furnished. Compared to the average household it was extremely basic in its provision of household items. That said, what was there was expensive. Most items and pieces of furniture were irregular or mismatched, and the appliances seemed insufficient for daily living. But everything that was there was high quality. This imbalance suggested all the more to Kiriko that the house was used as a temporary meeting place for secret lovers.

Kiriko's eye alighted on a small object lying beside the body. It was metallic and shone silver under the light. It was a cigarette lighter, probably belonging to the dead man.

A pack of cigarettes lay open on top of the brazier. The ashtray was empty. Two or three cigarettes had fallen out of the pack.

"Please, hurry, tell me your name," said Michiko, speaking quickly. She was writhing like a person hanging onto the edge of a cliff, grasping desperately at a clump of grass.

"It's Kiriko Yanagida."

Kiriko answered calmly, her eyes fixed on the body. She hadn't so much as uttered a word when she first laid eyes on the deceased. There had been no perceptible change, other than her lips clamping together and her brow turning slightly pale.

"What about your address? Tell me your address," continued Michiko.

"I work at Bar Seaweed, in Ginza."

On hearing these words Michiko gulped. There was fear in her eyes as she looked at Kiriko.

"Bar Seaweed... You mean the place that Kenji's sister runs?" Michiko gazed at Kiriko's face.

"Yes. That's where I work," answered Kiriko slowly.

Michiko swallowed hard. "I see. And so that's why you came here, is it?"

But Michiko had misunderstood. She assumed that because Kiriko worked in Kenji's sister's bar she had come here to visit Kenji. Kiriko didn't attempt to correct the misapprehension.

"I see," repeated Michiko, looking at Kiriko with a pleading gaze. "Kiriko Yanagida, Miss Kiriko Yanagida, right?" Michiko said it twice so as not to make a mistake.

"Do you know who killed him?" muttered Kiriko.

"I don't. I've no idea who it might have been," said Michiko in a loud voice, shaking her head vigorously from side to side. "Let's go. It wouldn't look good if someone came. The housekeeper might come back. Come on, let's get out of here."

Michiko went out of the room first.

Kiriko walked from the six-mat room through the three-mat room. She put her shoes on where she had kicked them off in the entrance hall. Kenji's shoes had been left untidily in one corner.

Michiko was nowhere to be seen.

Kiriko found herself alone. She went back along the alleyway and came out on the street with the tramlines. There was no sign of Michiko anywhere. She was long gone.

To her front stood the public bathhouse. Peals of laughter echoed as two women carrying washbasins ducked under the hanging curtain. Three young men, towels in hand, came out of the male bathhouse entrance and onto the street. A tram went by and soon obscured her view of the building. Cars sped along. A truck lumbered past. The sidewalk bustled with people. It was an ordinary evening much like any other, the town blissfully unaware that somewhere in this neighborhood walked a murderer.

Kiriko began to walk towards the tram stop. Several people waited for a tram under the sign. None of them was aware that a murder had been committed.

She scanned the vicinity but she couldn't see Michiko. She had had a head start and was probably clean away in a taxi by now.

The scene of the murder was printed indelibly in Kiriko's mind. That scene, and the one she now beheld in front of her, seemed so different as to be literally worlds apart. Not three minutes from where she now stood lay a dead man whose lifeblood had drained away.

A man on a bicycle rode past singing a popular song. The image that remained in her memory seemed to fade slightly as she gazed absent-mindedly at the monotonous reality now surrounding her. Predictably, what she could see now was the more vivid image.

Kiriko started. Something had flashed through her mind. It was the lighter. The combination of colors—the deep red of spilled blood and the silver of the small metal object lying next to it—appeared strangely beautiful together.

She had thought it belonged to the deceased, but thinking about it, might it not have been dropped there by the murderer? This thought suddenly came upon her. The scene going on around her suddenly disappeared, and in her mind's eye the room and the blood came vibrantly to life again.

She thought about the time. It couldn't have been more than five minutes since she left the house. It was unlikely that anyone else would have been there since. It would take about three minutes to walk there. Kiriko turned around and entered the alleyway again. She turned the corner and for the third time that night came upon the apartment blocks. The lights were still on and laughter still resounded from the windows.

She arrived at the house and went through the gate. For a while, she stood and strained her ears, but all was quiet. The radio from before had been shut off. Like an invited guest Kiriko opened the door and slipped into the entrance hall. She calmly removed her shoes, and as she did so she suddenly noticed a black object lying on the floor. She bent forward and realized that it was a leather glove. She hadn't noticed it when she came in earlier. The glove bore an understated but stylish arabesque design. It was a woman's right-hand glove. Kiriko realized Michiko must have dropped it in her hurry to leave earlier. She picked it up and held it in her hand. She didn't know why exactly, but she simply stood there grasping the glove.

She passed through the three and six-mat rooms. She could feel the softness of the *tatami* on the soles of her feet more keenly than ever before. Her heels felt as though they were sticking to the surface of the mats.

She came to the eight-mat room. Both the body and the blood rested almost ornamentally still. The deceased had his eyes open, staring blankly at the ceiling above. Not the slightest movement. His mouth gaped open in a perpetual yawn, a gold-capped tooth glinting in the light. The only perceptible change while Kiriko had been away was the increased volume of blood pooled on the surface of his dress shirt. The lighter was still there.

Kiriko bent down and picked it up. A design of grapes and squirrels decorated its surface. Two of the grapes were scratched.

Kiriko recalled that night in the bar when Kenji sat there smoking cigarettes. He had fished around in his pocket and, she remembered, pulled out a box of matches. But Nobuko had lit his cigarette for him and he had returned the unspent matches to his pocket. She was sure he hadn't used a lighter that night, which made her think he didn't possess one.

The ashtray lay on top of the blanket, but it was empty of cigarette butts. There were cigarettes on the brazier, but no sign of anyone having smoked any of them.

It struck Kiriko as odd, therefore, that a lighter should be on the floor next to the body. Her intuition told her it belonged to the killer.

Without really thinking, she put it in her pocket. Her right hand still held the woman's right glove. She dropped it at the side of the body—just where the lighter had been. Kiriko arranged the glove, with its slender fingers, on the surface of the *tatami* as if it was an object of great value. Even though the black glove had been substituted for the silver lighter, the color still complemented the red blood.

Kiriko went back towards the entrance. She looked at the soles of her feet while putting her shoes on, but there was no sign of blood on her nylon socks. She closed the door behind her and went out onto the street.

There was no sign of life in the narrow, dark alleyway. Everyone in the neighborhood was home for the night. As she passed the apartment block, two young men opened a door and came out. They shot a fleeting glance in her direction. There was nothing to worry about as she wasn't known in this neighborhood.

She emerged onto the street with the tramlines and walked towards the stop. The people who had been waiting for the tram before had since gone, to be replaced by two new people standing around looking uncomfortable in the cold. Kiriko joined them. Nothing had changed—everything suggested a typical, uneventful night.

Kiriko stopped by Bar Seaweed. It was just before closing time and a few customers were still there.

"Oh Rie, is everything all right?" asked one of the girls.

Kiriko had taken the evening off, but Nobuko ought to have covered for her and explained her absence.

"I was supposed to be meeting a friend from my home town, but she didn't show up."

An accordion player struck up a song requested by a customer. Nobuko caught sight of Kiriko and came over from the customer booths.

"Rie, got a moment?" she asked, calling her over to a corner of the bar.

Kiriko remained calm and wandered over.

"Well?" asked Nobuko in a hushed voice.

"I'm sorry," replied Kiriko quietly, "but I didn't see Kenji at all." She continued, "I stood out front for a while and when he didn't show up I called the restaurant and asked about him. They said he'd left thirty minutes earlier. I guess I didn't notice him leave."

Nobuko clearly showed her disappointment. "And you've no idea where he went?"

"No. I asked, but they wouldn't tell me. I'm sorry. I've let you down. I really tried to pay attention but, well, I bumped into someone I know and while I was chatting I suppose Kenji must have gone by. The person was pretty persistent and distracted me."

"Who was it?" asked Nobuko, showing little real interest.

"Kenji's friend. The one who came here the other night. I just bumped into him while I was standing there. He asked me all sorts of questions, like what I was doing, and things like that. I did my best not to let on."

"You met Mr. Yamagami?" said Nobuko, looking distinctly uncomfortable. She didn't particularly care for him.

"When I telephoned they said Kenji wasn't there and so I decided to go and see a movie. Then afterwards I thought Kenji might have come back and so I called the restaurant again. But no one picked up."

"It's no wonder, calling at that time," said Nobuko, a little despairingly.

Kiriko was apologetic. "I'm sorry, I really am. Next time I'll do it right."

"Yes, I may ask you again sometime." Nobuko was dissatisfied, but couldn't bring herself to be angry with her friend.

"Hey, Rie!" called one of the customers from his table. "Why don't you join us?"

"Coming!" With a carefree, happy expression she walked over to the customer.

"What's this then?" teased the man. "I heard you were taking the day off today. Have you just gotten back from a date or something?"

"Not a chance! No one ever takes me out."

The customer joked around a little longer and then asked if she would like a drink.

"I'll have a gin fizz, please," replied Kiriko nonchalantly.

Kenji Sugiura's corpse was discovered by the housekeeper. He had died from a fatal stab wound with a dagger-like weapon to the back, through the heart. The weapon was not recovered from the scene of the crime.

The murder was reported widely in the press. A statement was taken from the housekeeper, and Michiko Kono was arrested as the prime suspect. The details were given as follows.

Kenji Sugiura was the head waiter at a restaurant owned by Michiko Kono. He had been working there for two years. When he came to Tokyo from Kyushu he came with the express intention of opening his own restaurant some day. In order to gain the necessary experience, he chose to work at Michiko Kono's restaurant rather than at his sister's drinking establishment, Bar Seaweed.

Within a year of starting work at the restaurant he had entered into a relationship with Michiko Kono. According to Michiko's testimony she had been seduced by Kenji. However, Kenji was younger than she. Of course, the dead couldn't speak, so it was impossible to know the truth. It was just as likely that he had been seduced by Michiko. Michiko had divorced her husband three years prior.

Michiko had testified before the public prosecutor as follows:

"My involvement with Kenji was nothing more than a mistaken impulse. Afterwards, I reflected on my past conduct and decided I had to somehow end the relationship and move on with my life. But Kenji was very attached to me and wouldn't listen. He was very young and I think he became infatuated with me.

"I really wanted to end the relationship but he was persistent and wouldn't leave me alone.

"We concealed our affair from everyone else in the restaurant, and our behavior was very circumspect. Nevertheless, it seems that some of the employees who have been with me for some time did suspect what was going on. I could tell from the way they were hesitant around Kenji. Because of our relationship, Kenji worked especially hard in the restaurant. It was almost as if he considered himself the owner rather than an employee. Perhaps he worked so hard simply for my sake. Although I thought this sentiment was touching, I knew our relationship couldn't continue forever, and I didn't think it was good for Kenji, either.

"We had rented that house so we could meet discreetly. I hired the housekeeper and made sure nobody else knew about the arrangement. I must add however that lately I had done my best to avoid meeting with Kenji. In fact, we hadn't been to that house much at all recently. I wanted to terminate the lease on the house, but I felt unable to do so until I was sure of how Kenji felt about things.

"What I mean is Kenji was obsessive and his mood swings could be pretty violent at times. Young people tend to give vent to their emotions and act on impulse. There was no knowing what he might do. I came to realize this recently.

"Since I have told you this much already, I may as well tell you the rest. Sometime later I became intimate with the lawyer Kinzo Otsuka, and this developed into a special relationship. This was also a reason why I wanted to bring my affair with Kenji to an end. I did my level best to keep my relationship with Otsuka secret from Kenji but before long he found out about it.

"Recently, Kenji seemed to understand my point of view and said he would be prepared to let things go. But then he flew into a rage when he found out about my affair with

Otsuka. He seemed to think that I wanted to split up with him because I was seeing Otsuka.

"Kenji frequently threatened me. It wasn't easy for him to do this with so many of the staff in the restaurant, but he would wait for even the slightest opportunity and corner me when nobody was around, saying he wouldn't be responsible for his actions if I didn't end it all with Otsuka.

"One time he waved a bottle containing nitric acid in front of me, and another time he flashed a pocket knife.

"I became afraid of Kenji. I shudder to think what he might have done at the time. I didn't tell Otsuka about it. He so believed I was a sincere and faithful woman and I didn't want to disappoint him. I didn't feel I could speak candidly with him about my relationship with Kenji. I agonized about it alone. I was forced to meet with Otsuka discreetly to avoid any suspicion. Even when I met with him I felt like I was walking on thin ice. I felt really bad towards Otsuka, especially as he genuinely believed in me.

"One time I went to play golf with Otsuka at Hakone. I made an excuse and told the staff at the restaurant that I had an errand to run some place. But Kenji must have realized it wasn't true, as he suddenly turned up at the hotel in Hakone. Just as we were eating dinner in the hotel restaurant, I caught sight of his pale features as he stood rigidly in the entrance hall and I could almost feel the blood drain from my face. He was trembling violently as he denounced me. He told me to come outside, and I tried to calm him down. But he'd caught me redhanded and it was no use.

"There were a lot of people in the restaurant and, particularly because Otsuka was looking over in our direction, I felt my head was spinning. Even so, I begged Kenji not to create a scene. Perhaps he felt a little sorry for me since he went over and said hello to Otsuka and then suddenly left the hotel. I smoothed things over with Otsuka by telling him that Kenji had come down from Tokyo with a message for me.

"After that incident, Kenji became increasingly jealous. He told me that when he came back from Hakone, he had intended to call Otsuka and tell him everything, but that he wouldn't do that if I promised to break up with Otsuka immediately. After that, he continued to intimidate me. He was young and strong and I really believed he could have killed me. I told him that even if we continued seeing one another, ultimately, because of the age difference, we could never marry. We couldn't live together either, for fear of what people would say. I told him that he was still young and would be happier marrying a younger woman. But he only had eyes for me. He said he found other women boring and that he would prefer to live alone for the rest of his life. He cried when he told me that. I felt sorry for him, but what could I do? I tried my hardest to persuade him to see sense. And then, at last, he agreed to end it.

"I told him that if we really did end our relationship, I would give him the money to set up his own restaurant in the future. But Kenji said he didn't need the money and that he wasn't short of funds. I don't really know what he meant by that. He said if he were to receive money from me, our

225

relationship would be only about money, and that was too horrible for him.

"Then he wanted to see me one last time, on that fateful night. I didn't really want to go, but I thought if I refused he would get really angry and cause trouble, so in the end I reluctantly agreed.

"We arranged to meet at nine in the evening. I took a taxi to the neighborhood and then walked to the house. We had an arrangement whereby the first to arrive would send the housekeeper out. When I reached the entrance hall I knew Kenji had arrived first because the housekeeper didn't come out to greet me. Also Kenji's shoes were there in the entry hall.

"Knowing Kenji would be waiting in the eight-mat *tatami* room as he always did, I went straight through to the back of the house. When I got there I saw Kenji's bloodstained body lying next to the brazier.

"I nearly collapsed the instant I saw him. I didn't know what I was doing and rushed out of the room back towards the entry hall. I couldn't get rid of the image of Kenji's bloodstained body.

"To be honest, I only thought of my own situation at the time. I was bound to be the main suspect. When I thought about how it must look if I were caught, it made my blood run cold.

"Then, when I ran out of the front entrance, I suddenly bumped into a young woman. I was pale and shocked. I didn't know who she was but she had definitely been watching the house.

"I thought she would think I'd done it, so all of a sudden I clung to her and told her that it wasn't me. She was stupefied.

"I carried on telling her I hadn't done it and asked her to be a witness. She agreed and came with me back into the house. She saw Kenji lying dead. I asked her for her name and address, because I wanted her to be my witness. She said her name was Kiriko Yanagida and she worked at Bar Seaweed. Bar Seaweed is a drinking establishment run by Kenji's sister. That young woman may have come to the house out of some connection with the bar. In any case, she agreed to testify to the effect that I was not the murderer, and I was greatly relieved to hear that. Then suddenly I became afraid of the body in the other room and I had to get away from there as quickly as possible. I didn't spare a thought for Kiriko Yanagida.

"I half ran along the alleyway, picked a taxi up and fled to my restaurant. I arrived there a little before 11:10 pm.

"I realized after I'd got back that I had lost my right glove. I didn't know where I had dropped it. I was surprised when I learned it had been found next to the body. I had no recollection whatsoever of dropping it there. In fact, there had been a lighter next to the body. It had a design on it of squirrels and grapes. Kiriko Yanagida must have seen it, too. You should ask her. She will testify and prove me innocent."

When Kiriko Yanagida was questioned, she refuted everything that Michiko Kono had said.

"I have never heard of, nor seen, anyone by the name of Michiko Kono. I didn't go anywhere near that house on the night in question. I went to the movies…"

Chapter 9

Michiko Kono's testimony and Kiriko Yanagida's witness statement completely contradicted one another.

The key points in Michiko's testimony were as follows:

1. Michiko Kono had a relationship in the past with Kenji Sugiura, the head waiter at the restaurant she owned. Michiko was no longer interested in Kenji, but he was infatuated with her, an older woman.
2. Michiko had since the previous year become involved in a relationship with the lawyer Kinzo Otsuka. However, she had concealed her affair with Kenji. Kenji was intensely jealous of Michiko's relationship with Otsuka. As a consequence, Kenji continually pressed Michiko to end her affair with Otsuka and threatened that if she refused to do so he would reveal everything to the lawyer and even subject her to physical abuse.

3. Michiko managed to appease Kenji.
   However, in order finally to persuade
   him to separate, she agreed to see
   him one last time at a house they had
   rented as a hideaway some time earlier.
   A middle-aged female housekeeper
   looked after the place while they were
   away.

4. At the appointed time on the evening
   in question, at about 9:00 pm, Michiko
   took a taxi to the neighborhood. When
   she entered the house she found that
   Kenji had been murdered, his blood-
   covered body lying next to a portable
   brazier in the eight-mat tatami room.
   She was scared and fled the house, but
   ran into a young woman as she was
   coming out of the entrance.

5. It dawned on her that this woman could
   prove her innocent and so she asked
   her to be a witness and guided her
   back to the scene of the crime. The
   woman agreed that she thought Michiko
   innocent. The young woman gave her
   name as Kiriko Yanagida, employed as a
   hostess at Bar Seaweed.

6. Michiko then fled by taxi to her
   restaurant in Ginza. She was confident
   that Kiriko Yanagida would prove her
   innocent. She had to recognize that
   Michiko had not carried out the crime.

7. She had no recollection of where she
   had dropped her right-hand glove. She
   was at a loss to explain how her glove
   had ended up next to Kenji Sugiura's
   body. She had no reason to have
   dropped it there.

Kiriko Yanagida completely rejected Michiko's story.

1. She didn't know Michiko Kono, either
   by name or in person. It followed
   therefore that she had never met her.
2. At about 9:00 pm on the evening in
   question she was watching a movie at a
   movie theater in Hibiya.
3. Furthermore, she had no reason to go
   to a house — the scene of the crime —
   that she had never heard of before.
4. Michiko Kono may well have heard her
   name before from Kenji Sugiura. Kenji
   frequently came to Bar Seaweed which
   was run by his sister, and he knew
   Kiriko worked there.

The public prosecutor in charge of the investigation considered both statements carefully.

Judging from her facial expression and the content of her written testimony, he didn't think that Michiko Kono was making a false statement. On the other hand, the witness, Kiriko Yanagida, stubbornly refused to concede that her statement was in any way untrue. She was still young and girlish, yet she had a strong sense of purpose and character and flatly refused to change her statement.

The public prosecutor, faced with little alternative, recommended that corroborative evidence be sought.

There was found to be no witness that Kiriko Yanagida had been in the movie theater at around nine on the night in question. However, she was familiar with the plot of the movie she claimed to have seen. Since Kiriko had only recently come to Tokyo, it was hardly surprising that she knew no one in the audience that night.

There was also no evidence to suggest she had been at the scene of the crime. There were no eyewitnesses. In fact, there was no evidence, as Kiriko herself had contended, that she knew of the house at all. The house had been especially rented so that Michiko and Kenji could conduct their discreet liaisons. It was fair to say therefore that nobody else ought to have known about it. Michiko's contention that she ran into Kiriko at the house that night simply didn't stand up as a credible story.

However, Kiriko's friend Nobuko had asked her to keep an eye on the movements of Kenji, her boyfriend. It was confirmed that Kiriko had taken the day off from Bar Seaweed in order to carry out this surveillance. Kiriko Yanagida had the following to say about the matter:

Nobuko asked me to watch Sugiura and see where he went, so I waited for a while at the front of the restaurant where he works. I think that was around 7 pm. Even though I waited a long while, he never showed up. I started to become a little self-conscious standing there alone, it was also boring and my feet were aching, so eventually I changed my mind and went to the movie theater instead. That would have been around 8:40 pm, if I'm not mistaken. There was an old woman in the tobacco shop opposite who saw me and she will probably remember.

The old lady from the tobacconist was duly questioned and, while she wasn't able to say with certainty whether or not it had been Kiriko Yanagida, someone very much resembling her had been there for about an hour from around 7:00 pm pacing up and down as if waiting for someone.

Kiriko had not been on particularly friendly terms with the victim. She knew him simply as the younger brother of the owner of Bar Seaweed who used to stop by there from time to time. Again, as Kiriko had said in her statement, she didn't know Michiko Kono at all. There was nothing to suggest she had any dealings with her.

Moreover, Michiko's assertion that Kiriko just happened to be at the scene of the crime appeared to be just too much of a coincidence, and so long as there was no evidence that Kiriko knew of the house, it seemed all the more to be a contrived fabrication. This point did not work in Michiko's favor.

The real problem was that Michiko's glove served to further implicate her. Michiko had categorically stated that she had lost her right-hand glove. She was questioned as to why she only removed one glove. According to Michiko, she was in the habit of taking off her gloves when she entered the house, and she had begun to do so on that occasion. But having taken one off, she then went into the *tatami* room, and after so unexpectedly witnessing the murder scene, she quite forgot to remove the other one.

This explanation seemed perfectly plausible. However, it remained a mystery as to why the glove was found lying next to the deceased's body.

Michiko stated that she had no recollection of dropping it in such a place and indeed there was no reason why she should have done so.

A further problem was raised following the autopsy carried out on Kenji Sugiura's body. The post-mortem results showed that the deceased had been stabbed once in the back with a sharp-edged instrument. He had died instantly from a wound to the heart.

There were also signs at the scene of the crime that Kenji had been sitting next to someone with their feet in the well of the portable brazier. In other words, it appeared that the murderer had been alongside Kenji talking with him when he suddenly stabbed Kenji with a dagger-like weapon. It could be inferred, therefore, that the murderer enjoyed quite a close relationship with Kenji. Furthermore, in order to grip the weapon properly, the murderer would have had to remove her glove. It was conceivable that having seen the victim collapse, the murderer panicked and in her desperate hurry to flee the scene of the crime, inadvertently dropped the glove by the body. This possibility worked against Michiko.

Yet the public prosecutor's attention was drawn to one issue in particular, namely, that part of Michiko's statement where she said, "There was a lighter next to the body. It had a design on it of squirrels and grapes. Kiriko Yanagida must have seen it, too. You should ask her."

When she was asked about this, Kiriko replied, "I haven't ever been to the scene of the crime, and so I can't have seen a lighter there."

But, somewhat curiously, the issue of the lighter stuck in the public prosecutor's mind. Upon further investigation, Kenji's friends and colleagues confirmed that he did not carry a lighter. In fact, a close friend who worked at the restaurant testified that on that particular day Kenji had used matches to light his cigarettes. If Michiko's contention was true, and a lighter had been dropped by the body, then it must have belonged to the real murderer.

Michiko also smoked, but she said she didn't possess a lighter. Furthermore, if Michiko were the real murderer, it was difficult to believe she would introduce the subject of the lighter in the first place. Of course, she could be doing so in order to obfuscate her crime and throw the investigation into a state of confusion.

The public prosecutor ultimately had no reason to doubt the veracity of Michiko's statement. She had also been bold enough to admit to the public prosecutor her relationship with the lawyer Kinzo Otsuka. The prosecutor, relying on his considerable experience in observing suspects under investigation, was able to tell intuitively whether or not a suspect was telling the truth. In this case, his intuition led him to believe that Michiko's statement was true.

The corollary was that he became more suspicious of Kiriko Yanagida's statement.

No matter how thoroughly the public prosecutor questioned Kiriko, she remained level-headed and exhibited an inner strength and resilience that was quite unlike that found in most young women her age. She simply asserted her own version of the circumstances of the case and refused to budge an inch.

"If you tell lies, you may be found guilty of perjury, do you understand? If you don't tell me what really happened, somebody may be given the death penalty," the prosecutor threatened, but Kiriko remained calm and collected throughout.

"Your honor, do you think I am trying to entrap Michiko Kono? I have no reason at all to do such a thing. What's more, I have no reason to hide anything with regard to this investigation. There is no connection between myself and Michiko Kono," she replied, glaring at the public prosecutor.

The arguments for and against were thus presented. No matter how thorough the investigation, however, there did not appear to be a hidden agenda between Kiriko Yanagida and Michiko Kono. Not only that, but the two had apparently never even laid eyes upon one another.

The investigation of Kiriko came to an end after three rounds of questioning.

The murder case was given wide coverage in the newspapers. The case was characterized simply as a crime of passion. Not only was the suspect Michiko Kono the owner of a famous restaurant in Ginza, but she was in a relationship with Kinzo Otsuka, one of the most renowned lawyers in the country.

Otsuka's name was well known not only in legal circles but also amongst the general public. He was known to be a top-class lawyer. His achievements in court were highly praised and his name was frequently in the press. He often penned articles for newspapers and magazines and spoke on the radio. He was, so to speak, a dignitary.

The murder case unwittingly exposed Otsuka's private scandal. Michiko Kono's insistence of innocence simply worked to fuel public interest.

There was a paucity of direct evidence in this case. There was no murder weapon. The results of the autopsy suggested it had been a sharp-edged blade such as a knife or dagger, but the weapon had not been recovered. In addition, there was no indirect evidence to suggest that Michiko Kono had obtained a weapon of the sort indicated in the post-mortem report. Looking at the position of the body, one would have expected the murderer's clothing to have been spattered with blood; however, none was found on Michiko Kono's clothing. No figerprints thought to be the murderer's were found on the brazier or any of the other articles at the scene of the crime. While a number of Michiko's indistinct prints had been found on several items in the house, it was clear they were not left there on the day of the murder, but rather during earlier visits.

This case aroused public interest because it relied on circumstantial evidence almost to the total exclusion of physical evidence.

Keiichi Abe had gone to Bar Seaweed to meet Kiriko.

"Oh, Rie? She quit," said one of the hostesses.

"When?"

"The day before yesterday." The girl had a sour expression on her face.

Kiriko had doubtless left partly out of consideration for the owner's feelings. It must also have become unbearable to work there any longer.

"Where is she now?" Abe scanned the room for Kiriko's friend Nobuko but was told that she too had handed in her notice.

"Rie isn't living with Nobu anymore, either. We don't know where she's staying right now."

"Can you tell me where she's working now?"

The girl could only tell Abe the name of the place where Kiriko had recently begun to work. She said it was Bar Lyon, located in one of the backstreets in Shinjuku.

Bar Lyon proved extremely difficult to find. A narrow alleyway led off from the rear of a department store. It was home to a myriad of small bars and drinking holes. Abe eventually found the bar tucked away at the end of the alleyway. It wasn't the sort of place you would pass by chance.

Bar Seaweed may have been a small place, but it was at least in Ginza. Somewhat dispirited, Abe couldn't help feeling Kiriko had fallen on hard times, having to drop out of Ginza and come to this small place tucked down a Shinjuku back alley.

Bar Lyon was a shabby place. Abe pushed the door open. The counter was immediately on his left. The walkway was so narrow, with customers taking up seats along it, that he almost had to turn sideways to get inside. As the place was so small Abe soon found Kiriko. She was towards the back, talking with a customer. When she caught sight of him she turned her head back, then looked straight ahead again. Abe remained silent. A customer was using the back of the only free seat to support himself with his elbow. Abe sat down there.

As he sipped his drink, Kiriko came over like a shadow.

"Hello. This is a surprise," she said in a low voice. With the gloomy lighting on her face, Kiriko looked more adult than she ever did at Bar Seaweed. It was probably due to the environment in which she now worked, but Abe had the impression it also had a little to do with being embroiled in a murder case.

"Why didn't you tell me you'd moved?" asked Abe, keeping his voice low so as not to be overheard by the bartender. It was partly a rebuke, but Kiriko just smiled and then apologized with unexpected gentleness.

"A lot of things have happened. I'm sorry."

"I read about you in the papers. I wanted to see you, but you had left the bar." Abe bought her a gin fizz.

"Yes. I had to see the police every day."

"I wish you'd called me and let me know," he chided.

Kiriko fell silent.

"So did you move here because you couldn't stand being in the other bar following the investigation?"

"Yes." Kiriko didn't disagree, but there was no sign of regret in her face either. She held her head up proudly.

It had been a long time since Abe had looked at Kiriko like this. He wanted to ask her so many things, but the bar was noisy with music and customers talking and he couldn't find a way to keep the conversation going.

"I'd like to talk to you," he said. "What time does this place close? When you're done for the night, shall we take a walk?"

Kiriko was chewing on a cherry that had been floating in her drink. "11:30. Can you wait that long?" she answered with surprising simplicity.

Abe met Kiriko at the agreed time on a corner leading from the alleyway onto the main street.

Kiriko joined him attired as she'd been back during her stint at Bar Seaweed. "Where shall we talk?" she asked.

The coffee shops were all closed at this late hour. In any case, Abe didn't want to talk in a place like that. "Let's just walk along and talk."

"Fine by me," she said cheerfully.

They avoided the main streets crowded with cars and walked along the quiet back roads. In one direction stretched the long wall of the Shinjuku Imperial Gardens. A prostitute waited in the shadows.

"I saw your witness statement in the newspaper," said Abe, his shoes resounding against the hard surface of the sidewalk as they moved slowly along.

"Did you?" Kiriko answered nonchalantly and without hesitation.

"Is that what you really meant to say?" He really wanted to ask whether or not her statement was true.

"I don't tell lies. I know myself better than anyone," she answered calmly.

"Yes, I suppose you do." Abe was quiet for a while. A cold wind blew around his feet.

"This will be the undoing of Otsuka-*sensei*, in the public eye, at any rate," muttered Abe.

"Do you really think so?" said Kiriko doubtfully. Or rather, she sounded as though she'd never given him a second thought.

"Yes, I do. That kind of scandal coming to light would be enough to sink anybody. Someone as well-known as Otsuka-*sensei*—he will lose his reputation."

They rounded a corner and followed the curve of the dark fence as it stretched ahead of them. In the other direction a line of red paper lanterns shone brightly from the various bars that flanked the street. A group of noisy young girls went by.

"Your revenge has worked splendidly, hasn't it?" Abe said this in an entirely casual manner, yet the words formed from an inner conviction.

"What on earth do you mean?" Kiriko's voice remained even. It was dark and not easy to see, but her gaze never seemed to flicker.

"You had begged Otsuka-*sensei* to defend your brother," said Abe, almost as if he were thinking aloud. "But Otsuka-*sensei* had turned down your request. His legal fees were too expensive for you, and he didn't know whether you would be able to pay them. You resented that, didn't you? After all, you'd come all the way from Kyushu especially to see him, to ask him to save your brother from the groundless charges he stood accused of. You must have been very upset going back to Kyushu."

"So what you're saying, Mr. Abe, is that Mr. Otsuka's possible downfall is my way of getting revenge?" she demanded in a calm and collected voice.

"Well, don't you think so?"

"No I don't," she replied, her voice resounding with confidence. "That's not enough to satisfy me. Mr. Otsuka will bounce back given time. But my brother is dead and buried with the stain of murder still hanging over him."

Kiriko uttered the last words with characteristic passion.

A group of youngsters came past them from the side. Kiriko and Abe must have looked like lovers out for a late night walk together.

"So you're still not satisfied?" asked Abe, seeking clarification.

"No, I'm not. If I were to tell you otherwise then I'd be lying."

"But," said Abe with renewed determination, "just supposing for a moment, and this is just supposition, that you deliberately plotted your statement to the public prosecutor, would that have got you your revenge?"

"I didn't plot my statement to the prosecutor." Kiriko's voice became calm again and she continued walking in an unhurried manner.

"I mean, it's purely supposition. I'm saying if you had planned it, what would it have achieved?"

"I wonder," replied Kiriko, turning the question back to Abe.

"I would say you had achieved your aim," said Abe.

"Well, I disagree. If you're asking me, I would say I was a long way off yet. Mr. Otsuka will recover his reputation. Someone of his standing can pick up the pieces and regain the public's respect. No, I would not be content, not at all."

Abe was wearing his overcoat, yet a shiver still went up his spine.

Kinzo Otsuka devoted all his time to Michiko's case. The incident had dealt him an extremely severe blow. To begin with, his relationship with Michiko had suddenly been made known to the world at large, and he was censured both privately and publicly.

There were some who were particularly candid in their condemnation of Otsuka. Until now he had been known as an upright lawyer not associated with scandals of this nature. He was now on the receiving end of scathing attacks on his character and felt like his mask had been torn off.

He also came under pressure from various cultural organizations he was affiliated with and withdrew from a number of them of his own volition. It was as if his opponents, hitherto lurking in the background, had suddenly revealed themselves.

The situation was also miserable at home. Once she found out he was seeing another woman, his wife went back to her family home. Otsuka's life became desolate. This sense of desolation manifested itself not only in his household. He had the feeling that his colleagues in the office also now looked at him in a different light. They fell to their work as usual, but they did their best to avoid making eye contact with him. These people, who thus far had demonstrated nothing but complete respect for him, now threatened cold-hearted revolt in the office.

There were undoubtedly a number of junior lawyers who, given the chance, would have left their posts on the slightest pretext. Some clients of the firm even came specifically to withdraw their cases. New briefs stopped landing on Otsuka's desk. He was the object of sarcasm in newspapers and magazines. The atmosphere in the office was gloomy and a chilling melancholy settled over the place.

Yet Otsuka was unbowed. He even felt somehow galvanized by the whole experience, a feeling similar to that he used to have when required to summon all his courage in facing a difficult case.

Furthermore, he believed in Michiko, and not just in regards to the case. He believed in her love, and he was prepared to sacrifice himself for her. Perched on the threshold of old age, neither his reputation, status nor glittering legal career mattered anymore.

Otsuka met with Michiko, who was on remand pending trial, time and time again. He researched the court records with a renewed level of scrupulousness.

He believed Michiko was innocent. He was convinced her statement was truthful, certain that his belief was not prejudiced by the love he felt for her. Under pressure as he was, he was determined that he would not lose his professional composure.

To add to the complications, there was the issue of the witness called by Michiko. Otsuka read Kiriko Yanagida's witness statement over and over again. His senses told him, intuitively, that it was a fabrication.

But that was an intuition. There was no proof that her statement was untrue in any respect. Her story seemed to make sense. It was constructed with no apparent faults and nothing in it called into question its veracity. Conscious of the futility of relying solely on his intuition, Otsuka somehow needed to find an objective way of cracking Kiriko's testimony.

He threw his whole being into this aspect of the case. He did not ask the help of his staff for even the most minute of investigations. He wanted to accomplish what he had set out to do on his own. It became a labor of love for Michiko's sake.

There had to be a way of finding fault with Kiriko's statement. Otsuka concentrated his efforts on this one issue.

Then suddenly something occurred to him—the name of a magazine journalist who had come to ask his opinion about a case involving Kiriko.

Hadn't he come to see Otsuka as part of Kiriko's plot for revenge? This, too, was purely an intuitive feeling. Otsuka looked into it and there was no evidence that Kiriko and Michiko were ever acquainted. Even Michiko had said they had first met at the scene of the crime.

The problem was how Kiriko knew the whereabouts of the house being used as a hideaway. Of course, this presupposed that Michiko's statement was true. This point troubled Otsuka. The public prosecutor had also drawn attention to the issue and censured this part of Michiko's testimony for deceit.

Even though Otsuka was now aware of Michiko's past relationship with the victim Kenji Sugiura, he didn't feel he'd been deceived by her. Michiko's mistake had resulted in intimidation by Kenji. Otsuka loved Michiko. He didn't blame her for what she had done in the past. Once she realized she was in love with Otsuka, Michiko had tried to end her affair with Kenji.

In a sense, it could be said that this unforeseen incident involving Michiko had occurred thanks to Otsuka himself.

He'd recalled Keiichi Abe's name in a last-ditch effort. Abe had come to the office to request Otsuka's opinion with regard to the murder in K-City, Kyushu, as an acquaintance of Kiriko. Otsuka now took it into his head to use Abe in a final attempt to find out the truth from Kiriko.

Abe met Kiriko again the night after Otsuka called him. He had decided to see her not only because of Otsuka's story, but because he, too, had doubts about Kiriko's testimony.

Abe was fond of Kiriko, but he wasn't about to delude himself and side with her to the exclusion of his own instincts. He wasn't about to cover up for her, but were she in danger, he would protect her. This time, for his own sake, he had to satisfy himself that the nagging doubt about the truth of her testimony was unfounded. Otsuka's request to pursue the matter wasn't the only reason he had.

Abe accompanied Kiriko from the bar in the back streets of Shinjuku at a little after 11:30 pm. They followed the same route they had walked before. On one side was the long dark wall of the Shinjuku Imperial Gardens.

"I'd like to ask you once more," said Abe, breaking the silence as they walked together. "You said that Nobuko had asked you to watch Kenji's movements, and that was why you were waiting in front of the restaurant that night, yes?"

Kiriko walked shoulder to shoulder with him. "Yes, that's right. That's what I told the public prosecutor, too."

"Yes, I know," said Abe, nodding. "It was also noted in the court records. The old woman from the tobacco shop testified to having seen you standing in front of the shop. You waited there from 7:00 pm for about an hour and a half. You stood there for the whole time before going to the movie theater, right?"

"Yes, that's right," answered Kiriko without hesitating.

"While you were waiting, did you bump into someone you know? This is important."

"Did I? I'm trying to recall," said Kiriko, appearing to think about it. Then suddenly, as if it had just occurred to her, she said, "Oh yes, I did meet someone."

"Really? Who?" Abe checked his step slightly.

"One of the customers I remembered seeing at Bar Seaweed. He was a friend of Kenji's. I'd only met him once before."

"What was his name?" pressed Abe.

"Yamagami, I think he said."

"Yamagami?"

"Yes. He said he was a friend of Kenji's from their junior high school days."

247

"What kind of person is he?"

"I don't really know what he does for a living. Apparently he was a member of a pro-baseball team in the past. He graduated from K Senior High School. Their baseball team is very good, you know."

"K Senior High?" Abe peered out of the darkness at Kiriko. "That's your hometown, isn't it?"

"That's right. Everyone at Bar Seaweed comes from K-City. Kenji was the same, so it's not surprising that he graduated from K Senior High."

"So this Yamagami fellow, he quit being a pro-baseball player?"

"I believe so. I didn't get this directly from Yamagami, Kenji told me. He said his friend had been talented at baseball and became a professional player but couldn't advance from the second team and eventually quit."

"Is that right?" said Abe. "I haven't heard his name before. What position did he play?"

"He said he was a pitcher. Yes, that's it, he said he was a southpaw pitcher."

"A southpaw pitcher?" Abe fell silent while he thought about this.

Kiriko, however, had not told Abe the whole story. She had seen someone very much like Yamagami that fateful night emerge from the dark alleyway onto the street with the tramlines, not 200 yards from the house, but she couldn't say with any degree of certainty whether it was him. Yet it was not this uncertainty that prevented her from discussing the issue. There was another reason why she had not mentioned this either to the public prosecutor or to Abe—not only would it reveal that she had been to the scene of the crime that night, but it would also provide Michiko—or rather, Otsuka—with the salvation they so badly craved.

Otsuka listened to Abe's report of his conversation with Kiriko and was startled to hear that Kenji's friend Yamagami had been a southpaw pitcher. This meant that Yamagami was left-handed. He was also interested to learn that he hailed from K-City.

There was something that Otsuka hadn't even mentioned to Abe. Otsuka had discovered, after a thorough review of the court documents, that the true perpetrator of the K-City moneylender murder case—the case that branded Kiriko's elder brother Masao a murderer—had been left-handed.

Masao Yanagida had died in prison while his appeal was pending. Otsuka had felt unable to relate this to Abe largely because his refusal of Kiriko's request for representation due to his high fees still weighed heavily on his mind. Were Masao Yanagida still alive, he would tell him so, and he would undertake his defense pro bono as he'd done on numerous occasions since he first started out in the profession.

But Masao Yanagida was dead. That, plus the fact that he had turned down the deceased's sister's request after she had travelled all the way from Kyushu to see him, represented a considerable burden on his conscience.

Otsuka knew that Kiriko resented him and he understood her feelings, but he didn't have the courage to try and set the record straight after all this time.

The court-appointed lawyer in K-City had not been able, ultimately, to make the discovery that he himself had made. As a result, Masao Yanagida had been found guilty. This was something that only Otsuka knew about. Something he couldn't disclose to anyone. It was a secret which he had to live with.

The realization that Kenji's killer was left-handed suddenly led Otsuka to a new train of thought. He had overlooked it the first time round, but it occurred to him that Kenji's killer had been sitting next to him in front of the brazier. He would have been on Kenji's right side. According to the post-mortem, the fatal wound was the result of a single stab to the heart from the victim's back. Supposing that someone sitting on the right side were to stab a person sitting on his left in the back, logically he could not use his right arm to do the deed. If he were to stab someone from a sitting position without attracting the victim's attention, he would have to use his left arm.

The fatal wound to the heart had been inflicted by a single stab from the back, and this clearly required a fair degree of strength. Whoever it was must have had a considerable amount of muscular strength in his left arm. In other words, the killer had to have been left-handed. Michiko was not left-handed. In that instant Otsuka thought he detected a single ray of hope.

However, from his considerable experience dealing with the court, Otsuka knew only too well that his discovery was, as yet, inadequate to challenge the prosecutor's concluding remarks. He could imagine what the prosecutor would be likely to say: "Assuming for the moment that the murderer was right-handed, it is conceivable that he could make the attack by shifting his sitting position and using his right hand. Perhaps he had stood up and momentarily moved away from the brazier on some pretext and then attacked from the rear once his victim's guard was down."

Otsuka could almost hear the prosecutor's counter-argument as he thought about it. Nevertheless, Otsuka was sure about his left-handed theory.

In order to shore up the deficiencies in his defense, he had to find some proof, some ironclad physical evidence that would succeed in proving Michiko innocent.

Even if the prosecution were able to add circumstantial evidence in convicting Michiko, they had no physical evidence. Conversely, if Otsuka could find physical evidence supporting her statement of innocence, it would constitute a compelling defense.

Otsuka was at his wits' end. Then something flickered in his mind—the image of the lighter referred to in Michiko's testimony.

She had said it was lying next to the body, but when they arrived at the scene, the police had not found it. Yet Otsuka's belief in Michiko's testimony was not swayed.

The fact that the police were unable to find the lighter that Michiko saw when they arrived at the house suggested to Otsuka that someone had taken it. It seemed obvious to him that the lighter belonged to the murderer. The question was, who took it?

According to Michiko's testimony, she and Kiriko had been standing together by the deceased's body. Then Michiko, gripped suddenly with fear, had fled the house first, leaving Kiriko there alone. Wouldn't it have been possible for Kiriko to pick up and pocket the lighter?

It certainly wasn't inconceivable. Even at their first meeting it was clear to Otsuka that the young woman, who looked barely out of adolescence, possessed a rather unusual character. Indeed, it seemed all the more possible considering her eccentric nature.

And if that were the case, why would she have done it?

Kiriko Yanagida was plotting her revenge against him. She believed that because he had turned down her request on account of his fees, her brother had been unfairly accused of murder and died in prison. It was a hell of a pretext. It was a deeply troubling matter for Otsuka.

He was not the judge who had handed down the guilty verdict to her brother, and he was perfectly entitled not to take on a case.

That was the logical standpoint, but Kiriko seemed to believe that the decision of the eminent criminal defense attorney Kinzo Otsuka not to represent her had directly brought about her brother's guilty verdict. This had dealt Otsuka quite a psychological blow.

Otsuka believed Michiko's testimony and would do so to the bitter end. Based on this conviction, he played over once more the events of the recent murder in his mind.

Having been asked by her friend Nobuko to watch Kenji Sugiura's movements, Kiriko waited in front of the restaurant

252

where he worked. She was there from 7 pm for about an hour and a half. She had been seen by the old woman in the tobacco shop and by Yamagami, who just happened to be passing by.

Kiriko had said that since there had been no sign of Kenji and she was tired of standing there, keeping watch, she'd gone to the movies, but Otsuka was sure she hadn't. Kenji had come out of the restaurant at about 8:30. He'd taken a taxi and gone hurriedly to the house they'd set up for their clandestine meetings. Kiriko must have hailed another taxi and tailed him to the house.

Which meant that Kiriko knew about the house, notwithstanding her insistence that she had never been there. The sequence of events after that were as stated in Michiko's testimony. While Kiriko was prowling around outside to get a better view of the house, Michiko, who had just come across the body in the back of the building, came running out of the front entrance.

Michiko was in a confused state, psychologically, on account of her desperation to avoid being implicated in the murder. She returned to the scene of the crime with Kiriko and begged her to be her witness. Kiriko was a complete stranger as far as Michiko was concerned, but in those circumstances anyone would have behaved in the same manner. As things began to unfold, a dark idea began to weave itself into a sinister plan inside Kiriko's mind.

Kiriko had agreed and given Michiko her name. Michiko couldn't stand to be beside the body any longer and left the house first. It was then that Kiriko picked the lighter up from where it had been next to the body and slipped it into her pocket—the lighter that bore the design of squirrels and grapes. Furthermore, she must have picked up Michiko's right-hand glove as she went out through the front. Another dark idea arose. She picked up the glove and laid it next to the corpse, and then left the house…

Likely as not, Kiriko must have suspected a relationship between Otsuka and Michiko. She had tried her level best to deal a blow to Otsuka by destroying the thing most precious to him—Michiko.

If that were the case, then the planned attack had been spectacularly successful. Michiko stood accused of murder. Otsuka had been censured by the public. His home life lay in tatters. His reputation had suffered a severe blow and he found himself in bleak and desolate circumstances.

And yet Otsuka displayed nothing but courage. The problem was always going to be how to save Michiko. He no longer cared about his own situation. For the first time in his fifty-odd years he was seized with a passion for the sake of the woman he loved.

The lighter with squirrels and grapes had belonged to the murderer. Kiriko had hidden it. He was sure about that. Otsuka wanted somehow to retrieve the lighter from Kiriko and get her to tell him what had really happened. Then he wanted her to testify truthfully in court and present the lighter. Otsuka was determined to make any sacrifice necessary to see that happen.

He was prepared to disregard his honor, his career and his age, prostrate himself at Kiriko's feet if necessary and beg her to do as he asked. She could denounce him if she liked. He didn't care that she may speak ill of him or that he would suffer humiliation. He would absorb all of this and more if she would only do as he wished.

Informed by Abe, Otsuka went to the bar in the back streets of Shinjuku just after 11:00 pm.

Initially he considered arranging a meeting with Kiriko through Abe but changed his mind thinking that she wouldn't show up. Plus, Abe's presence would no doubt make it difficult to talk. As he suspected, there was no alternative to confronting her directly.

Otsuka had chosen to go there just after 11:00 pm because he had learned from Abe that the bar closed at around 11:30 pm. Since Otsuka didn't know Kiriko's address, he could do little else than wait for her to leave the bar and try to talk to her, as Abe himself had done previously.

He wandered down the narrow alleyway and searched for Bar Lyon. It was a small place. He pushed on the door and went in.

The bar was narrow and filled with cigarette smoke. A fleeting glance told him that the clientele was not particularly high class, very different from the sort of people he was used to mixing with. They were low-grade businessmen and day laborers. Knowing that the surrounding area was seedy, it took a considerable amount of courage on Otsuka's part to come to this place and sit down at the bar.

He looked for Kiriko's face as soon as he came in. He had only a faint recollection of her appearance, yet he knew he would remember her if he saw her. There were four or five hostesses in the bar busy attending to their customers. The lighting was dim and it was difficult to make out faces in the gloom, so for the time being he propped himself up at the counter.

It seemed the bartender had also noticed how out of place Otsuka was. His age and the good quality and cut of his clothes gave him away. His build was somewhat portly on account of rich living. The other customers in the bar found themselves looking over in his direction.

Otsuka felt himself shrink under such scrutiny and distracted himself by staring at the shelves of drinks in front of him.

"Good evening. What can I get for you?" asked the bartender politely.

The shelves were full of bottles of cheap liquor. There was nothing there that Otsuka was familiar with.

"I'll have a scotch and water," answered Otsuka.

He drank the cheap scotch and took a furtive look around. Next to him sat a fairly drunk businessman, his elbows jutting out. Being careful not to brush against him, Otsuka took a look around the bar, searching the gloom for Kiriko, yet he needn't have spared the effort. From out of the midst of the smoke-filled bar appeared a slightly built girl.

"Welcome, good evening."

It was Kiriko. Her face looked just the same as he remembered it from her visit to his office. With a slight smile on her face she sat down by Otsuka's side. She was playing her role of bar hostess thoroughly.

"Hello." The words didn't come easily and he was troubled as to how to greet her.

"It has been a long time, *sensei*," said Kiriko.

Otsuka was slightly startled. Kiriko looked completely at ease, almost as if she had been expecting him to show up. Otsuka could feel his heart thumping. He was compelled to play along and act like a customer. He had completely lost the opportunity to say what he had intended to say. His discomfiture was also due in part to his unease with his surroundings.

He had arrived late and before long, preparations were begun for closing time. Kiriko drank a cocktail.

As the other customers began to leave, Otsuka steeled his nerve and said to Kiriko, "I'd like to talk to you. Can you spare me some time on your way home?"

Kiriko suddenly fixed her eyes on the liquor bottles lined up on the shelf. Her profile was just as it had been in his office the first time he met her—a hard, set expression, as she chewed thoughtfully on her lip. A pale blue vein stood out on her forehead. She nodded quietly in affirmation.

Otsuka went outside first and waited for her. He couldn't relax in such alien surroundings.

He stood there, watching and waiting. A constant stream of inebriated men staggered past, gibbering to one another in loud voices. Several odd-looking youths walked past and looked him up and down.

Ten minutes later, Otsuka finally found himself side-by-side with Kiriko, walking along a deserted street. He wanted to walk somewhere with few people around and she chose this route for him.

Otsuka didn't know this area at all; he'd only ever travelled by car on the main streets.

"*Sensei*. From the moment you came into the bar I knew we'd end up talking properly like this," said Kiriko, breaking the silence. She spoke directly and with confidence, which made it easier for Otsuka to begin talking.

"Really? If that's the case then I feel I can speak freely." Otsuka was inwardly relieved. Since he left the bar he had been planning how and in what order he would broach the subject of conversation he had in mind, but that was no longer necessary.

"You don't have to explain. I already know what you're going to say. It's about the latest murder, isn't it? You want me to testify that I was at the scene of the crime, with Michiko Kono, don't you?"

Otsuka was taken aback at how grown up she suddenly seemed to have become. The Kiriko he knew had been an immature, innocent young girl fresh from Kyushu. Her experiences since arriving in Tokyo—working in bars and such places—had no doubt turned her into the woman that now walked confidently by his side. Yet her innate strength of purpose and sense of resolution that he'd witnessed in his office had not changed. That characteristic ran through her whole being like a length of wire.

"That's exactly right," said Otsuka. "I didn't come here to criticize you. I came here to ask you a favor. You already know about my relationship with Michiko Kono from the

258

newspapers, and probably even from before the murder," said Otsuka as they walked along. "I want you to tell me what really happened. I know you dislike and even resent me. I can understand that. But I will do anything to make amends, to show you how sorry I am. All I ask is that you please tell the truth in front of the public prosecutor."

"The truth?" repeated Kiriko. "I already told the truth to the public prosecutor."

Otsuka thought he detected a note of cynicism in her tone of voice.

"I don't believe you did. I have practised as an attorney for many years. I think what Michiko said is the true version of events. And I'm not simply saying this because of my relationship with her. Furthermore, I have a pretty shrewd idea who the real killer is."

"What did you say?" Kiriko's face loomed out of the darkness and stared at Otsuka. "If that's true and you think you know who did it, then surely it would be better to look for that person?"

"Of course, I intend to," answered Otsuka assertively. "However, that'll be quite difficult. I need to find evidence. Before that, I must prove that Michiko is innocent. The reason I have asked you to tell the truth is twofold. The true murderer dropped a lighter at the scene of the crime. Michiko says she saw it there. But later when the police arrived, it was gone. Someone had taken it away. I think that you have the lighter."

Kiriko didn't answer. She continued to walk alongside him, unflustered, with an even step. There were few pedestrians about and the shops on both sides of the street were closed. Occasionally a taxi drove past.

"Michiko testified that the lighter bore a design of squirrels and grapes. If only I had that lighter, I'm confident I could reveal the identity of the real killer. And if I'm right, there is a possibility that it's the same person who framed your brother for the murder of the old woman. In fact, there are definite indications that it's the same person."

For the first time Kiriko stopped momentarily in her tracks. "Is that true?"

"I wouldn't lie about something like this. I reviewed the paperwork and discovered this myself. You weren't to know this, but I had the official court transcripts sent up from Kyushu and I studied them as closely as I could. My conclusion was that your brother was innocent and that someone else is the killer. The circumstances are very similar to those in the recent murder of Kenji Sugiura."

A hysterical laugh exploded in his ear.

Kiriko was gripped with anger. "Why didn't you undertake my brother's defense at the time? What's the point of identifying the true killer now? It won't bring my brother back to life. I don't care who the real killer is. I wanted to save my brother. I wanted to help him while he was still alive. And for his sake I spent what little money I had and came all the way to Tokyo—you were my only hope. Someone without money, like me, could only afford two nights in Tokyo. I threw myself on your mercy. And then on the second day, what did you do? Why, you left to play golf, saying that you couldn't take my case on because I wouldn't be able to afford your fees. The whole court system is at fault if poor people can't get justice. And yes, I do resent you, even now. I don't want to know who the real killer is. I haven't got that lighter, and there's no reason why you should think I have. If you want to save Michiko, then that's up to you. Go do it yourself!"

Otsuka went into the office, but there was no work for him to do.

The younger lawyers came to work and did their jobs as before, but there was an almost perceptible sense of malaise permeating the atmosphere. An increasingly conspicuous element of shoddiness was apparent in their work. Since the murder incident had been reported in the press, an increasing number of clients had withdrawn their cases from his firm. This was something Kinzo Otsuka had never before experienced. Up until now, even if he had declined to undertake their work, clients would arrive at the office anyway and implore Otsuka to accept their cases. Everything had been turned on its head. Needless to say, there were no new clients.

That was fine. It didn't matter anymore. What Otsuka wanted more than anything else at the moment was Kiriko's truthful testimony and to obtain from her the lighter for use as evidence. There was absolutely no other way of saving Michiko. Even if he relied on his vast experience and weaved together his most compelling legal logic, it wouldn't come anywhere near the efficacy of the young woman's testimony reinforced by the physical evidence.

However, now Otsuka had nowhere to turn. He had read all the court records exhaustively and considered all possible lines of defense, but to no avail. He had no more energy left to fight this case. He simply sat, absent-mindedly, in an office that was filled with an all-pervading feeling of decline and gloom. The sun shone in through the window, its light touching the lawyer's sagging shoulders. His slouching form, sitting motionless in his chair, made him seem as if he were casually sunbathing.

It was the same when he was walking along or riding in his car.

When he returned home at the end of the day, there was nobody there to soothe his anguish. His wife had left him and gone back to her parents' home. With the exposure in the press of his affair with Michiko she'd refused to return. She was evidently bitter about the ongoing betrayal.

However, Otsuka had reconciled himself to all this. Now that his wife was gone, he considered marrying Michiko. But at this point, Michiko was out of his reach, and it was useless to think of such things. First, he had to secure her release from prison.

Otsuka believed wholeheartedly in Michiko's innocence. It had become a kind of conviction for him. But mere conviction and faith would be of no assistance in a court of law.

Otsuka's house and office were piled high with documents for Michiko's murder trial. His briefcase was also filled. Yet there was no need to read them anymore. He had never before spent so much time reading and re-reading and committing to memory each line and paragraph of each court record in a single case.

He sat quietly, his head bobbing slowly to and fro. He knew he was mentally exhausted. He felt seized by a great irritation, as if he were walking across hot sand.

Late that night Otsuka went again to Bar Lyon.

He opened the narrow door and went into the gloomy interior of the bar. It was about an hour before closing time. He sat at one corner of the counter, propped himself up on his elbows, and ordered a highball.

"Good evening!" the bartender, proprietress and the hostesses all welcomed their high-tipping customer. He was the perfect middle-aged gentleman, well behaved, who liked to sit and drink his liquor quietly.

Whenever he came, the proprietress, the girls and Kiriko would come over and join him. They knew that this reticent gentleman came here to see Kiriko.

"Good evening," said Kiriko. She came close to Otsuka, nearly brushing his shoulder as she sat down next to him. "May I have a drink?"

Otsuka agreed and Kiriko ordered a brandy.

The drink arrived and Kiriko offered it to the lawyer. "*Sensei*, will you warm it for me?"

"Yes."

Otsuka took the glass in both hands and gently swirled the yellow liquid around. The fragrance drifted to his nose.

He cradled the glass, staring at it in silence for a couple of minutes. In this world of nightclubs and bars, a woman asking a man to warm a glass with his hands implied she liked him.

"Your hands are warm, *sensei*," said Kiriko, taking the glass from Otsuka, and feeling its warmth.

"You're so kind, *sensei*," she said, swilling brandy round her mouth and then taking a drink of water. "But they say people with warm hands have cold hearts." She said this in an unremarkable manner, but her subtext had particular meaning.

"That's not true. I would stake my life on a woman I loved."

The bartender heard Otsuka's words, but he took them for nothing more than the mutterings of a pleasantly tipsy customer.

"Well, of course. That's the sort of person you are. Yet you sacrifice so many for your cause. It isn't all about you. Wouldn't you agree?" Kiriko peered at Otsuka's profile from the seat next to his, just as a hostess is wont to do.

"There's nothing I can do about that. I haven't got much time left. I won't get a second chance in this world. My time is precious. I don't want to die having stood on the sidelines doing nothing of importance about a sordid and terrible mess."

"That's very admirable. I really envy how fortunate people like you are. There are those who don't even get the chance to live ordinary lives, whose lives are cut short prematurely." Kiriko was of course referring to her brother, and Otsuka knew as much.

Whenever he came to the bar, Kiriko would smile at him in a familiar manner and show him affection and consideration in everything she did—so much so that the other bar staff began to suspect the pair were in a relationship.

When it was closing time, Otsuka settled the bill and made ready to leave. Kiriko helped him on with his overcoat, slipping it over his shoulders from behind. She even held his hand. He was, after all, a valued customer.

"Rie, it's okay, we can manage now. Why don't you go along?" said the proprietress tactfully.

"I will, then," she replied, unashamedly. If anything, Kiriko seemed to be enjoying herself.

They walked out into the dark street together. From the moment they left the bar Kiriko kept a slight distance between herself and the lawyer and let go of his hand.

"You're always talking about your brother, aren't you?" said Otsuka as they walked along, his shoes resounding on the sidewalk. "Look, it was wrong of me. I've said it a hundred times already, and although I can't make it right, I admit I was wrong and I regret that now. I will do anything to make up for it."

Kiriko moved away from Otsuka, thrust both hands in her overcoat pockets and increased her pace.

It was dark and so he couldn't see her face clearly, but he heard her ice-cold laugh.

"Kiriko, I'd do anything to make up for my error. But Michiko hasn't committed any crime. You must understand that. Just look at your brother's case. Michiko is innocent.

Please, for her sake, can't you somehow bring yourself to tell the truth?"

Kiriko remained silent.

"I understand your feelings as if they were my own. But just think for a moment about Michiko's position. It's one thing to exact revenge on me, but there is no need to sacrifice her like this."

"I'm not sacrificing her," replied Kiriko lightly.

"That's as may be, but if you don't change your mind, Michiko will be charged with murder."

"If you're so very fond of her, why don't you save her? She deserves a top-notch lawyer."

"Of course. But in order to do that, I need your testimony and the lighter the murderer dropped at the scene of the crime. If only I had those two things I could save Michiko. I'm begging you, please, give me the lighter," Otsuka repeated his request. He was so strained blood seemed ready to burst from his eyes and ears.

"I don't know anything about it. Everything is as I told it to the public prosecutor," answered Kiriko, turning into the wind.

The street was dark and cold, but Otsuka was prepared to prostrate himself before Kiriko and beg her.

Otsuka visited Bar Lyon on three further consecutive nights.

He knew now that Kiriko was behaving in this way purely out of spite, but there was nothing else he could think of. There seemed to be no alternative to persuading Kiriko to comply with his request. Although Otsuka cursed Kiriko, he needed to hold on to her. If he let her get away from him, it would consign both him and Michiko to the depths of despair.

The Kiriko he met in the bar was all smiles and a picture of friendliness. She had wholly absorbed what was required of her as a hostess. She was indulgent to a degree, and positioned herself in a moderately flirtatious manner close to Otsuka's shoulder.

Even though Otsuka came each evening to drink at the bar, none among the staff suspected his real motives. It was not uncommon for middle-aged customers to become infatuated with young hostesses.

Otsuka was spending his money freely and the proprietress was in high spirits. When Otsuka left the bar for the night, he didn't forget to take Kiriko with him, but once they were out on the dark street, the daggers were drawn. There was nothing surprising about that. Otsuka detested Kiriko, and yet he still pleaded with her.

"You're here nearly every night, aren't you?"

As usual Kiriko walked apart from Otsuka.

"It won't do any good turning up so often, you know. Once I've decided something, I don't change my mind so easily."

The sidewalk was still wet from the morning's rain. A cold wind blew through the night.

"Don't say that. I've no choice but to keep on asking you. I've been a lawyer for years, but this is the first time I've come up against anything like this."

"Fine," said Kiriko coldly. "If you've been a lawyer for years, then of course you've gained a reputation and saved up a lot of money. I'm sure you're very capable. In all your time as a lawyer I should think you've saved scores of people. All for the sake of money…"

Kiriko placed particular emphasis on the last word.

"I bet you've refused to defend people and left them to die because of money before. It must be so unbearable for the families of those people. You take on cases because you can make lots of money. But if a client has no money you show them the door. That's just business, isn't it, *sensei*? So I guess that's okay. You can live with that. But what about the families of those people who have been put to death despite being innocent? They'll always resent you. However much they may have pleaded with you, you refused to help them."

"I know that. You've said that over and over again, and I have apologized over and over again. But I have to beg for your help. For Michiko's sake you have to tell the truth to the court. Please give me the lighter to use as evidence. In return, I will do anything you ask to make things better for you. In fact, I would go down on my hands and knees, right here, right now, in front of you."

"Oh?" sneered Kiriko. "But that's got nothing to do with what I'm talking about. What I'm talking about is the feelings of all those people you have turned your back on. That has nothing to do with Michiko's predicament. Nothing whatsoever."

"Kiriko," Otsuka clenched his fists as anger welled up inside him. What he did next was unconnected with his pent-up feelings of frustration. "I beg you Kiriko," he said, taking hold of her hands, in spite of himself.

"What are you doing?" asked Kiriko, looking down at her pinioned wrists. "We're not in the bar anymore."

Taken aback, Otsuka let go and drew his hands back. "I'm sorry, that was wrong of me. I didn't mean to do that. I wasn't thinking, I just meant to ask you to help me. I'm impatient, that's all. I've never been in a fix like this before. Please, help me, I beg you." Otsuka bowed his head repeatedly in front of her.

"*Sensei*, you ought to be ashamed of yourself."

"No. I'm no longer a lawyer, I'm nobody. Just a person begging for mercy, that's all."

"It's no use," said Kiriko, turning and walking away.

Otsuka, prone now to making earnest statements, pursued her. "Kiriko. Michiko is innocent. I know the identity of the real killer."

Kiriko suddenly stopped walking. "What's this again? You know who it is?"

"All right, I'll tell you everything. The person who murdered Kenji is the same person who killed the old woman in K-City and framed your brother. I reviewed the records and discovered that the old woman was killed by a left-handed person. I've kept it to myself until now, because it's too late to do anything about it. I realized this while reading through the court transcripts. The court-appointed lawyer didn't figure that out. What I mean to say is that the murder could not have been committed unless the culprit was left-handed, which rules your brother out. He was most definitely right-handed."

Kiriko seemed to have turned to stone as she stood bracing herself against the wind.

"The murder that Michiko now stands accused of was also committed by a left-handed killer. I can prove that from a number of different angles. I can prove it, but my contention alone would not be sufficient. If I am to successfully challenge the prosecution's conclusion and convince the judge, I need to present physical evidence."

Kiriko's face turned pale as she listened. Her eyes sparkled in the dark and she stared fixedly into the distance. Her face was set and motionless.

A vision of Takeo Yamagami rose before her eyes. She gazed at him, the left-handed pitcher from Kyushu.

"The left-handed man," resumed Otsuka, "murdered that old woman in K-City. Afterwards, he came to Tokyo, and killed Sugiura, also from K-City. The murderer was an acquaintance of Sugiura's. At least, he was probably from the same city. There is no contradiction in the killer first murdering the old woman in K-City and then killing Sugiura following his arrival in Tokyo. As to why he murdered Sugiura, well, that question will need to be asked once he has been arrested. At the moment, I don't know what his motive was. However," continued the lawyer, "while it is true that Sugiura was the head waiter in a restaurant, he was also a good-for-nothing hoodlum."

Otsuka paused for a moment. He suddenly had a vision of Michiko and Kenji Sugiura together.

"The murderer was also, in all probability, a delinquent friend of his. A quarrel started between them. I have the feeling, intuitively, that I know what it was all about. I think it had to do with the murder of the old woman in K-City. At the time of the murder, Sugiura had returned temporarily to K-City, and he was probably aware that his friend was the killer. He may even have been an accomplice. The friend would have been the offender and Sugiura an accessory to the crime. Two guest cushions had been placed on the floor in the old woman's house. Sugiura and his friend both left for Tokyo, and I think they kept in touch. It was probably after that time that their difficulties began."

Kiriko recalled something while she was listening to Otsuka's story. She couldn't remember when exactly it was, but it was after Kenji and Yamagami had been at Bar Seaweed together. Kenji had been intimidating Yamagami. Even though they had been drinking at the bar together, Yamagami acted cautious around Kenji…

Assuming that Yamagami was the principal offender in the murder of the old woman, and that Kenji had gone along with it at Yamagami's request, Kenji, as a mere accessory to the murder, would always have been in a position to blackmail Yamagami to wring money out of him.

But Yamagami didn't have any money left. It was possible that Yamagami somehow managed to raise funds and pay Kenji for a while; when he no longer could, Kenji began a campaign of intimidation.

Although it had been several years since Kenji moved to Tokyo, he probably happened to return to K-City at around the time of the murder. He would have been invited to take part in the crime by his friend Yamagami. Sometime later, Yamagami also went to Tokyo.

Kiriko saw in her mind's eye Yamagami drifting to and fro between the two murders.

"Kiriko," said Otsuka, peering into her face. "If you testify in favor of Michiko, I will pin down the real murderer. The key to all of this is that lighter. Michiko testified that it bore a design of grapes and squirrels on its side. It must have been you who picked it up at the scene of the crime. If you would just give me that lighter, I'll be able to prove your brother innocent too, in addition to having Michiko acquitted. I'm asking you, Kiriko—for your brother's sake, testify, and hand over the lighter."

"It's not fair." Kiriko's words slipped out from her mouth.

Otsuka couldn't believe his ears. "What?"

"It's not right. It's fine for you to prove my brother innocent. But he's already dead. Whereas Michiko is still alive, isn't she?"

Otsuka was aghast.

"Were my brother still alive, I would probably do what you have asked. But he died in prison. It's unfair if Michiko is the only one left alive of the two. You might think that's all right but…"

She let the words die on her lips.

The following night it rained.

Around 11pm Otsuka pushed on the door to Bar Lyon. Droplets of rain had collected on the shoulders of his coat. His hair was wet.

"Oh, quickly, come in!"

Kiriko came over to his side. "You'll catch your death of cold, *sensei*. Come on, let me have your coat."

She worked briskly, taking his overcoat off and placing it by the heater to dry. She brought a towel over and wiped Otsuka's head and face.

"You poor thing. Have a drink before you catch cold."

The lawyer remained silent. He stared fixedly into the mid-distance and placed both elbows on the counter. His hair was graying and his cheeks sunken.

"Will it be your usual? A highball?" The bartender took down from the shelf the only bottle of Johnny Walker in the establishment. It was red label, but expensive nevertheless, for this place.

"Here, please have a drink."

Kiriko took the glass and put it to the lawyer's lips. She kept one hand resting on his shoulder.

Anybody looking on would have simply seen a hostess entertaining a man she was fond of. Otsuka looked like a customer enraptured by the attentions of his favorite girl.

This particular customer came every night. When he left, he always did so together with Kiriko. Their relationship had the virtual blessing of the bar staff.

Otsuka sat at the counter for almost an hour.

Kiriko hung around continually, indulging him. Otsuka wasn't very talkative. He wasn't usually one for saying much at this place, but this evening he was particularly taciturn. He kept his eyes downcast. It was difficult to see in the dimly lit interior of the bar, but Otsuka's eyes had a monomaniacal look about them.

The bar closed and, as always, Otsuka and Kiriko left together. The rain was teeming down outside. Otsuka didn't have an umbrella.

Kiriko turned up the collar of her overcoat and pulled her hood up. She didn't seem at all concerned that Otsuka was getting drenched. When he had come into the bar earlier she had been the personification of kindness and consideration, cheerfully drying his overcoat and rubbing his wet hair with a towel.

They took the usual path. The ring of light thrown down onto the sidewalk from the street lamp highlighted the slanting rods of rain.

On one side of the street was the long fence, and the branches of trees nodded and peeped over its parapet. On the opposite side of the street was a row of houses. They were shuttered up for the night due to the lateness of the hour as well as the rain. Nobody was about, no cars went by. The sound of pelting rain filled the air and ricocheted off the tin roof on a house to one side.

Without warning, Otsuka stopped and squatted down in the mud. Before Kiriko's very eyes he bent his knees and placed both hands flat on the muddy ground.

"See, I told you I would do it. I'm past saying anything now. I understand how you feel. I just want you to help me, listen to what I have to say. I beg you." Otsuka's voice sounded muffled in the driving rain.

Kiriko stared down at the lawyer kneeling at her feet.

"Kiriko, I beg you to help me. I know this alone won't ease your pain, but I don't know what else to do anymore. If you help me, then I'll do anything you like in return. Please, tell the prosecution the truth and let me have the lighter."

Kiriko stood there in silence. The rain beat down on the ground. She continued to stare at his pleading form. The rest of Otsuka's words were drowned out as he bowed his head repeatedly like some kind of cowed animal.

"*Sensei*," said Kiriko at length. "All right, I understand."

The lawyer raised his bowed head.

"But please, get up."

"You understand?" Otsuka peered up at Kiriko from out of the darkness. His voice seemed suddenly full of hope. "You understand? You mean you will testify in front of the public prosecutor? Really you will?"

"Yes I will. And I'll give you the lighter too."

Otsuka almost jumped for joy. "You… You really will testify?"

He peered at Kiriko half in disbelief.

"Yes, that's right."

The lawyer breathed out a deep sigh of relief.

"Anyway, please get up. We can't talk with you on your hands and knees."

"But, do you really forgive me? I will stay like this until you did."

"Let's not talk about that anymore. Come on, stand up."

Otsuka's face was full of hope. He staggered to his feet in the sludge. "W-When can you give me the lighter?" He formed his dirty hands into fists and pressed Kiriko for an answer.

"Tomorrow night," replied Kiriko, swallowing hard and adding, "Tomorrow night, come to my apartment. I'll give you the lighter then."

"Thank you."

The lawyer's muddy hands came together in an attitude of prayer. "Tomorrow night? That's fine. It doesn't matter where, I'll be there. You really will give me the lighter, won't you? And you're sure you are prepared to testify to Michiko's innocence in court?"

"I promised, so you can be sure I will."

"Thank you, thank you so much." Otsuka's grayed head bobbed and his eyes were full of tears. "Where is your apartment?"

Kiriko told him her address for the first time and added, "The bar closes at 11:30, so tomorrow don't go there, go straight to my apartment. If you get there just a little after midnight, I'll definitely be home by then, waiting for you."

Standing there in the rain and covered in mud, Otsuka felt beside himself with joy. The absurdity of going alone to the apartment of a single woman late at night didn't even enter his mind.

Next evening Otsuka went to the address he was given. It was the first time he had been to the area. Plus, it was the middle of the night.

It was a district on the outskirts of Tokyo. The apartment building was located in the backstreets. The entrance fronted the street. Thinking it would be locked he pushed on the door, but it was open. It looked as though Kiriko left it unlocked for tonight.

Otsuka saw that there were stairs off to the right. This was just how Kiriko had described it. Footwear lay scattered about in the entrance hall. Otsuka wondered whether to remove his own shoes but then decided to keep them on and climbed the stairs.

It was a steep incline to the second floor. A corridor led away from the landing. The passageway was dimly lit. There were doors on either side, like in a hospital. Kiriko's room was on the right at the end of the corridor.

Otsuka felt like a burglar. He did his best to tread carefully and reach the apartment door without making any noise. He kept thinking someone might suddenly come rushing out of one of the doors as he went past. He came to Kiriko's door and knocked softly.

He heard a low voice from inside. The door opened a crack and Kiriko's face, darkly silhouetted against the light behind her, appeared in the doorway.

"Welcome." She greeted Otsuka with the etiquette normally reserved for one of her customers.

Otsuka slipped inside the room. It was barely a six-mat room. The atmosphere was fragrant from an incense burner that stood on the desktop sending a wisp of smoke upwards. On the opposite side were curtains. A single cushion had been placed in the middle of the matting.

"I've just got back. I've been expecting you."

Kiriko had changed into a kimono. It was brightly colored, but the sort of garment that would be worn about the house. She brought over a bottle of whisky and a glass.

"I don't have much, but please, drink this," said Kiriko, smiling at the lawyer.

It seemed strange to Otsuka how very grown-up Kiriko appeared to be. It was probably due in part to the kimono she had changed into, but also due to her makeup, which she wore only infrequently. She had clearly spent some time preparing herself for his visit.

"Please, don't go to any trouble," said Otsuka looking over at Kiriko. "Will you give me the lighter? And then testify that Michiko's innocent, as you said?"

"I will, as promised. But if I give you the lighter now you'll go home right away. Why don't you stay a while and relax."

Kiriko spoke to Otsuka in a tone of voice very much unlike that with which she normally spoke. She gazed at him with glistening eyes.

"*Sensei*, please have a drink. You needn't worry, I haven't poisoned it." She sounded so mature. Her words were those of a well-practised bar hostess.

Otsuka decided not to resist. Kiriko's manner was assertive. Having come this far he didn't want to offend her. He suppressed his feelings and put the glass to his lips. The neat whisky burned on his tongue.

"It's okay to get tipsy, *sensei*," said Kiriko. She sidled up and leaned towards him. "You have a car waiting outside, don't you? Then there's nothing to worry about. I want you to drink a little and enjoy yourself."

"Give me the lighter!" cried Otsuka. "Give it to me now!"

"There's no need to hurry. Won't you stay just for a while longer? How about another drink?"

"I've had enough," said Otsuka, exhaling forcefully. "Now if you don't mind I would like to leave. Please give me the lighter."

"Oh, but I can't do that," laughed Kiriko. "Is that all you care about, the lighter? Have one more drink and then I'll let you go home. Okay? When you leave I'll put the lighter in your pocket."

Otsuka steeled his nerve and drank another whisky. It was a strong brand and he wasn't used to drinking so much.

"Give me the lighter," he repeated, holding out his hand.

"You're so hasty." Kiriko's voice slipped out amid a haze of red anger surging before him. His vision seemed filled with bright dazzling color.

"*Sensei.*" Kiriko's voice sounded close in his ear. She slipped her arms around his chest. Otsuka later remembered being pulled along in front of the curtains on his unsteady feet. The curtains he had seen when he first came into the room were yanked noisily apart. The image of a bed reflected in Otsuka's eyes.

He stood and stared in disbelief. The bed had been prepared for him.

"What's going on?"

"*Sensei*, please."

Kiriko lauched herself at him and pushed him down onto the bed. Otsuka fell backwards with his back landing against the duvet quilt. The back of his head touched the pillow.

Kiriko clung fast, embracing him with strong arms and shoulders.

"W-What on earth are you doing? Give me the lighter!" he shrieked.

"I told you I'd give it to you. But first, *sensei*, listen to me!"

"What?"

"I love you." Kiriko took a handful of his gray hair and fastened his head to the duvet, and then began licking him all over vigorously—on his lips, nose, eyes and cheeks. Her mouth and teeth roved his face with frenzied movements and he thought his skin would break with the intensity.

"I loved you all along."

She climbed astride him and pressed down with her weight. "I'm sorry for saying all those spiteful things. But I said it because I love you. You understand, don't you?" she said and chewed on his earlobe.

Sweat ran down Otsuka's face. He tried to push Kiriko aside but his strength gave out and he was unable to resist. He stared helplessly at Kiriko's lips hovering above his face. From somewhere within he discovered renewed strength.

Slowly he moved his hands round to her neck. He felt almost unconscious as though after a prolonged struggle.

For the first time now, Kiriko began to shake with fear. Still, she refused to move away from Otsuka's body and clung on with all her strength. Keiichi Abe's figure flashed through her mind.

The following day, Kiriko Yanagida sent a certified letter to the public prosecutor who had been investigating the murder case involving Michiko Kono.

Recently, the lawyer Kinzo Otsuka has persisted in visiting me and asking me to testify to Michiko Kono's innocence. It became so bad that I quit my job at Bar Seaweed, the bar managed by the elder sister of the murder victim, Kenji Sugiura, and moved to a different bar. However, Otsuka showed up there as well. He would turn up late every night, walk me out after closing hours, and ask me to testify that Michiko Kono is innocent. He wanted me to say that I was at the scene of the crime with Michiko, and that the victim, Kenji Sugiura, had already been murdered before she arrived there. He then accused me of taking and hiding the lighter that is supposed to have belonged to the murderer, saying that I should hand it over to him because he could use it to prove Michiko not guilty. As I stated to the prosecution, however, I have never been to that house. How could I have known about the secret rendezvous place of Michiko and Kenji? Nevertheless, Otsuka insisted that if I did as he said, then Michiko would be found not guilty, and accordingly that is how I should testify in court. In other words, he

ordered me to testify that I had been
to a house I have never been to and
met with Michiko when I have never in
fact met her.

I question whether this sort of
behavior is appropriate for a
first-class lawyer. Clearly Otsuka
was attempting to coerce me into
committing perjury. But I refused to
do so. He would wait for me time and
again on my way home from work and I
was afraid of him. But the one thing I
couldn't bring myself to do was lie to
the court and so I flatly refused his
requests.

Yet because this involved saving his
lover, he started to torment me.
Finally, last night, he came to my
apartment. No matter how many times
I refused him, Otsuka wouldn't leave
me alone. He forced his way in and
repeated his demands that I should
tell lies in court. This happened
after midnight.

I continued to refuse his demands.
Then Otsuka suddenly dragged me to
bed and forced me to have sexual
intercourse with him. He no doubt
thought that if he won me over,
I would testify in the manner he
had been demanding. I put up as
much resistance as I was able, but
eventually succumbed to his advances.

My complaint is not that I was defiled
by a cunning and experienced lawyer.
Of course, that is a disgrace I will
have to live with for the rest of my
life, but what I mainly take issue
with is the way he tried to compel me
to commit perjury. I feel revulsion
at the underhanded way this top-class
lawyer tried to win me over as a
witness and persuade me to tell lies
by taking advantage of me. The world
would surely be a better place without
lawyers like him.

I am prepared to reveal my humiliation
for the sake of exposing this well-
known yet wholly unscrupulous lawyer.

I trust that once you have had an
opportunity to read the above, you
will take all the circumstances into
consideration.

The public prosecutor summoned Kinzo Otsuka and notified him of the contents of Kiriko Yanagida's letter.

Otsuka ran his eyes over the letter then froze as if his blood started to flow backwards.

"Well? Is it true, what it says in this letter?" asked the public prosecutor.

Silence.

Otsuka didn't have the courage to deny it. He knew this was Kiriko's revenge. Even so, he couldn't bring himself to refute the letter's contents.

Otsuka also knew that Kiriko had staked her body. She had been a virgin. Guilt over this weighed on him, deeply.

It would have been easy enough for him to relate his seduction by Kiriko to the prosecutor, but that was something that was between only the two of them. He would not refute the contents of her letter and advance his own, correct version of the events. That he was unable to muster the courage to do so had less to do with his own shame and embarrassment than the knowledge that he had despoiled a young woman.

Otsuka looked at the letter and neither refuted nor affirmed the accuracy of its contents. An uncertain smile settled on his pale, trembling face.

Inducing a witness to commit perjury was the ultimate disgrace for a lawyer and meant the end of his career.

Otsuka resigned from his various positions within the legal world and as a lawyer. While he did this of his own volition, those around him who knew only of the reported facts of the case opined that he had painted himself into a corner by his own mistakes.

Kinzo Otsuka put himself through purgatory. It was a harsher punishment than the confines of the prison cell where Michiko Kono spent her days.

Kiriko disappeared from Tokyo without a trace.

THE END

About the Author

Seicho Matsumoto (1909-1992) was a native of Fukuoka Prefecture and prolific writer of socially-oriented mystery novels. Formerly a journalist, he debuted as an author after reaching the age of forty with the historically-based *Saigo Takamori Chits* (1951) and *The Legend of the Kokura Diary* (1952), which earned him the 28th Akutagawa Prize. He then went on to establish his unique style of crime fiction with works such as *Points and Lines* (1958) and *Zero Focus* (1959) to become Japan's pre-eminent name in the field.